CW00493260

This is a work of fiction. Similarities to are entirely coincidental.

LOCAL KILLER

First edition. May 20, 2023.

ISBN: 978-1915981110

Written by Paul Trembling.

Table of Contents

Real CSI meets fictional in the new addition to the Local series. Such a gripping read following Alison through some truly page turning situations. Get a little look into the real CSI with nuggets of actual forensic processes enhancing the reality of the storytelling. From a real CSI reading it, it really adds to the authenticity of the story, although we don't usually get in as much trouble as Alison, honest!!

Helen Berry, British CSI

WITH CHARACTERS THAT intrigue and a plot that mesmerises, from first to last page Local Killer is a triumph of crime writing.

Wendy H. Jones, multi-award winning author.

A 'JUST ONE MORE CHAPTER' crime novel of the best kind! Prepare for a late night turning pages. This linked series just keeps getting better!

Alison, the CSI expert is an engaging character whose first-person viewpoint puts the reader smack in the action. She needs her personal rituals to get her through daily contact with other people, and I warmed to her courage, both in coping with everyday intrusions on her sensibility and in following up on a murder that her police colleagues have classified as solved. But Alison was a witness and the murder victim nearly became a friend so this is personal.

The forensic puzzles are brilliant, the red herrings are plausible and the resolutions to both the crime scene anomalies and the overall whodunnit and why, are all highly satisfying. Some heart-thumping action and danger scenes, and a special friendship, all add to a story which never feels forced. Trembling's ability to turn ordinary people inside out and show the human failings which lead to murder is once again evident but this novel followed darker twists in the human psyche than in previous 'Local' books. This time the victim is of less interest than the murderer. Light-touch details of place and background make every scene come to life, from the court-house to the rough moorland, and I feel I know this shabby English town and the people in it, so completely has the author created its streets and buildings, the neighbours and officials.

As each 'Local' novel focuses on a different main character, this works as a standalone while giving extra entertainment to readers who recognise the other residents from previous books.

Jean Gill, author of the 'Troubadours' Quartet.

Other books in the 'Local' series by Paul Trembling
Local Poet
Local Artist
Local Legend
(All published by Lion Hudson Limited)

Paul Trembling
LOCAL KILLER

DEATH IS CLOSE TO HOME

Resolute Books

Published by Paul Trembling with Resolute Books
First Edition 2023
Cover Art by Liz Carter

Being a writer is a bit like being a zombie: you achieve nothing without picking a lot of different brains.
With grateful thanks to all those who have allowed me to pick their brains!
Your advice, encouragement and gentle nudges in the right direction have made this a much better book than I could have managed on my own.

Chapter 1

CSI Kit Checklist: camera bag, fingerprint Case, DNA recovery kit.

Out of the last ten minutes of her life, Ruth Darnley spent five of them talking to me.

Is that significant? Or just coincidental? It feels significant, but I can't always trust feelings like that.

I'd just come out of Court, and was standing on the back steps checking my keys, my phone, my radio and so on, when I heard her call my name from the corridor behind me.

"CSI Kepple?"

I turned round as she came out of the open doors. I was used to seeing her on the Bench and out of that context I didn't recognise her at first. A short, dark woman with a surprisingly gentle smile. "Yes?" I asked cautiously. Then recognition kicked in and I hastily added "Your Honour?"

She waved that away. "None of that, please. Ruth to my friends when I'm not in court. And you're Alison, right?" She put out a hand to shake. "There, that's the formalities over!"

I'd heard this about Ruth Darnley. In the courtroom, a stickler for protocol, very strong on upholding the dignity of the court. Outside it, friendly and approachable.

But still retaining a sense of authority and presence, I realised. I'm not a particularly tall woman and I was looking down on her head. Yet at the same time I felt very much the inferior. It was confusing. Not knowing what to say, I said nothing.

She, however, had no such problem. "I'm glad I caught you, Alison. I wanted to say how much I appreciated your evidence. Not just today. You've given evidence before me on several occasions, and it's always excellent. Clear, factual, precise. So many people, even professionals, seem to feel the need to pad things out, but I've never had that from you."

I wasn't sure how to answer that. "I'm only there to say what I know. So that's what I say." Did that sound rude, I wondered? People think I'm rude, sometimes, though I don't mean to be. "Not much point in saying anything else." Oh, heck, that did sound rude! "I mean – I'm sorry – I..."

"No, no. You're absolutely right and I wish more people would think like that. It would make my job a lot easier!" She gave me a shrewd look. "You find it easier talking in Court than outside of it, don't you?"

Not many get that. "There are rules, in Court," I explained. "I know what I'm there for. It's defined. Outside, well – I..."

Ruth Darnley smiled. "Outside, the rules aren't clear and they're always changing."

"Yes," I agreed.

"Then stick to Court rules, Alison. Be clear, concise and accurate. People appreciate that more than you realise, and don't waste time on those who don't like it."

She held my gaze for a moment, and nodded as if she approved of what she saw. "I hope we can talk again, Alison. With more time. But I have to be going. If I can find my car in this mess!"

The main car park was being resurfaced. A yard at the rear of the Courthouse, once intended for service access to the old boiler-house, had been pressed into temporary car park duty, but even though it was supposedly restricted to court officials and police officers on court duty, it was totally inadequate. All the marked out spaces had long since been filled, but vehicles had continued to drive in and park up wherever they could.

The situation was made worse by the lack of security. There were no actual human guards available to cover the gates – budget cuts had seen them replaced with CCTV and automatic barriers a year ago. And of course, the yard had neither. Just a set of gates which, with the volume of traffic going in and out, had to be left open.

Which meant that anybody could drive in and take up space. And apparently had. The Judge let out a word which I would have expected her to know but never to use.

"Looks like someone's blocked me in! That's my car, behind that rusty old Transit. I'm sure that shouldn't be here."

My CSI van was parked a short distance from Darnley's Mercedes – thankfully it seemed to be clear of obstructions. We walked in that direction together, whilst I considered her words, and my reaction. It seemed like she was offering a friendship, which I suppose should have made me feel flattered, or even happy. Instead, it started my stomach churning with worry.

"It looks like they've left a note on my windscreen," the Judge observed as we drew closer. "Good, I might be able to get out of here after all."

Something was bothering me, quite apart from the conversation. I glanced over towards the entrance. There had been someone standing there, watching us, when we came out. They weren't there now. But why should that bother me? There were people passing by all the time, often glancing in as they did so. I didn't understand why I felt uneasy about it, and not understanding made me feel worse.

We reached my van. "I have to go," I said.

"Yes, of course." Her attention was on her own car and the vehicle blocking it in. "Thank you again, Alison."

I opened the van, put my folder with all the court paperwork on the passenger seat. Ruth Darnley had reached her car, and was reading a sheet of paper that had been placed under the wipers. She took out a mobile.

I went round to the side door and slid it open. I had a job to go to, burglary on the north side of town. I'd checked all my kit was there before I left the station, but I checked again anyway. I always do.

Fingerprint kit, camera bag, DNA recovery kit, all lined up in size order, just inside the door, just as I'd left them. I opened the camera bag, checked camera, spare battery...

There was a thunderclap, the loudest I'd ever heard, and the van jerked sideways and flame poured round it, over it, even under it, licking up past my boots. The door sill hit my legs and I thought for a moment that the whole vehicle was going to fall over on top over me, but then it righted itself, rocking back on its suspension.

I was screaming. Crouching down, arms over my head, screaming and shouting "Whatwhatwhat?" Because it didn't make sense, that noise, it didn't belong, and I didn't know how to process it.

Until habit asserted itself. When in doubt, list. When I don't understand what's happened, I go over what has happened.

"Loud noise," I told myself. "Flames. Van rocking like something hit it."

That was all I knew. I needed more, so I uncurled myself and stood up.

The flame was gone, but there was an acrid smell in the air, strong enough to have me coughing. And light, a colour of light that didn't belong, flickering on the back wall of the Court buildings.

I stepped out from behind the van, and saw flames climbing furiously into the air for twenty feet or more before turning into thick black smoke.

They were coming from Judge Darnley's Mercedes, or what was left of it. The car parked next to it was on fire as well. There was nothing visible of the van that had been blocking her in, though some of the burning wreckage could have been tyres.

In the midst of the flames, apparently embedded in the Merc's windscreen, was a roughly human shaped figure. It wasn't moving. It was never going to move again.

Behind me there was shouting, panicked screams. My radio had been turned off while I was in court; I clicked it on. "9818 to Control."

"Control, go ahead."

"Explosion in the temporary car park at the courthouse. Several vehicles now on fire. At least one casualty, believed to be Judge Ruth Darnley. Fire Service required ASAP."

There was a short pause. But Control Room staff are used to dealing with emergencies.

"9818, can you confirm the cause of the explosion?" A different voice, probably the Control Room Manager cutting in. The 999 calls were probably already starting.

"It appears to have been a vehicle that had been parked in front of Judge Darnley's car. A white Ford Transit, VRN unknown."

"Confirm your own status, 9818?"

"I'm unharmed." I thought I was.

"Good. Do not approach the scene. Stay clear and keep other people clear. Is Judge Darnley visible to you? Does she appear injured?"

What did he think casualty meant? "She appears dead."

Long pause. "Stand by, 9818, Fire and Ambulance are on their way."

I replaced my radio on its clip. Then went back into the van for my camera. I'm a CSI. We photograph things.

I started with wide shots of the general area, moved around for different angles, then zoomed in on details of burning wreckage. Especially Ruth Darnley's car. The flames had spread to other vehicles, it was hard to make out much even with the zoom, but there was still a human shaped figure just visible through the conflagration. I was still taking pictures when the fire service arrived. There were police officers there as well. They ushered me away, took the camera off me, led me over to some paramedics.

It was only then that I realised that I was in pain from my legs, and that my eyes were aching from staring into the flames, and that my cheeks were wet with tears.

THEY MADE ME GO TO hospital. I didn't want to go, but a Chief Inspector who had turned up to take charge ordered me. One of our Senior CSIs was there by then as well, and she confirmed it, so I had no choice.

I don't like being touched, but doctors and nurses have their jobs to do, so I put up with it. I insisted on undressing myself, though, telling them all the time that I wasn't badly injured. I'd stopped crying by then, and was able to talk clearly and calmly. Repressing the irritation I felt at being fussed over, the feeling of confinement at being forced to stay in the little cubicle of an examination room.

Eventually, it was agreed that I wasn't seriously hurt. Some superficial burns, from staying too close to the fire for too long. Grazes to my lower legs from where my van had hit me – there'd be some bruising coming out there, no doubt. My boots had protected me from the flames that had flashed under the van in the initial explosion. I had a few minor cuts, on my forehead and on the back of my right hand. I didn't remember how they had happened, but it didn't matter anyway. There was nothing that needed more than some antiseptic and a plaster.

In spite of which, they wanted to keep me in – for observation. "You're in shock," the doctor told me. Middle-aged man, firm manner, not accustomed to disagreements. "We'll need to monitor you for at least twenty-four hours."

There was no way I was going to do that. Staying overnight would mean waking up there in the morning. Waking up in a strange bed, a new place. For me, that was a nightmare - literally: it had been a recurring dream when I was young, one that made wake up screaming. Even now the thought made my stomach clench.

"I'm going home," I told him. "You've got better uses for the bed, and I don't want to be here."

The doctor argued, but I was already getting dressed again. He soon realised that, short of physical restraint, he had no way of forcing me to stay.

"Very well then. You do have someone to keep an eye on you? Friend, family?"

I have a cat. We mostly ignore each other.

"Yes."

"Have them bring you back in if you experience any of these symptoms..." he reeled off a list. "Or call an ambulance if need be. And go to your GP as soon as possible. Is that clear?"

I agreed that it was, and he finally left, off to find some more amenable patient. I signed some things, accepted a packet of painkillers, and was finally allowed out.

It was dark by now, and the sharp November air cut through my fleece. I had a coat back in my locker at the CSI office, but I now realised that I actually felt quite unsteady on my legs and incredibly tired. The walk back to the station for my things seemed too much to consider, so I took a taxi home. I hate taxis - a vehicle I don't know, a person I don't know who might want to talk. It's always a tense, nervous experience. But there was nothing else for it - and at least this driver didn't try and start a conversation. Perhaps respecting the fact that I'd just come out of hospital.

Stepping back through my door, enfolding myself with familiarity. My space, my safe space at last.

Exhausted, I went straight to bed.

DULL GREY LIGHT AND throbbing headache woke me. Not just my head, either. As I struggled back to consciousness I discovered a range of other aches and pains. Legs and face mostly. And hands.

And something inside, not a physical pain but a hurt, all the same. The image of Ruth Darnley walking towards her car was vivid in my mind. "*Thank you again, Alison.*" Her last words.

No point in dwelling on it. No point in letting the tears start again. I began my morning list, concentrating with more than usual intensity, despite the headache.

Phone on the table by the bed.

Dressing gown hanging on the back of the door.

Clothes for the day on the chair... No! I hadn't put them out last night. Of course, I had some excuse for not following routine. But it was annoying.

I checked my phone again. I'd turned off the alarm last night, on the very reasonable grounds that I needed the sleep and I wouldn't be expected to turn up for my shift anyway. All the same, the break in routine was disturbing. As was the long list of texts and voicemail messages. I don't usually get many. Mostly just reminders from the dentist. Or ridiculously cheerful messages from the phone company boasting that they'd taken another months payment for services I barely used.

Most of these names were colleagues, which wasn't surprising since (apart from the dentist and the phone company) only colleagues had my number. I checked a few, and they were all variations on "Wow, gosh, heck, how awful, terrible, shocking, hope you're OK, glad you survived, get well soon, etc." Of course, the news would be all round the department by now.

I couldn't cope with it all at the moment. I put the phone down, dragged myself out of bed and got back into routine.

Shower.

Get dressed. Black uniform trousers, black uniform polo shirt, black uniform fleece. All clean. Everything I'd had on yesterday smelt of smoke, so it all went in the wash.

Hair. No longer smelling of smoke, fortunately. Brushed back and in a pony tail. I keep thinking I should get it cut short, but it's just not something I've got round to.

Breakfast. With the TV on. Not surprisingly, the bomb was national headline news. They had a reporter in the street outside the courthouse, but of course there was nothing to see apart from the crime scene tape and a bored PCSO on cordon duty. So they switched quickly to shaky mobile phone footage. Big clouds of smoke billowing up over the car park wall, excited shouts.

And on the other side of the wall I was in the middle of that smoke. Well, not quite in the middle. Ruth Darnley had been in the actual middle.

I switched it off. They didn't know anything, anyway. It was mostly speculation, the only definite fact they had was that a Judge had been killed.

Clean teeth. Check the mirror. Same face – long, pale, unremarkable. A bit red round the eyes, perhaps? And the cheeks, the nose. Was that from the fire? They felt tender, but not painful. Whatever. People were always saying I needed more colour in me, anyway.

Outside, the rain had set in, not heavy, but a persistent drizzle that had obviously decided to stick around for a while. Normally I go into work on my moped, but that was still at the station and I wasn't sure that I'd care to use it anyway. So it was the bus, then.

Fortunately, the service is regular and the stop is only a short walk away. Unfortunately, there's no shelter at this stop. So, moped or not, I pulled my waterproofs – leggings and jacket – on over my uniform, and did my going-out list.

Phone.

Keys.

Spare house key, in a concealed pocket inside my belt. (Yes, I know it's overkill. But I might need it someday).

Wallet. (Not a purse, they tend not to fit well in pockets and I don't use a handbag. I've got enough things to carry around already).

Change. (Always have some, but especially when catching the bus. Some of the local buses take plastic, some still do not).

Packet of tissues.

Small bottle of water.

Painkillers – for today only. The headache had subsided now, the other pains weren't significant, but just in case.

And finally...

"You OK, Alison?" I whispered.

"I'm OK." I answered. Checked the time, there was a bus due in ten minutes, which would mean five minutes waiting in the rain if it was on time, but you had to allow two or three minutes either side. I needed to get going anyway, so I left my flat, went downstairs and out of the house, checking all the doors were properly shut behind me.

Chapter 2

Friends Checklist: Sam, Helen...Ruth?

The bus was three minutes late, which was long enough to be very thankful that I'd put on the waterproofs, especially as the rain was getting heavier. It was full, of course – the route comes in through several outlying villages and although it was now a bit late for people going in to work, the first wave of morning shoppers was settled in with their empty bags, wet coats and glum expressions. The most cheerful face on the bus belonged to an excited spaniel (is there any other sort?) who filled the air with constant yapping and a strong odour of damp dog.

I don't like taking the bus, but it's endurable, if I can find a seat. I've found that the best strategy is to concentrate on my phone. The mobile phone is the greatest invention ever. No one tries to talk to you if you're looking at your phone. Especially if you put some earplugs in.

There was a space, near the back. The teenage girl in the seat next to it should probably have been at school, but instead she was on her phone, so we were able to happily disregard each other's existence. Getting out my phone wasn't entirely pretence, either: I had a lot of messages to answer. There were even more of them now, news had got round to other shifts and other stations. Some were from CSI colleagues who I hadn't seen for months. There were even a few from police officers I'd worked with. It was quite touching, really. And a little disturbing. I hadn't realised that so many people knew me. I sent back variations on the theme of 'Thanks, I'm fine, see you soon.'

One of the texts was from Helen, who was probably the closest thing to a friend I had in the department. I get on OK with my colleagues – most of them, most of the time – but Helen and I had started on the same day and I'd had a bit of a social life with her at one time. Not so much since she'd got married, and even less once she went on maternity leave. She still kept in touch, though, and I'd had two texts and an email wanting to know all about it and how I was. I sent a longer message back, giving her some extra detail. She wouldn't leave me alone otherwise. And besides, I missed her. She had a ridiculously bright and cheerful attitude on life which often gave me a lift. Logically, I should have dragged her down by an equivalent amount, but that never seemed to happen.

More messages came in while I was doing that. Too much to cope with, especially as my headache was coming back. If I answered them, I'd be rude about it. So instead I switched off the phone and spent the rest of the journey sitting with my eyes shut, listening to the dog and wondering what it must be like to be so relentlessly happy.

The CSI base is in an industrial estate on the edge of town, a full mile from the main police station and the Courts. We're housed in a re-purposed industrial unit. We were promised that we'd have the entire site to ourselves and that the old warehouse would become a proper forensic vehicle examination bay. Getting the facilities to do vehicle examinations in a suitable environment has been an on-going issue for years – the back of the local garage with a plastic sheet separating it from where they were doing oil changes just didn't cut it.

Of course, when it came to it, we found that we were sharing the office block with Traffic, who had taken over the warehouse for their vehicles. The room that had been intended as our equipment store was allocated to CID for some task force unit, which meant that our gear had to go down in the basement. There was another office building on site, but Special Branch had got that, all three storeys, with mirrored windows and extra security added on.

So the Southern County CSI Hub now had one large room for a general office, a small one for the Senior's office, a cubbyhole in the basement for stores and equipment and another at the far end of the building for recovered evidence. And that had to be shared with Traffic and CID, and was usually filled with their junk.

This is what the police call efficiency. Don't get me started.

There had been a bus stop right outside the office when we were based at Central Police Station. Now it was a ten minute walk through the industrial estate, which was enough to reactivate some of the aches and pains from the previous day. I finally arrived at the office, damp and hurting, to be greeted by 'What the heck are you doing here?'

Charlie Flynn. It would be. The rest of the shift were out and about examining crime scenes, but Charlie was working on a statement for court. He often did when the weather was bad. Rumour was that he had been writing that statement for the last five years.

"Hello, Charlie." I started to struggle out of my waterproofs. We didn't even have a proper cloakroom; I'd have to hang the wet things up in the ladies'.

"Thought you'd be off for a month," Charlie grunted.

"I'm fine."

"No you're not. After that thing yesterday, you've got to have PTSD or something. Plus all sorts of physical symptoms. Some of them might not come out for weeks." He gave me a sly wink. "Milk it, girl!"

"Like you would, you mean?" Charlie is one person I don't have to worry about offending by mistake. Hide like a rhinoceros. You'd have your work cut out to offend him on purpose.

He nodded enthusiastically. "Exactly! Play this right and you might not need to work for years!"

The door to the Senior's office opened, sparing me the need to find a suitable reply. Derek looked out, frowning.

"Alison? I thought I heard your voice. What are you doing here?"

"Well, I..."

"Never mind." He jerked his head to indicate I should come into the office, so leaving my waterproofs making a wet patch on the carpet tiles, I went over and followed him in.

Derek Guysler. A dapper little man, always neatly turned out, quite good at a crime scene but more inclined to be dealing with something administrative. A stickler for proper procedures and not, by and large, someone I got on with. It didn't look like today was going to change that.

The Senior's office had two desks between three people, so it tended to look a bit cluttered. Except for where Derek sat: he always started his day by tidying up his part of the surface. The space in front of him had several sheets of paper laid out on it, all of them squared up and an equal distance apart.

"I was supposed to spend today catching up on the Annual Performance Reviews. But that thing at the Courthouse has put a spanner in the works. We've got half the shift working on that, the other half trying to cover all the burglaries that came in last night, and of course there was a miniature crime wave. So all morning I'm getting calls from injured parties and police officers wanting to know when CSI are going to be there. And in the middle of all that, Special Branch are asking me – no, *telling me*, top priority, to find out where the heck you are! A bit difficult to answer, since you were not where you were supposed to be, which was in hospital. Furthermore you're not answering your landline and your mobile's been switched off. We were just about to assume you'd been kidnapped and were poised to hit the panic button, then here you are, wandering in like Lady Muck visiting the peasants!"

I ignored most of that to concentrate on the interesting bit. "Special Branch have taken this one?"

"Of course. Bomb attack. Judge killed. Reeks of terrorist! They're not even leaving it to the locals, there's a full team coming up from London. Some hot-shot DCI, a complete set of forensic experts, and probably a few MI5 spooks. So our home grown people are keen to get everything neat and tidy for when the big boys arrive. They had someone at the hospital first thing this morning to get your statement – the only eye-witness they've got, mind! - and there you were: gone! They even sent someone round to your home address, where you also weren't, and now they're on my back about it."

Derek seemed more bothered about the disruption to his routine than Ruth Darnley's death, or even any injury I might have had. I struggled to find something diplomatic to say, couldn't think of anything, so remained silent.

"Nothing to say for yourself, eh?"

"Sorry, I didn't mean to get blown up." It came out of my mouth without passing through my head. I realised at once that I should have stuck to my silent policy. Too late.

What Derek might have said to that I don't know, but from the look on his face it wasn't likely to be gracious. Fortunately, his phone rang at that moment. He answered it without taking his glare off me.

"Yes sir. She's here – that's right, in the CSI office. Just walked in. Yes, seems to be OK. Right away, sir."

He put the phone down forcefully. "Get yourself over to Special Branch now." He waved at the door. "On. Your. Way."

I got on my way. I picked up my uniform coat, hung my waterproofs in the ladies, and made a dash across the car park to the Special Branch hide-out.

And stood there for a minute. And another. In the inadequate shelter of a small porch, getting wet all over again as regular gusts of wind blew the rain in and swirled it around. But I still stood there, trying to ease the knot in my stomach. Telling myself that it was just another office, just another part of the police station. Nothing I couldn't handle. Sure, Special Branch. Yes, that was a bit unusual. But still, just another office.

I hated going into other offices. Different offices, full of different people. With the rooms and the desks and the doors all laid out differently. Different voices, different talk. All the little office jokes, the internal politics and the finely tuned levels of interaction that I'd managed to learn my way round in my office – all different. The fact that it was Special Branch wasn't a big thing. The fact that it was different, was.

Not like I had a choice, though. I took a deep breath, and ran my ID card through the gadget on the door. Of course, it being Special Branch, it wouldn't accept my I.D. card for entry, so I had to lean on the buzzer and wait for an answer to get in. Which took several further minutes of standing in the gusting rain until someone answered it and reluctantly released the lock.

It was just another office, despite being Special Branch. Desks, computers, paperwork on desks, paperwork stuck on noticeboards, more paperwork coming out of printers. And a few coppers - plain clothes, of course - wandering round, shifting paperwork from one pile to another.

I was ushered into a side office, offered a cup of coffee, logged in to a computer and told to write out a full statement.

"I think I told most of it to someone last night."

"Yes, we've got that, but we'd like to get it in your own words please, Alison." The young woman who'd taken charge of me seemed pleasant enough, but distracted, she obviously had more important things to do. "Just whatever you can remember. Come back to the main office when you're done and let me know. I think the DI wants a word with you."

She rushed off, and left me wondering why I couldn't just have done this in my own office. Perhaps they had special software which would detect if I was lying while I typed.

I settled down to it. The promised coffee never appeared; the headache was getting worse. I struggled to focus. What had been the exact sequence of events? I couldn't remember the address of the courthouse. I couldn't even remember the date.

What I did remember was the incredible noise of the explosion. When I thought about it, it still echoed in my ears and jarred through my body. I could remember the flames, their vivid colours. Their heat on my skin. Ruth Darnley's body embedded in her car windscreen.

I closed my eyes, took deep breaths. Drew up a list in my mind. Starting with the basics, and got those down on the screen first.

'My name is Alison Kepple. I am a Crime Scene Investigator.

On (date) at approximately 1400 hours, I exited the courthouse (full address) by the side entrance into the temporary car park on (name of street). I did so in company with Judge Ruth Darnley, who had been presiding over the court case in which I had been called as a witness. We had a brief conversation.'

I paused. How much of that conversation was relevant? I wasn't sure I could remember every word. The Judge had congratulated me on the quality of my evidence and had intimated that we should meet up sometime. Nothing of significance there.

'We had a brief conversation about the case.'

That should be sufficient, I decided.

'We walked towards our vehicles, which were parked fairly close together in the North-West corner of the car park. At this time, Judge Darnley noticed that her car was blocked in by a white transit van. The van looked to be an older model and in a poor state of repair, with significant rusting on the bodywork. She also noticed and remarked on the fact that a note appeared to have been left on the windscreen of her vehicle.

At this point we parted company, and I went to my vehicle (CSI Ford Transit Connect. Vehicle Registration Number...)'

No, that was gone as well. I'd only been driving it for the past two years... I'd obviously been more affected than I realised.

Deleting the bit about my van – if they really wanted to know, they could ask the CSI office, it was all on the allocation board – I carried on with a bare-bones summary.

'I opened the sliding side door in order to check equipment. At this point the van was in between myself and Judge Darnley, so I did not see what she was doing.'

Which seemed like stating the obvious, but that's how you had to do it with statements. Making everything crystal clear avoided having to explain yourself in court, possibly several months later when you'd forgotten the details anyway.

'There was then a very loud explosion, which rocked the van quite violently. When I moved round the van to a position from which I could see Judge Darnley's car, it was fully ablaze. The car next to it was also on fire. The white Transit was no longer visible.

I could not see Judge Darnley. However, there was a human figure on the windscreen of her car, and appearing to have been pushed some way into it. This figure was almost obscured by flames but I believed that this was probably Judge Darnley and that she was probably dead.

At this point I contacted the Control Room on my personal radio and reported the incident.'

I had to stop for a moment. Trying to remember details without thinking too much about them was exhausting, and no help to my headache. Trying to put it into the proper language for a formal statement was even more so. What had happened next? I couldn't remember, exactly. I'd taken pictures until someone had stopped me. I knew that because I remember them taking the camera off me. But what pictures I'd actually taken... I knew in general terms, but I couldn't remember any specific shots.

'I got my camera from the van and began taking a series of images of the scene. I continued to do this until help arrived. My camera was taken as evidence by attending officers.'

I couldn't remember who they were. I hoped I'd get the camera back.

'I received initial medical treatment from paramedics at the scene, before being taken to hospital by ambulance.'

And that was it. That was all there was to say. I looked at the few short paragraphs, slightly stunned. I'd written longer statements for walk-in burglaries. Was this really all that I saw? Was that all there was to say about the end of Ruth Darnley's life?

I closed my eyes, visualising the events, scene by scene, frame by frame. I pictured Ruth Darnley, standing talking to me just outside the door. Then walking across the car park. She'd seen the Transit, remarked on it. She'd said there was a note on the windscreen... I couldn't remember seeing it myself, but I was looking the other way at that point.

I'd been looking at the gate. Thinking that there was someone watching me, but I didn't see anyone. Should I add that?

I typed

'Whilst approaching my van I had the impression that there was someone watching me from the gateway, but when I looked there was no-one visible.'

I considered it. There was no trick of wording or way of expressing it which did not sound ridiculous, especially in the context of a formal statement. I deleted the sentence

I spent another ten minutes trying to think of anything else that should be included, after which I remembered that the temporary car park opened onto Rosamund Street. I amended the statement accordingly, saved it to my drive, logged out and wandered back to the main office.

I found my minder sitting at a desk well covered with the usual police paperwork and frowning at a screen, which appeared to show some grainy CCTV images.

"Anything on there?" I asked.

"Nothing useful. But I don't suppose there would be. This is from a newsagents two streets away." She looked up and did a double take when she saw who it was, before hastily turning the screen away. No way was an unauthorised person like myself allowed to see any CCTV, even totally irrelevant CCTV. "Oh. You've finished your statement?"

"Yes. It's on the shared drive."

She frowned. "No, delete that. There's a dedicated drive for this operation. You'll find it on the Force LAN under 'Operation Blaze'. The access code is 'Opblaze#1' - capital first letter, no spaces."

My turn for a double take. "Operation Blaze? That's insensitive."

"Operational names are computer generated," she said defensively. "Chosen at random from an approved list. It's nothing to do with me!" she added, her frown intensifying towards a glare.

Another person I'd managed to offend with a random remark. "I wasn't suggesting otherwise," I said, trying to sound placatory but probably coming off as prickly.

"Just save it under 'statements' then print off a copy. Send it to that printer over there. Hurry it up, the DI is waiting to interview you."

"Right." No point in asking for that coffee, then.

I went back, logged in, found the Operation Blaze drive and the Statements folder, copied my statement across and sent it to the printer. I hesitated before deleting the original copy, not liking the idea of not having access to my own statement, but the instructions hadn't let much room for manoeuvre, so I reluctantly complied, and headed back to the main office, collected the hard copy off the printer, signed it and dumped it on my minder's desk. She was still watching CCTV footage of a street where nothing ever happened, and barely glanced up. I found an unoccupied chair and sat down to wait.

The DI who had been so keen to interview me had apparently found something more interesting to do. Minutes ticked by. My headache wasn't getting better, and there was still no sign of any coffee. I was probably suffering caffeine withdrawal.

On the other side of the room was a little nook. Partially hidden behind a row of filing cabinets, but I could see a sink and a scattering of mugs. It looked promising. I stood up and casually wandered in that direction.

Nobody took any notice. They were all far too busy. I'd always imagined that Special Branch offices would be all smooth efficiency, but that wasn't the impression I was getting here. More borderline panic, if anything.

I reached the nook, and peered in. Sure enough, there was a kettle, and cups. And even a coffee filter machine, unfortunately empty, but there was a jar of instant and a small fridge with – on investigation – some milk. It was on a shelf labelled 'Office Team Only' but I decided I could legitimately call myself a temporary member of the Office Team. I had used the printer, after all.

The big problem was finding something to drink out of. It appeared that everyone was too busy to do the washing up, and the sink was well stacked with dirty plates and cups. However, up on a shelf I found a clean mug. Quite a nice one, a bit pink for my taste but with lots of little red hearts, very lovey dovey. I took it down and scrubbed it out with hot water and a bit of washing up liquid I found under the sink. Rinsed it out several times, then made myself a drink and sipped it slowly as I walked back to my borrowed chair.

The instant coffee was a disappointment – one of the cheaper brands, and it tasted like it – but at least it wasn't decaf, and my head was clearing already.

The frantic activity hadn't eased up. Looking round, I could see at least three people fast forwarding through CCTV tapes, several others making phone calls, some searching through paperwork or scrolling down computer screens. I supposed they could be excused a bit of stress, considering that they'd just had a terrorist incident dropped in their laps. And – I recalled what Derek had said – they had the A team coming up from London to take over. Even more stressful, and they'd be frantic to show that they were on the ball when the big boys and girls rolled in.

"CSI Kepple? The DI will see you now." My minder called across from her desk. "Interview room 1 – down the corridor, first on the right. Take your statement with you." She waved it at me, eyes already back on her screen.

I took the statement and my half-drunk mug of coffee and went dutifully on my way.

The door to Interview Room 1 was open, so I knocked and stepped in. It had the standard layout. Table, four chairs and recording equipment. Full video, it looked like, with multiple cameras – nothing but the best, it seemed.

Two people sitting behind the desk – a bulky dark-featured man and a hard faced blonde woman. Bottle blonde, her roots were showing. They were sitting behind a pile of papers and deep in discussion when I entered and announced myself.

"CSI Kepple. You wanted to see me?"

They looked up. The man's eyes fell on my borrowed mug and he frowned.

"CSI Kepple," he said. "I hope you've been made comfortable." There was a sharp edge to his voice, but perhaps he spoke like that all the time. "Enjoying your coffee?"

"Not much," I said honestly. "But I was gasping."

"Sorry if it's not up to your preferred standard, but we are a little busy at present."

There was definitely an edge. Had I upset him already? How? I'd said barely a dozen words to him yet – was I about to set a record?

"That being so," he continued, "perhaps you could find time to wash my mug up when you've finished?"

His mug? Oh. Crap.

"Your statement?" he continued, before I could come up with an explanation.

I handed it over. He flicked a hand at one of the chairs and I sat down as he and the woman read through it.

It didn't take them long.

"Is this it?" he asked.

"Yes. There wasn't much to say."

"Very well." He nodded to the woman and she pressed a button on recording equipment. "Operation Blaze Interviews," he continued. "The time is 10:05, the date is 14th November 2018. Present are myself, Detective Inspector Martin Halse, Special Branch."

The woman chipped in. "Detective Sergeant Marie Johnstone, Special Branch."

They looked expectantly at me.

"Um – CSI Alison Kepple."

Halse proceeded apace. "CSI Kepple, according to your witness statement you spoke with Judge Darnley as you were leaving the building. What did you talk about?"

"We discussed the case that I had just given evidence in. And which the Judge had presided over."

"Can you be more specific?"

"She congratulated me on the quality of my evidence." I hadn't wanted to go there, it sounded like I was bigging myself up. But

Halse and Johnstone were still looking at me expectantly. "She said it was 'clear'. And 'factual'."

"What else?"

"That was it, really. She – she called me Alison and asked me to call her Ruth, outside of court."

Inwardly, I cringed. I really had no need to say that. Now it really sounded as if I was boasting.

"Who initiated the conversation?" asked Johnstone. She had an intonation that suited her appearance, hard and flat. Not actively hostile, but it felt like it was about to slip over the line.

Or was I just imagining it? "She did. She called to me as I was walking out of the door."

"How did she seem?" Halse again. "Her manner?"

"Friendly," I said, off the top of my head. I thought of the moment. Her eyes were brown and they had crinkles round the edges as she looked at me. She was smiling. Suddenly I found myself choking up. "Excuse me. Sorry. Yes, she was friendly. Cheerful."

"Not tense? Did she appear worried? Apprehensive?" Johnstone again. She sounded like she wouldn't believe me whatever I said.

"No. Nothing like that. She was annoyed when she saw that she'd been blocked in."

"That was by a Transit van?" Halse. They were tag-teaming smoothly, had obviously done this before.

"That's right. The one that exploded."

It continued like that for several minutes. They took me through the events in fine detail, questioned even finer details, went back over things, probed for anything I'd forgotten. Or hidden.

Finally, they began to wrap it up. "Are you sure that there's nothing else you remember?" asked the DI. "Any detail, no matter how small?"

The vague feeling of being watched – was that a detail? I'd already dismissed it once, but perhaps it might mean something to the DI.

"Well," I began, then DS Johnstone's mobile, sitting on the table next to her, buzzed. She checked it, and nodded to Halse. "They're here."

"Right then. CSI Kepple – I don't think there'll be anything else. We'll contact you if there is. Interview concluded at ... 10:40."

He was already standing up as he spoke and was out of the door a moment later. Johnstone switched off the machine and gathered up the paperwork before following him at a rush.

I sneaked a look out of the door. A large group of people were being ushered into a room I hadn't visited. I waited a few minutes to allow the corridor to clear, before heading for the exit and making my escape.

Once outside, I took a few moments to stop and catch up with myself. And to run through my checks.

Phone. Keys. Wallet. Change. I'd left my painkillers and water in my waterproofs, which had been a mistake. If I hadn't, I might not have needed to pinch – well, borrow - DI Halse's pink heart mug.

At that point I remembered that I'd left the mug in the interview room, half full of cold coffee.

Chapter 3

Personal Checklist (Priority items): keys, wallet, phone

If it had been any other office I could have just gone back. But it had been hard enough to get in when they wanted me there. I couldn't imagine they'd let me back just to wash up a mug.

I took a deep breath, forced myself to focus on basics. Keys, phone and wallet were where they should be. That much was all right.

"You're OK, Alison," I whispered to myself. I had probably just ensured that DI Halse would always think of me as a mug-thief, but what was new? I've always been good at first impressions.

Back in the office, nothing had changed. Charlie was still working on his statement – though it looked more like playing solitaire on his PC. And Derek was still in his office and still pissed with me. He came bustling out before I had even had chance to sit down.

"Right then, all finished with Special Branch?"

"Yes."

"In that case, get off home."

"I thought I'd just..."

"Never mind 'just'. Go home, rest, whatever. If you won't go into hospital, at least see your GP and get yourself checked out properly. You're officially off sick, and you don't come back to the office for at least a couple of days. After that, we'll see. There is counselling available, and I'd advise you to make use of it. In fact it might even be mandatory, I'll look into that. But for now, get yourself off."

He hesitated, then stepped closer and put a hand out towards my arm. I stepped back quickly before he could reach.

"Don't touch me!" I said. I'm not usually so abrupt, but he'd taken me by surprise.

"Oh. Sorry." He dropped his hand, looking annoyed and embarrassed. "I didn't mean... look, Alison, all I wanted to say was that you've had a terrible experience. Take that seriously. Look after yourself. Right?"

He disappeared back into his office, leaving me with a confusing array of emotions. Angry. Scared.

And aware that I'd just managed, yet again, to upset someone who was only trying to be kind to me.

"Wow." Charlie had looked up from his 'statement'. "First time I've ever seen Derek getting all warm and fuzzy. That was frightening. I may need to take a day off myself."

Surprisingly, it was the right thing to say at that moment. I stifled a laugh, just in case Derek heard it, and it came out as a snort. "Oh sod it," I answered. "I'm going anyway."

The only problem was, where?

Back outside the rain had thankfully eased off, leaving gloomy clouds wandering listlessly across the sky, still blocking any sunshine there might be on the other side. I put on my waterproofs anyway – it wasn't weather to trust – and got my moped out before I considered that question.

Back home, was the obvious answer. Or I could go and visit my parents, but that was an hour away, and I didn't fancy that.

Putting off the decision, I pulled out my phone and checked messages again. There were a lot I should answer, at least to reassure people that I was OK, so that was probably what I should do. Go home and spend the rest of the day texting.

Exciting prospect.

One name on the list caught my attention. Not one of my colleagues, not family, and not a lot of other people had my number. Sam.

A message of three emoticons. A shocked face, a sad face and a telephone. Which I translated as "Wow! Sorry to hear about what happened. Give me a call".

And how had he heard, I wondered. My name hadn't been in the news, Sam wasn't police. He shouldn't know I was involved.

But Sam had a way of knowing about things, and about people. And he was one of the very few people in the world who I had not managed to offend, at least not yet. Not for lack of trying, I was as socially maladroit with him as with the rest of the world, but he simply refused to take umbrage.

Being with Sam was like stepping into a pool of calm, and he was absolutely the right person to talk to just now. Besides, I wanted to find out what he knew and how.

I called him. He answered on the second ring. "Alison – what a truly crap thing to get caught up
in!"

"Yes. It was. How did you know?"

"I'll tell you over lunch. The Nook in twenty minutes – that OK?"

"Er – yes, OK."

"Great. See you then."

He hung up. Only then did I realise that I'd just agreed to a lunch date and I was wearing my uniform and soggy waterproofs.

No time to go home and change. And in any case, I knew it wouldn't matter at all with Sam.

The Nook is a hidden gem. It doesn't even have a permanent sign outside, just a board that leans up against the wall. A chalked arrow leads you down a side alley. I'd worked in this town for years without knowing about it – though that's something in its favour, since most of the places I do know have been crime scenes. It was Sam who had introduced me to it, and he'd learned of it through his Dad, who had been a local reporter and who knew not only the Nook, but all the other nooks in town. Every nook, every cranny, and the spaces in between.

The alley emerges into a beautiful little walled garden. Red brick walls under a luxuriant growth of ivy. Small, well-tended flower beds, a short stretch of lawn, a pond with its own waterfall, a couple of apple trees. There are only about half a dozen tables, and a few more in the adjoining conservatory, but they aren't crowded together, and as soon as you step out of the alley you can feel the tranquillity. All the more remarkable for being so near to the busyness of the town centre, and just a few streets away from the massive building project at Delford Mills.

It wasn't at its best this time of year – the colours were muted, the perfume of flowers replaced with a musty (but not unpleasant) whiff of damp earth and composting leaves. I took a moment to stand and look and smell and listen, and let the balm of the place touch me.

It was, however, a little too cold and still too damp to be sitting outside today, so I went into the conservatory and was glad to see that my preferred table was free. It usually is, being tucked away round a corner and therefore less noticeable – which is why it's my preferred table. It's a deal breaker, to be honest. If that table is taken, I'll leave. Since I was meeting Sam and therefore didn't have that option, it was a great relief to sit in my normal seat.

I nodded politely to the elderly couple sitting near the heater, was ignored by the student-looking girl with her laptop open, and ordered a coffee – I was desperate to get rid of the taste left by Special Branch's cheap instant. Before it arrived, Sam slipped into the chair opposite.

"Hi," he said, running a hand through his already tousled blond hair. A couple of shades darker than my own, and always just a fraction short of untidy. He smiled.

Sam has the best smile I've ever seen. He's not the most handsome man in the world, features too irregular for that, but when he smiles he dazzles.

"Hi yourself." I answered. "So just how did you know? Spying on me?"

Which isn't a great way to start a conversation, without even an attempt at small talk or a glance at the menu. However, it is the way I usually start, and I usually follow by cringing inside at my own rudeness. Often confirmed by a look of shock or annoyance from the other person.

Sam just shrugged. "Didn't take much spying. The story's all over the news – including a clip from someone's mobile showing you being helped into an ambulance."

"What? I'm on the news?"

"Relax. You're name isn't mentioned and your face isn't shown. Just a glimpse of a blonde pigtail. And they do say that a CSI suffered 'minor injuries'. It didn't take much detective work to put those things together."

My coffee arrived, and we took the opportunity to order some lunch. Mixed grill for Sam, thick vegetable soup with crusty rolls for me, which is what I always have. They do a very good range of soups at The Nook, someday I shall have to try one of the others.

I sat back and sipped coffee.

"Did you know Judge Darnley?" asked Sam.

"Not really. I'd been in court with her a few times. But I think – I think I might have got to know her..."

I heard her words again. *'I hope we can talk again Alison. With more time.'*

But she hadn't had any time left.

I didn't notice when I started crying, but my face had gone wet and I was dripping over the table. Sam silently handed me a tissue. Then he put his hand on mine and gave it a gentle squeeze. I gasped and pulled my hand away so suddenly that the table rocked and coffee slopped into my saucer.

"Oh! Heck – Alison, I'm sorry. I wasn't thinking." Sam was holding his hand back as if it had been burned. I could feel every eye in the Nook staring at me. Everyone wondering "What is that silly girl doing?"

Too much. Ruth Darnley. The horrendous noise of the bomb echoing through me. Sam's hand on mine. Too much. I had to get out...

I was pushing my chair back, preparing to stand up, run away. But then the waitress arrived with our food. Giving me a curious look as she put my bowl of soup in front of me. "Everything all right?" she asked, and I faced the horrible embarrassment of leaving the food on the table, untouched and unpaid for, if I ran out just then.

"Yes, yes, fine thank you," I muttered, sitting down again. "I just – spilt the coffee, that's all."

"No problem," she said cheerfully. "I'll get a cloth."

She bustled away, and we sat in silence. I risked a glance round. Nobody was looking at me.

When she'd come back and wiped up the spill, and offered a refill which I declined, I was able to look at Sam again.

"I'm sorry," I whispered. "I over-reacted. I do that sometimes."

"No, not your fault." He spoke very softly as well. I was glad of it. "I forgot."

"But... I know you were just being comforting. Only, I find it difficult."

"Of course. I understand. It's OK."

"I embarrassed you."

Surprisingly, he laughed at that. A gentle chuckle. "Oh, I've embarrassed myself a lot worse than that! I'll tell you the stories sometime. That was nothing. And my fault anyway."

"If you want to leave..." I was afraid he would. Which was ridiculous, since I'd just tried to do exactly that myself.

"Of course not! I'm hungry! And I do want to hear what happened. If you want to talk about it. But let's eat first."

He started in on his mixed grill. Making careful slices through sausage and bacon. Not rattling or banging his cutlery.

I could still feel his touch on my hand, but I made a conscious decision to ignore it, and after a moment I picked up my spoon and tasted the soup. It was, as usual, very good.

We ate in silence for a while, and then I began to tell Sam all about it. In more detail than I had in the interview room.

"This person watching you," he asked after I'd finished. "Was it male or female, do you think?"

I shook my head. "No idea. I didn't even look that way, really. I was in the middle of a conversation, I was looking at – at Ruth... It was just out of the corner of my eye that I saw, well, had the impression of someone standing watching me. Then, when I glanced in that direction, they were gone."

"People often see more than they realise." Sam scratched his chin thoughtfully. "It's just a matter of accessing the memories. Tell you what, try this. Sit back, relax, close your eyes."

"I've tried already."

"Won't hurt to try again."

"OK." I swallowed the last spoonful of soup and sat back; eyes closed.

"Just think about your breathing for a moment." Sam said. "Feel the air coming in – out – in. Feel your lungs filling, emptying. Just be aware of that and nothing else for a moment or two."

I tried. Taking my mind away from the courthouse, the bomb, and everything since. Even away from Sam and the Nook. Trying to think only of my breath, coming in, going out.

It wasn't easy. There was an itch on my left leg, and the elderly couple were rattling chairs as they stood up to leave, but I persisted.

"Now think about the court. Being in court, giving evidence. Remember what you said."

There hadn't been too much for me to say. Just to confirm the details of the investigation. And to explain exactly where I'd recovered evidence from, and why I'd looked there. Nothing that wasn't in my statement or scene report, but the earnest young man wearing the wig was very keen to make sure it was all clear.

"Then you leave court. Down the corridor to the door."

The older part of the court building. A lot of oak, a lot of cracks in the plaster.

"You meet the Judge."

"She called me. I was in front of her and she called me. I was already outside on the steps. I turned round and she caught up to me."

"What was she wearing?"

"I..." I could remember her face, her eyes... but not her clothing. "Something dark."

"Coat? Jacket?"

"A coat I think."

"OK, that's good. Now, think back to when you're talking to her. Did you stand still or did you start to walk?"

"We stood on the steps at first. Then she said she had to go and we began to cross the car park."

"And you felt like someone was watching you? While you were talking or when you started to walk?"

"I... think it was before we walked. Yes, because it was when I was going to my van that I looked over at the gate. So they must have been there when we were standing on the steps and talking."

"Great! Concentrate on that moment. You're talking to Judge Darnley. You're looking at her and someone is standing in the gateway, looking at you."

"Yes..."

"Where they tall or short?"

I didn't answer, trying to capture the moment.

"Male or female? What were they wearing?"

I shook my head and opened my eyes. "Sorry, Sam. I can't come up with anything more than that."

"No problem. I expect that CCTV will have picked them up anyway. They're probably being interviewed now!"

"I doubt it. I don't think Special Branch have got that far. They were falling over themselves trying to get things sorted before the 'A' team from London arrived." I waved a finger at him. "I shouldn't have told you that. I don't know if it's public domain yet."

Sam mimed zipping his mouth shut, and winked.

"In any case, there isn't any CCTV covering the entrance, or the street outside as far as I know. When I was in the office they were looking at footage from a shop in the next street."

"You'd expect them to be thorough. I should think they've pulled in everything they can find for miles around."

I nodded agreement. "Yes. But they'd want to review the closest cameras first. So that they can show the visitors the best bits. But in any case they'll be looking for the van, not some random individual."

"I suppose you're right." He sat back in his chair. "I'll have a think, see if there's any other way to jog your memory. If you want to, that is. You might prefer to put it all behind you?"

I thought that over. "No. If I can dig something up, it might be helpful. Probably won't make any difference to the investigation – it probably isn't connected at all – but it might help me."

"OK, then. Are you going to be all right?"

"Yes. I think so. Thanks, Sam. Thank you for understanding me, and for being patient. This..." - I gestured round, to indicate the entire experience – "has been just what I needed. And so have you."

He smiled. Not his full-wattage charm-attack grin, but a gentle, caring smile that was if anything even more powerful. "Any time, Alison. Look, I've got to go – I'm doing a bit of part-time work with a photo studio. There's a big wedding out in one of the villages and they want me on hand to carry bags or something. Maybe even take a few of the easier pictures! But keep in touch. Perhaps we can have lunch again tomorrow?"

I nodded. "That sounds good."

"What are you going to do with yourself now?"

"Go home. And probably sleep." I was feeling a weariness starting to roll over me like a thick blanket, in spite of the coffee.

"Good plan. Sleep's the best cure for everything – or so my Mum always said!"

I laughed. "So did mine."

"Must be something they teach in Mum School. I'll pay up on the way out, and I'll see you tomorrow."

I shook my head. "We'll go out together and I'll pay!" We ended up splitting the bill. I went home and slept.

THE MUMS KNEW WHAT they were talking about. When I woke up my head felt clear and my various aches, largely ignored but still present, had all but vanished, as long as I didn't touch certain places.

It was still dark. Hardly surprising as it was only just past four o'clock in the morning. I'd been asleep for over fourteen hours, which was something of a personal record. And I was desperate for the loo and for coffee (in that order).

It was while I was dealing with the first of those needs that I had a thought. More than a thought. A revelation. An epiphany. Something so sudden and so clear that I almost gasped with the shock of it.

My first instinct was to call Sam and tell him. Fortunately I'd left my phone by the bed, and so had time to realise that he might not want me calling him at that time of night. But the more I thought about it, the more excited I was.

What time would Sam get up? I wondered, as I sat on my sofa, wrapped in a duvet and sipping coffee. He wasn't the sort to lay in. Well, I didn't think so. But he'd be up and about by seven, wouldn't he? Or eight at the latest.

Even seven was two and a half hours away. I couldn't wait that long.

I sent a text. He'd get it when he woke.

"Sam, just had a thought. Call me when you're up!"

That should do it.

I made some toast, and thought some more. Perhaps he'd need a bit more information than 'I've had a thought'.

I sent another text.

"I know why someone was watching us!"

Was that enough? I wiped toast crumbs off the screen and thought again. Might as well tell him the whole thing. Then when he did call he'd be up to speed and ready to discuss.

"They must have been watching to see when Ruth came out and went to the car. The bomb must have had some sort of remote detonation device, but they had to know when to set it off. So they were watching for her. Not watching me!"

After I'd sent it, I finished the toast and decided that my reasons for bothering him needed clarification.

"Does that sound reasonable?"

Then, just to emphasise the point,

"Because if it is then it might be significant for the investigation, and I need to tell Special Branch ASAP."

And finally.

"So please call me when you're able. Let me know what you think. Thanks."

I put the phone down, determined to leave it at that, but it rang almost immediately.

"Hello? Sam?"

"Morning, Alison." He sounded slightly less than half-awake. Understandable since it wasn't even five o'clock yet.

"Oh – Sorry, did I wake you?"

"Nah... No. 'S OK. Was awake anyway. Somebody kept texting me."

"Oh. Yes, sorry – I didn't think it would wake you."

He chuckled. Sleepily, but at least he wasn't annoyed. "No big deal. I can always go back to sleep. How are you?"

"Good. Better, anyway. And I had this thought... you read the texts?"

"Yeah. Sounds very possible. You should probably tell someone. But wait until I see you again, I've had another idea about how to jog your memory."

"OK, that sounds good. Lunch at the Nook?"

Another chuckle. "Well, might as well be breakfast now, don't you think? How about eight-ish? I think they open about then."

"Right. Fine. See you at eight then."

"I'm turning my phone off now and going back to sleep! Bye for now."

"Bye, Sam," I said, but he'd already dropped out.

I spent the next half hour going over events, obsessively trying to pull out more details, before resolutely putting it out of my head. I'd give Sam's idea a chance, but till then there was no point in wearing my brain out.

Instead, I switched on the TV and watched some news. Judge Darnley's murder was still headline. The Home Secretary had made a statement last night – nothing remarkable, just making the proper noises about 'Barbaric act' and promising 'Full resources deployed to bring the killer to justice'.

More interesting was a brief clip of a statement from a DCI Brodun. Not for what he said, which was a standard request for anyone with information to come forward, and an assurance that 'there is no indication of any danger to the general public' with a promise that 'several lines of enquiry' were being pursued. What was interesting was that he was apparently in charge of the investigation. Not one of our local coppers, so this was probably the Big Man up from London.

I recalled the crowd in the corridor yesterday. Brodun had presumably been part of it, though I couldn't remember seeing him.

That reminded me of D.I. Halse, and his pink mug. If I did go back to Special Branch with this extra information, it would probably be better to avoid him. Perhaps I should speak to the DS – Johnstone, was it? Except that she hadn't seemed very friendly, either. I wish I'd got the name of the other woman I'd met there. But come to think of it, I'd upset her as well.

Life would be so much easier if I could stop doing that.

Chapter 4

Personal Interests Check list: Photography, Science Fiction, Walking, Classic Rock.

Predictably, Sam had a full English breakfast. Like the mixed grill, only with fried bread. If he has a fault, it's his appetite, and if he has another, it's that he never seems to put on an ounce of weight. The first is minor, the second is almost unforgivable.

They didn't have soup on yet, so I had scrambled eggs on toast. A safe option. Which, counting the toast I'd had at 4 a.m. was my second breakfast, but so what? It works for Hobbits.

"How was the wedding thing?" I asked.

"Good!" Sam beamed enthusiastically, dribbling a bit of egg yolk down his chin as he did so. He dabbed it off with a napkin as he continued. "Very formal sort of event, usual set piece shots – bride and groom, bridesmaids, groom's family, bride's family and so on – and of course Archie – the photographer – did all those – but he gave me one of his cameras and gave me carte blanche to wander round and take informal shots of whatever caught my eye. We went over them afterwards; he pointed out some errors but was generally very encouraging and even said he'd use some of my pictures in the final album!"

"That's great! What camera did you use?"

"The one he loaned me was a old Canon 450d – he's a bit of a Canon enthusiast..."

We talked cameras all through breakfast.

It was cameras that got us together. We'd met at a wedding – June Henshaw, June Seaton now, one of the coppers that I know and get on with better than most. I normally avoid social occasions, but I was surprised and rather touched to get an invitation, so I screwed up my courage and went along. And, as normal, found myself hanging around, sipping drinks and trying to make painful small talk without offending anybody. Actually, trying to avoid talking as much as possible, whilst wondering when was the earliest I could leave without causing offence.

Then Sam came over and started a conversation – something like "I hear you're a CSI. You must know a bit about cameras, and I've been wondering..."

Yes, I know a bit about cameras. We talked cameras all evening. Then he called me a few times to ask technical questions, and in conversation we found other shared likes. Science Fiction. ("Seriously? You've read *all* the Dune novels?"). Walking. Classic rock...

We were onto our second coffee when we got the camera talk out of the way and were able to focus (see what I did there?!) on the main point of our meeting.

"It's a good theory," he agreed. "They had to have some way of knowing when to set it off – assuming that the Judge was the specific target, and it wasn't just a random act aimed at anyone who was there."

"If you're going to do something like that you'd do it in a public place. Maximise the body count.

That's what terrorists aim for, isn't it?"

"Good point," Sam agreed. "I don't think there's any real doubt that Judge Darnley was the target."

"The only thing that's bothering me about this as a theory is that that the bomber would have had to have stayed in the vicinity until the device exploded. You'd have thought they'd prefer to be as far away as possible."

"Yes, but think about what happens in such an event. A bomb goes off – or a fire breaks out, a serious traffic accident, anything like that – and you get panic, confusion, crowds of people. Some run away, some try and see what's happening. Emergency services turn up and that brings more crowds, more people milling around. Very easy for anyone to lose themselves in the crowd."

"They might be spotted, though. I mean – I did spot them. Perhaps. Almost. And there could have been CCTV."

"If they'd done their reconnaissance they'd know what the CCTV coverage was. And they'd probably have a change of coat, a hat perhaps, anything they could slip on to alter their appearance. Even easier if there was a team of them. One to plant the bomb, one to watch the scene, another ready to detonate it on command. No obvious connections between them."

"So it's plausible." I shook my head in frustration. "If only I could remember more details, I might have something to take to Special Branch."

"Ah, well, I've had an idea about that." Sam looked pleased with himself. "Want to try something?"

"OK..." I said, warily. "What, exactly?"

"Well, first off, sit back, close your eyes, get comfortable and relax."

"We did that yesterday."

"I know, but try it again, anyway."

I dutifully sat back and closed my eyes. He took me through the same preparation as before, talking me through the events leading up to the explosion.

"So now you and Ruth Darnley are standing just outside the door, talking. Someone is watching you from the gate. Concentrate on them... now open your eyes!"

I opened them. He was holding up a sheet of brown card.

"What's that?" I asked.

"Colour prompt. Does 'brown' link to anything in your memory of that moment?"

"No." I gave him a suspicious look. "Is this a real interview technique?"

"Might be," he said breezily. "I'm sure I'm not the first to have thought of it. Now concentrate. Go back to that moment... how about this one?" He showed a light blue card.

"No."

"This?" Dark blue.

"No... hang on!" I closed my eyes again. Not trying to dredge up specific memories, just aiming to be there, in that moment. "Show that again..."

"You've got something?"

"Her coat. The Judge's coat. It was dark blue."

Sam grinned. "Yes! See – that triggered a memory. Yesterday you only remembered it was something dark."

I nodded my head, conceding the point. "Let's try the rest of them, then."

Sam started flipping through the colours. Red – nothing. Brown – nothing. Orange – flames. Fire and heat... I put that aside, and Sam continued. Green, purple, yellow...

"Hold on – go back a bit. No, one more. That's it."

Sam was holding up the green card. In my mind, a figure stood in the gateway, shadowy, only glimpsed, but wearing green.

"It was darker than that," I said.

"I couldn't get any other colours," he said apologetically.

"Don't worry about it. That's enough. They were wearing something green. Something like a coat or a jacket. But definitely green."

Sam shuffled his coloured cards. "I wonder if I can patent this idea?"

AFTER BREAKFAST, I went back to Special Branch - avoiding the CSI office in case I ran into Derek again - and called from the car park.

"Hello? This is CSI Alison Kepple. I was in your office yesterday to make a statement about the bomb. I've remembered something else since. Can I talk to DI Halse."

"I'm afraid DI Halse is out of the office just now." A man, not a voice I recognised.

"DS Johnstone then?"

"She's not available. Hold on a minute..." The phone went on hold for a few moments, then another voice came on. The woman who had met me yesterday. "CSI Kepple? This is DC Dothridge. I understand you've got something else to tell us?"

"Yes. I've remembered something else. It might be important."

"OK." She didn't sound very excited about it. "Come over to the office, then."

Going into Special Branch was a little less nerve racking than before. After all, it was no longer completely new territory. On the other hand, my previous visit hadn't exactly covered me with glory. I was actually quite relieved not to be seeing DI Halse, and so avoiding any mention of the mug.

Dothridge let me in and ushered me into the same room that I'd used to write up my statement previously. She was looking just as harassed as before, and possibly even more tired.

"I wanted to get this information to DI Halse or DS Johnstone," I began, but she cut me off.

"They're very busy. Tell me, I pass it on if it's important," she said, without either enthusiasm or conviction. "In any case, I doubt if the DI would want to see you personally."

"Oh, he's not still upset about me using his mug?"

Dothridge glared at me. "He is directly assisting DCI Brodun, and the investigation has reached a critical phase. We'll be making arrests shortly, so he does have other things to attend to. Now, what's this information?"

It didn't take long to tell her that I'd seen someone wearing green watching us from the gate as I was talking to the Judge. She was not much impressed.

"Is that it? You saw someone?"

"Yes. But I think it could be important because they would have been waiting to see when the Judge went to her car so that they knew when to set the bomb off. So it is possible, likely even, that the person I saw was the bomber, or was in touch with the bomber and let them know when to

detonate it."

"No, it wasn't," Dothridge said bluntly.

I stared at her. "You can't know that for sure. Shouldn't you at least consider it?"

"No. It's a waste of time. We've had forensics back and we know exactly how the bomb was set

off."

I gave her a sceptical look. "Really? But..."

"The initiator was just a box of ordinary matches tied to a cheap mobile phone that had been set to vibrate. We believe that the mobile's number was on the sheet of paper that Darnley found on her car." Dothridge sighed. "OK, we wouldn't have known about that if it wasn't for you, so thanks for that at least." She forced a smile: it looked painful. "When Darnley dialled the number, the vibration of the phone set off the matches. It was in the cargo area of the van, which had been sealed up, air-tight, and half-filled with propane gas. Maybe a few other things as well, but mostly it was a propane bomb. And the Judge set it off herself. So the point is, the bomber didn't have to wait around to set it off. They were long gone by the time that happened."

I felt suddenly deflated. I'd been trying so hard to remember the details, and it turned out that they were meaningless.

"Look, just add an addendum to your statement, and I'll let the DS know about it. She can decide if the DI needs to know. But honestly, I doubt if it's important. Just a random passer-by. See yourself out, please, I've really got to go."

She fired up the PC and put in the access code to get me into the dedicated drive for Operation Blaze – having apparently forgotten that she'd already told me what it was. For a Special Branch officer, DC Dothridge seemed very relaxed about giving away information. I wondered if she'd been in the department long – and how much longer she might last.

Left to myself it only a took a few minutes to attach a paragraph about the person in green. Properly speaking I should have printed off a copy and signed off on the addition. But it didn't seem like it was going to be important enough to bother with. They could always get back to me if they wanted.

I closed the document, but hesitated before I shut the PC down again. My eye was drawn to the folder marked 'CCTV'.

OK, so it was just a random passer-by I'd seen glancing in at the gate.

No, not glancing in. I was pretty sure they'd stood there for a moment, staring in. Staring at us.

But in any case, nothing to do with the bomb.

All the same, I couldn't quite let it go. I still wanted to get confirmation, to be sure about them...to know who it was.

It came to me, quite suddenly, that that was the reason why I was obsessing over this person. Apart from my normal obsessiveness, that was. There was the feeling that I knew this person, or that I should know them.

Of course, it was just me being me. I get these things in my head, sometimes, and I can't get any peace until I've chased it down, found out exactly what or who it was. I'd once spent the best part of a week combing through music files to track down one particular little guitar riff that I was sure I'd heard and that I knew, but it was out of context...

If I could just get a clear picture of this person in the green coat, enough so that I could confirm that I either knew them or didn't, then I could put it out of my head. And of course, there was no CCTV of the gate itself, but they might have been picked up walking towards or away from Rosamund Street.

I opened up the folder, and was daunted by the huge number of files. And the size of them. Hours and hours and hours of footage. From traffic cameras and shops and houses and flats...

I found the closest one, which covered the traffic on the road outside the main court entrance, and after a bit of searching came to the footage taken just before the explosion.

There was only a short stretch of pavement visible, and it wasn't very busy. I fast forwarded through an hour, without seeing anyone wearing green.

It was a pointless exercise, I told myself, and came out of the CCTV folder. And dangerous, in that I had no business snooping around in these files. If discovered, I would be in deep trouble. People had been dismissed for less.

On the other hand, this was the best chance I'd have. Theoretically, I could access the drive from anywhere on the Force Local Area Network, since I had the codes. But if I did it would be logged. So if I was going to check anything else, it would have to be now.

I looked at the other folders. A lot of scene photographs, of course. Mine would be in there, and I was tempted to take a look. Not that it would show me anything relevant, but I had a professional interest in checking the standard of my own work.

On the other hand, considering what I'd been taking pictures of... in my mind I saw the figure of a person surrounded by fire. No, I didn't want to go there again.

More promising was the selection of mobile phone pictures and videos. Obviously none from before the bomb went off, but it was amazing how soon afterwards people had begun to gather round, mobiles out to record the event.

I opened one of the files. Disappointing. Blurry images of smoke billowing up from the car park. So much smoke... I didn't remember that much smoke. But then, most of it was going up and the breeze was taking it away from where I had been. Otherwise I'd probably still be in hospital with serious lung damage.

Another file showed much the same, from a different angle. The wall prevented any sight of the actual fire, though some flames were flickering above it. Access to the car park had already been blocked off, presumably by police who had been in court and were on scene within moments of my call.

I switched the sound on. The person with the phone was providing his own commentary, but since he didn't know anything it wasn't much help. He was basically repeating the obvious - "There's a fire, something blew up, someone's hurt..."

Another file, another view. Same scene from further back and a bit higher up – on top of a car, I thought. The commentary sounded like a young man with a couple of mates interjecting. They seemed more excited than alarmed. Like it was the most fun they'd had all day. There was a lot of speculation about how many coppers had been killed. They'd already concluded that it was a terrorist bomb, and that it must have been Muslims. They didn't need evidence, prejudice filled in all the blanks.

I turned the sound off again, but kept watching the video. It was the best view I'd seen yet. A considerable crowd had gathered by this point, and I was trying to see if there were any green coats visible. There might have been a few, but the picture was too shaky to get a good look at any of them.

police cars started to arrive, Officers tumbling out to extend the cordon out from the gate, pushing the crowd back up and down the street. A panicking girl, waving her hands wildly at the smoke, tried to push her way in and was led away. Probably someone who had a relative in court.

Fire engines turned up, their crews dragging out hoses and other equipment.

It had been a fireman who had led me away from the scene, I remembered. I'd still been taking pictures.

I ran the clip forward, wondering if it would show me coming out. Not sure that I wanted to see it if it did. But the police were still clearing people back, and the person taking the video was ordered off the car and sent on his way. There was a glimpse of an ambulance arriving – and a TV crew! then it finished.

I sat back and was surprised to find that I was shaking. My eyes were starting to tear up again.

"Get a grip!" I snarled at myself. And shut the PC down. Enough of that.

I got up to leave but as I opened the door, the corridor suddenly filled up with people coming out of a room further up. They were all pulling on coats and obviously heading somewhere, looking tense and excited.

What had Dothridge said? "We'll be making arrests shortly." It didn't take a detective to put the pieces together: the briefing had just finished and everyone was heading out on a raid. Or raids, there looked to be enough officers to cover several locations, and you'd have to factor in uniformed police as well. Armed Response would certainly be involved. Plus which the Army would be on hand – Bomb Disposal, just in case there were any other devices found.

The main rush passed, but then DCI Brodun and DI Halse came past. They were deep in conversation, but Halse saw me in the doorway and stopped.

"What are you doing here, Kepple?"

"I came to..."

"Never mind!" He cut me off with wave of his hand. "Your part's finished, you stay out of it now, understand?"

He carried on along the corridor without waiting for a reply. Brodun gave me a curious glance, and I heard him asking "Is that the CSI who..."

Then they were gone, the corridor was empty.

So they were off to make arrests. The investigation side of things was all but over, and as he said, my part was finished. It didn't matter about the person in green who'd been watching us. They weren't relevant.

Perhaps I should have felt relieved. I didn't.

I left the station, and headed back to the Court.

FROM THE FRONT IT LOOKED no different – an imposing modern glass and concrete edifice apparently pasted onto a red-brick Victorian monument to Justice. It was a building with a split personality.

I went past the entrance, round to the side. Rosamund Street. Allegedly named after the first female Mayor of the town, but someone had spelt it wrong.

The cordon was long gone, the rear gates closed. I wandered down to them, and stood there for a moment.

The watcher would have been about... here? Just outside the gateway, on the left as I'd been looking at it.

I looked around. On the court side of the road the blank wall continued on until it changed to a slightly different coloured blank wall. There was some sort of industrial premises there, I thought.

On the other side of the road a row of terraced houses gave way to a newsagents, a greasy-spoon cafe, a charity shop, then a succession of small businesses. "Adi's Auto Repairs". "Extra-Value Double Glazing". "Treble-A Taxis", and so on, right down to the end of the street.

I considered the greasy-spoon. "The New Dreadnought". It had changed hands recently – the last time I'd noticed it had been "The Chirpy Chicken". Incongruous name, I'd always thought. The prospect of being served up deep-fried and extra-crispy (there were no other options) wasn't likely to make any chicken feel chirpy.

The name wasn't important. The location was. Anyone sitting in one of the table windows would have had a good view of the gate, and therefore of anyone who might have been loitering around in front of it. If they'd noticed.

"Simple enough," I said to myself. "Just go and ask. Can't do any harm."

But asking meant talking to people. Which was OK when I had a reason to talk to them. An official reason. I had no problem with knocking on the doors of complete strangers and expecting them to invite me in to cover their windows with fingerprint powder. That was the job, after all. Talking to them wasn't a problem when I was asking the standard questions - "What was the point of entry, what was touched, moved, taken..." and so on.

But talking to people outside of that, without the cover of being On Police Business – that was social interaction, and that was when my talent for annoying people really shone.

Was it worth it? After all, it meant nothing.

I turned round and walked back up the street.

But... I still wanted to know. It was an itch in my head. Had we been watched? Was it someone I knew?

I swore at myself, quietly. Trapped between opposing failures in my own psyche!

Taking a deep breath, I quickly checked my pockets. Keys, Wallet, Phone, and other bits and pieces. All there, list complete. Reassuring.

What was the worst that could happen? So I might offend someone. Not a big deal. I'd probably never see them again anyway. Better than offending half of Special Branch and my own Senior, which I'd already done. So it couldn't be worse, could it.

"I'm OK," I said firmly. "Alison, you're OK." Repeated, for emphasis.

I walked on down to The New Dreadnought.

Chapter 5

Eating out checklist: price, menu, quality, atmosphere – familiarity.

In keeping with the name, the interior of "The New Dreadnought" was mostly grey. I wasn't sure if that was by design, or just years of inadequate cleaning that the new owner hadn't yet caught up on.

Other than that it was pretty standard. Formica-topped tables, plastic chairs, and tomato ketchup in large plastic tomatoes. The name was supported by various black and white pictures of battleships and their crews. A faded White Ensign was draped over the back wall, and the counter (which started half-way down on the left) boasted a large model warship, between the till and a display of dispirited looking cakes.

A wizened little man was lounging behind the till, flicking through a newspaper. He seemed familiar, which might be good or bad, depending on whether or not I'd offended him in the past.

"Hello," I said. Cleared my throat and started again. "Uh, hello? Can I have a coffee, please? Americano?"

He gave me a sad look. "Sorry love. In here, coffee comes black or white, with sugar or without it. Them's your options."

"Oh. OK, then, white with sugar."

It came in a large mug. "Sugar's on the tables," he said. "In the bowls," he added, making it clear that this was an establishment with some class.

"Thanks." I remembered where I'd seen him before. "Didn't you used to have another place? Over in the old Victorian Market?"

He nodded. "Yeah. Got closed down because the building's unsafe. There were bits falling off it – someone even thought they saw a body once." his eyebrows went up. "Here, ain't you the CSI what came out to look at it?"

"Yes, that's right. But I didn't have anything to do with it closing," I added hastily. "My examination was – ah – unofficial. Favour for a friend." Sam, actually.

"Well it was always going to happen sometime." He shook his head, resigned to the cruelty of fate. "Place was deteriorating for years. They say that they're going to renovate it, but that depends on someone putting up the money. Till then, if it ever happens – I've got this."

"Not the same." I injected a little sympathy into my tone, wondered if it just sounded sarcastic.

Fortunately, he agreed with me. "No, nothing like the old place," he agreed. He leaned forward, and dropped his voice a tone. "Most of my customers here, they're – dodgy."

"Dodgy?"

"Dodgy. They come in here waiting for news from Court. Who's gone down, who's got away with it, and so on. Only most of them wouldn't go inside the court themselves. Not voluntary, like!" He grinned. "On account of they might be recognised, and they wouldn't want that! That's why there's no CCTV in here. If I put up a camera, I'd lose half my business overnight. And the place would probably get done over as well!"

"Oh. I see." Now I came to think of it, I'd heard similar stories about the café's previous incarnation. As a Sergeant had once told me - 'If you want to see what a collection of criminals looks like, go into the Chirpy Chicken while there's a big case on. But don't go in uniform or you'll empty the place in thirty seconds flat!'

"Must have been a problem after the bomb," I continued. "Didn't you have a lot of coppers in here then?"

He nodded. I remembered his name now. Ward. "I was pretty well full before that happened. Then there was this huge bang and a load of smoke and everybody rushed out. Of course, your lot turned up and started cordoning the street off, so none of my customers came back. Most still haven't. It's just my old regulars from the Victorian Market I've got in now." He gestured round at the nearly empty tables. "The detectives were in here asking questions, of course, wanting names and so on. But I couldn't help them. Nobody gives names in here – not real ones, anyhow."

"Mr Ward, isn't it?"

""Call me Sharkey. Everyone does. Me old nickname from my time in the Mob." He saw my expression. "No, not that Mob. The Royal Navy. That's what we used to call it – The Mob."

"OK. Sharkey – you don't happen to remember seeing someone in here wearing a green coat? Just before the bomb went off?"

He raised an eyebrow. "Is this part of the official investigation?"

I shook my head. "No. Not at all. Just... trying to find out if a friend of mine was here."

Sharkey snorted, letting me know how weak that sounded, then shrugged to say it didn't matter. "Can't remember anyone in particular. But I know a man who might. Hey, Ed?"

An elderly man sitting by the window looked round.

"Ed spends more time in here than I do!" Sharkey said in a stage whisper. "And spends less money!" He returned to his normal voice. "Ed - the young lady here is in inquiring about a friend of hers, in here just before that bomb went off. Wearing a green coat? Do you remember anyone like that?"

"Aye."

"You do?" In truth, I hadn't been expecting anything, and this sudden breakthrough caught me by surprise. "Well – um – do you know who it was?"

"Naw. Never seen 'em before in me life."

Of course not. Stupid question. "Right. OK – what did they look like?"

Ed said nothing, but looked sadly into his mug, and swirled it around.

"Perhaps if you offered him another cuppa?" Sharkey suggested.

"Oh. Yes, of course. Can I get you something, Ed?" First name terms already, my social skills were improving.

"Another mug of tea, since you're offering." Ed was quick to take up the offer, and also to expand on it. "And a bacon butty if you don't mind."

"No, no – of course not. Sharkey?"

"Right with you," said Sharkey with a grin. "Ed, why don't tell the young lady what you remember – I'll be there in a minute."

I took my coffee over to Ed's table, sugared it and took a sip. It wasn't great, but definitely better than in Special Branch. "This person in a green coat?" I prompted.

He shook his head. "Naw. Didn't have a green coat. They was wearing one of them waterproof thingy's. A cagal?"

"A cagoule?"

"That's it. One of them."

"A green one."

He shook his head. "Naw. Sort of muddy brown colour, it was."

I frowned, wondering if this was a wind up, and if there was still time to cancel the bacon butty. He must have seen the intention in my eye, because he added hastily "But when she took it off, she had one of those green sleeveless things on underneath."

"Green? Sleeveless – like a gilet?" Clearly, fashion wasn't Ed's area of expertise.

"Aye. That sort of thing. Never saw the point of 'em meself. Who wants a jacket with the arms ripped off? But I did wonder why she'd bothered with the cagal thing, being as it wasn't raining. Even had the hood up when she came in."

"She?" And even as I said it, I realised that yes, it was a she, it had been a she watching us from the gate, and that I'd known that all along but only just realised.

"Yeah. Young woman, 'bout your age? Short dark hair."

Young woman. Short dark hair. Wearing a brown cagoule with a green gilet underneath. This was huge progress.

"So what did she do, Ed?"

"She got a cuppa and sat down there, next table along. Took off her waterproof, and just sat there staring up the street. Had her phone out and kept looking at it, like she was checking something. I reckoned she must be waiting for someone who was in court. Get a lot of that in here."

"So I hear. How long did she stay?"

"She wasn't long. About half-an-hour, perhaps." To Ed, thirty minutes sitting in a café with a cup of tea was no time at all. "Then she gets up and goes out, went back up the street."

"Towards the court?"

"That's right."

"Before the bomb went off?"

Ed nodded vigorously. "Oh, aye! I remember that, an' no mistake! Nearly made me spill my tea, that did!"

"You couldn't have spilt it, it had been empty for an hour!" Sharkey put in, coming up to the table with a fresh cup and a bacon butty. "There you are, Ed. Has he been helpful?" he asked me.

"Yes. Very. Thanks. Oh – one more thing, Ed. Did she put her coat back on?"

Ed scratched his chin. "Don't know as I noticed. I think she might have been carrying it, though. No, wait a minute – she folded it up and put inside a pocket or something. I remember thinking it was amazing how small it folded up." He took a bite out of his sandwich and began chewing. "Thanks for this," he added.

I overlooked the damp crumbs which he'd just sprayed over the table. I was leaving anyway. "That's OK. You enjoy it."

I WALKED BACK UP ROSAMUND Street, my head buzzing with a deluge of new thoughts. While I'd been in court, the mysterious watcher, the woman, had been sitting drinking tea. As I'd walked down the corridor towards the exit, she had been walking this street, just as I was doing now, putting her feet on the same paving stones.

I stopped outside the closed gates, with the police tape still draped across them. When I was standing on the steps talking to Ruth Darnley, she had been on this exact spot. I could almost feel us touching, brushing against each other, separated only by a few days' worth of time. The synchronicity of it made my head spin.

I took a deep breath. "Get a grip!" I muttered to myself. I didn't even know if this was significant. There was no good reason to believe that this woman was anything to do with the bomb – not even a theory as to how she could be connected, now that the forensic evidence had shot down my idea.

I have a bad habit of seeing significance where it doesn't exist.

But.

But I still felt that I knew who this person was. It was there, in my head, tantalisingly close, still out of reach. If only I'd found a bit of video that showed them, if I could have just one frame of their face, then I was sure that I'd be able to put a name to them.

Of course, when I'd looked at the video files I'd been looking for someone in green. They could have put their brown cagoule back on.

I might have actually seen them on the monitor but not recognised them. If I'd known then what I knew now..!

Was there a way to have another look? Yes, but not without having to answer some difficult questions about why I'd accessed a supposedly secure Special Branch LAN drive. Potentially a criminal offence, so probably not worth the risk.

I needed to talk to Sam about it, but his phone went to voicemail. Probably doing another wedding or some other photography thing. I left a message for him to call back asap, and went home.

My mind was still on the brown cagoule when I got there. Consequently I nearly walked into someone coming out of the ground floor flat. A short woman with frizzy red hair and a dog collar. "Oh, hi!" she said, thrusting out a hand. "I've just moved in – are we neighbours?"

"Uh, yes, I'm on the top floor. Alison." I struggled to refocus my thinking on the here and now, and the first thing in my mind was "Do jeans really go with a clerical shirt?" Fortunately I managed not to say it.

"I'm Patricia. The new Curate down at St Patrick's. So Pat from St Pats!" she laughed at herself whilst withdrawing the hand which I'd not thought to take. "I always think I should say that with an Irish accent!" she added, grinning.

"Oh, yes. Right." I nodded, wondering how rude it would be to just stop talking and carry on upstairs. Probably too rude, since she was a neighbour and I'd have to see her regularly.

"I haven't really got to know anyone round here yet," Pat continued. "Do you go to St Patrick's at all?"

"Never been inside it," I admitted. Thinking as the words left my mouth that a polite lie might have been more socially acceptable.

She was unfazed by my honesty. "Oh, OK. Well, if you're at all interested, I'm running a little series of, well, not exactly meetings, more informal get-togethers. My first church project, you might say! Just making an opportunity for me to get to know people and talk over things."

"Talk about God, you mean." It came out a bit more hostile than I'd intended, but I really wanted to get back to my own train of thought.

"God, the Church, the weather, the price of chips – whatever you like really. I'm just trying to find out where people are at in their lives, what they really think about these things. Here, have a leaflet."

I glanced at the flyer she'd thrust into my hand, big black letters on the front, something about 'Do you deserve God's love?'

Great. Invitation to a cosy little guilt trip.

"I've got other things to do." Sod neighbourliness, I thought, and carried on up the stairs.

"Nice meeting you," Pat called behind me, but I ignored her.

As if the new neighbour hadn't been enough, I found a visitor waiting for me – my cat, Oliver. I say my cat, but it would be more accurate to say my occasional flat-mate, who sometimes happens to be in at the same time as me. He has his own means of access, and comes and goes as he pleases. Often the only way I know he's been in is that his food bowl has been emptied. And heaven help me if I don't top it up again as a matter of urgency!

Today, however, he was waiting for me in the hallway. As soon as I stepped through the door, he came up to me with a loud miaow and rubbed himself against my legs.

"What's got into you, Oli?" I asked. I tossed the flyer onto the nearest surface and leant down to stroke his back.

He hissed at this unwanted familiarity and stalked off, affronted.

I have no more success at getting on with cats than I do with people.

I wondered if he had been expressing a measure of sympathy for recent events. But that was probably yet another example of me reading meaning into random events. If he was glad to see me, it would be because his food bowl was empty.

A sudden yowl from the kitchen supported that theory. I sighed, and attended to my duty.

SAM DIDN'T GET BACK to me until the evening, when I was eating beans on toast and thinking that I should go shopping. Not that I've got anything against beans on toast, but it's nice to have a choice. "Have you got the TV on?" he asked before I could say anything. "Get the news, quick!"

I fumbled for the remote, and switched in on just in time to catch the tail end of an item. A reporter was standing in some nondescript suburban street, with a background of police vehicles and flashing blue lights.

"...more than twenty arrests have been confirmed from all across the country. The Home Office has issued a brief statement which says 'Today's prompt and efficient action by the police sets the standard for this country's response to any and all acts of terrorism. This is a message not just to those who perpetrated the murder of Ruth Darnley, but to any who think that they can intimidate this country by cowardly acts of violence.'"

The reporter signed off and the studio moved onto the next item. I muted the TV and picked up the phone again.

"That was quick," I said. "Though I did see them heading out on a raid today. I didn't realise that this was countrywide, though."

"It was well co-ordinated. I'm looking at it on the internet now, and they're saying that there were arrests in London, Birmingham and Manchester, as well as locally. But something interesting... Hang on, I'll email you a link, see what you make of it."

I went to my laptop, switched it on, and found Sam's link. It took me to a news site that listed some of the raid locations in detail.

"OK, I've got it, what should I be looking for."

"Notice anything about those locations? What sort of areas they are?"

"Well, one's a mosque – so is it Islamic extremists that they're targeting?" I thought of the comments made on the mobile phone video I'd seen earlier. "I know a lot of people assumed that's what it must be."

"Some of them are in Muslim areas," Sam agreed. "But not all of them. "See that local pub that got hit? The Royal Oak? Am I right in think that was a hang-out for the extreme right?"

"Yes. Well, there was a local group who met there – called themselves English Patriots or something like that. More into racist talk and a bit of graffiti than anything serious, though."

"But not a Jihadi stronghold, though."

"No, of course not... Oh, I think I see what you mean. They've gone after Muslim extremists and some hard right groups – but how would they be linked? Except... Ruth Darnley sentenced people from both sides at one time or another."

"I presumed so. But apart from that there's nothing to tie them together. There's no realistic scenario that has people from both groups working together for anything. Not even murder."

"You're right." I scanned the website again as I spoke. "This doesn't make sense. What sort of evidence are they working from?"

"They're not working from evidence at all." There was a grim note in Sam's voice. "This is political."

"How do you mean?"

"I mean that it's a very bad time for the Government to have a terrorist incident come up. They've just been making a big thing about how they're 'Winning the War on Terrorism' and talking about budget cuts to the security services. So they'll be keen to get this sorted fast. And cheaply, if possible. That means huge pressure on the police to do something quickly. Don't waste time with proper investigations, get out there and make arrests."

"Round up the usual suspects."

"Exactly. Someone has decided – probably on the basis of who the Judge has sent down in the past – that this is either Jihad-inspired Muslim terrorists or some hard-right knuckleheads. So they've drawn up a list and gone out to pull them in. In the hope, no doubt, that once they've got them banged up, someone will talk."

"But that's assuming that they've got the right people. Or even the right groups. Ruth probably upset a lot of people over the years."

"Any judge who was doing their job properly would upset people. But there's not many who would go to these sort of lengths to get revenge."

"But terrorist groups, extremists of any persuasion, they would. I suppose there's a certain logic to it."

Sam chuckled. "The logic of Government embarrassment. Anyhow, what have you been up to today? Sorry I didn't pick up your call. The boss gave me a job to do on my own, would you believe? Nothing very exciting, publicity shots of some local business premises, but the client was following me all over, telling me exactly what to shoot and how to do it. Didn't get chance to check my messages till later."

"Sounds like I had a more interesting time!" I recounted the day's events.

"So that's where Sharkey went. I knew that the old Dreadnought had closed down, but I thought he'd retired." Sam paused, then went on in a thoughtful tone. "So we're looking for a brown cagoule now? A dark-haired young woman in a brown cagoule."

"Yes. But it doesn't really help. I still don't have a name, and I can't get access to all the recovered video files. Not without a good reason, and I don't think I've got one to give."

"There is some footage we might be able to look at."

"There is?"

"TV. The cameras were on the scene pretty quickly. Perhaps while this person was still in the area."

I recalled some of the mobile phone pictures had shown the TV van arriving. "I suppose it's worth a look. There can't be much of it, though."

"More than you'd think, perhaps. The bits that go out on the news won't be the whole thing. The raw footage will be a lot longer, might show more."

"Special Branch will have that."

"They'll have copies. The TV company would keep the originals. And my Dad might have a few contacts. He knew a lot of people when he was a local sports reporter – probably still does. I'll have a word with him."

"OK. Thanks Sam. Are you around tomorrow – lunch, maybe?"

"Sorry, can't do that. The boss wants me to help out on another commercial job, but it's out of town and I'll be away all day."

"Right. No problem, see you whenever, then."

Actually, it was a problem. I was surprised to suddenly find that not seeing Sam would be a problem. It shouldn't be that much of a problem. He was just a friend, after all.

"We should be back late afternoon, though, so how about dinner?" Sam continued.

"Dinner? Yes, that sounds... OK." Great, I'd been about to say. But I didn't want to start gushing.

"Good. Well, I'll call you tomorrow then. Any preferences?"

"Preferences?"

"About where to go."

Somewhere familiar. Somewhere I knew. A very short list. "Oh. No, not really." I hoped I wasn't going to regret that.

"Then it'll be a surprise. Probably for both of us! See you then."

"See you."

I put the phone down and considered my feelings with some alarm. Just when, exactly, had Sam gone from being a friend to being... whatever. A friend plus? Being ready to risk going somewhere unknown was a big commitment. Huge. How much of a friend was he?

I quickly shelved that thought, before it started a chain of circular thinking and worrying that might take me hours to get out of. Better to just keep thinking of Sam as a friend, end of story. Anything else would be too complicated, and I had enough complicated in my life just now.

I needed something else to do quickly, so I began searching online for news footage from the explosion. I hadn't even looked at the headlines before.

"Massive Explosion in Court Car-Park!"

"Bomb Blast Wreaks Havoc in Court!"

The earliest reports were short on facts but long on emotive language.

"Judge Killed, Police Officer Injured in Terror Attack!"

I puzzled over that one for a moment, before realising that the 'Police Officer' in question would have been me. The reporter hadn't been told that I was actually a CSI. Or perhaps they just thought that 'Police Officer' looked better in a headline.

I came across the first TV report from the scene. A crowd milling round in front of police tape. I wondered how many of them were Sharkey's customers? Beyond that the street was packed with emergency vehicles. Mostly Fire Service – there was still some smoke rising above the wall. Police cars, of course, and one ambulance – with someone being helped into it.

I paused it at that point, and looked more closely. The camera had zoomed in on that bit of action – there wasn't much else to look at, to be honest – and although my face wasn't shown my ponytail was briefly visible before I was surrounded by paramedics. I understood how Sam had known it was me.

I let it play again. The picture pulled back and panned round to bring the reporter back into shot and I hit pause again. Ran it back a few frames.

Just there. On the edge of the crowd, walking off to the right as the camera panned left.

Brown cagoule.

Chapter 6

Walking Checklist:
food, water, spare clothing (if required) maps (as necessary), torch,
compass, phone, keys.

I t wasn't a great picture. For one thing, they had their hood up,
only a glimpse of white flesh showing as they turned their head
slightly. Not enough for recognition. I took a freeze-frame and tried
to zoom in, but I didn't have either the technical skills or the software
to do a proper job, and only produced a blurry, pixelated image.

I went back to the original, and played the short segment again.
And again. Looking for something that would point me to a name.
But all I could say for sure was 'brown cagoule.' With the hood up
– but several other people in the crowd had hoods up, it wasn't that
unusual.

Yet, as I watched it, I was more certain than ever that I knew
that person. I wasn't sure why. Something in their walk, perhaps?
They seemed to be in a hurry, moving as fast as they could without
breaking into a run. Which would have attracted attention. Perhaps
they'd just registered the TV camera and were keen to avoid being
caught in the picture?

I shook my head. That was a lot of speculation from a second or
so of footage.

I picked up my phone to call Sam, then put it back again. I'd see
him tomorrow. In the meantime, no point in bothering him. There
wasn't much to say, after all. And I didn't want him to get fed up with

me intruding into his life all the time. I still felt embarrassment over my stream of texts that had woken him up that morning. He'd been really good about that, but there was no point in pushing my luck.

I spent another hour searching for any other pictures or TV footage of the scene, but none of them showed the brown cagoule or anything else of interest. Eventually, I gave up, and went back to the current news.

Reporters had begun picking up on what Sam had noticed. As one of them said "This could have been the work of one group or the other, but not both." Their conclusion, like Sam's, was that this was political. Opposition politicians were already making a big thing about interfering with an active police investigation.

Nothing that helped me. Perhaps a good night's sleep would.

THE NEXT MORNING BROUGHT the best weather we'd had for a while, fine and clear, though with a sharp bite still in the wind. Good walking weather, I thought.

There was nothing new on the news, and no new ideas in my head. So a walk it was, then. I put water and sandwiches in my small backpack, ran through my walking check list.

"You OK, Alison?"

A day out in the countryside, on my own. It doesn't get better.

I rode my moped over to the North side of town, and parked it just round the corner from the bus stop. Then caught the number eleven out to Frayhampton, and began walking.

Further north at first. Following a well-marked path alongside the river up to the top of the valley. In the summer, it was often no more than a stream, tinkling demurely along the bottom of its bed. But now it was a torrent, roaring over the rocks and hammering against the tree roots that held the banks together. At some points it was washing over them and swirling round on the path.

My boots were well waterproofed. I splashed on through, enjoying the power and exuberance of the water.

As the valley became steeper and narrower, the path diverged, climbing up the side and over a low ridge. The valley beyond was even narrower, just a dip down to a lane before the path went up again, higher this time. I came out on the top and hesitated for a moment. To my left was open country and part of me was drawn to that, wanting to be up in the high hills and the moorlands. But I wasn't equipped for that sort of expedition, so I stuck to my plan, turned right and followed the Ridgeway south, back towards town.

It was a familiar path, but I checked the mapping app on my phone now and then out of habit, and to confirm my progress. I hadn't been that way since spring, and the seasons had wrought subtle changes, with the first hints of autumn starting to show in a slight shading of leaves here and there.

I lost myself in the landscape, in its slowly changing views. And in the steady rhythm of walking. Not thinking about bombs or brown cagoules. Not even thinking about Sam. There was just my boots on the path, one in front of the other, and the world shifting around me as I moved.

I passed Frayhampton again, a little cluster of grey stone buildings down in the valley, huddled around the squat tower of the church. Across a road, then up onto the highest point, buffeted by the wind that still had enough edge to cut through my clothing. Not unwelcome, though, after the stiff climb. Beyond that the path ran through woods for a while, more sheltered. Then out at the stone circle – part of the landscape for over a thousand years – and on, a level stretch along an increasingly narrow ridge with wide views opening up east and west.

I drank it in. The space, the emptiness. I had the path to myself; I was alone and at peace in the world.

The path eventually came to an end at The Bowl. The official name is Monument Hill, but nobody local uses that. It's what its name says, a deep bowl cut out of the hillside where the ridge finishes, so one side is open and you can stand there and look down on the town. There's a war memorial right on the edge, in the form of a Celtic cross, and at Easter the local churches put three wooden crosses up on the ridge above.

There's also a road that comes up the side of the ridge from a car park. In summer the place is full of families, often with organised events happening on the grass in the bottom of the bowl. Now I was the only one there.

I stood by the War Memorial, leaning on the safety fence and looking down at the town. Almost directly below was the Monument Hill suburb, an untidy sprawl of terraced and semi-detached houses clustered loosely round a school, a shopping area and two pubs. Further away, the huge building site of Delford Mills was the most prominent feature, but there was a lot more I could recognise. There was the silvery glint of the canal that circled the town. Off to the right, the football stadium. In the centre of town I could make out the Victorian Market where Sharkey used to have his place. Then further to the left, the Courts.

It was sheltered in the bowl. A good place to stop for lunch. I took out sandwiches and bottled water, and was about to take my first bite when my mobile rang.

The world always manages to intrude. I was tempted to ignore it, but then thought that it might be Sam, so I got it out and checked the screen.

Not Sam. My mother. I experienced a guilty moment - I hadn't been in touch with my parents since before the bomb, and they probably didn't even know I'd been involved. So perhaps I'd better answer it.

"Hello Mum."

"Alison!" she always sounded slightly surprised when I spoke to her, as if she'd been expecting someone else. "At last! I've been calling all day."

All day? "Sorry, I've been walking, probably didn't have a signal. How are you?"

"Oh, can't complain." She always said that. Just before she started complaining. I settled myself more comfortably to hear about her back, her knees,what someone said to her at Church last week and my sister's concerns about her youngest.

Which led inevitably to how well my sister's eldest was doing, and then what a marvellous parent she was, and how wonderfully she coped and... and I listened politely, made appropriate noises, and took deep breaths to damp down the familiar feelings. Resentment, which in the past had sparked major tantrums. Still worse, the crushed feeling that came with realising that a tantrum would get me punished, but not noticed.

No, I would not go there. I would not have the day spoiled by the things I'd put behind me.

"And what about you?" she said at last. "It's been so long since I've spoken to you." (Spoken *at* me, mother, I corrected mentally) "Anything exciting happened lately?"

"No, not really," I lied, unable to cope with a long explanation. I knew I'd have to do it sometime... but not today. Maybe when I was ready for the questions. And the blame. ("Oh, Alison, how do you get yourself into these situations?" And so on). Instead, I switched to a safe topic. "How's Dad?"

"Oh, he just keeps going, much the same as ever. He's sitting out in the garden now. I keep telling him it's too late in the year for that, but he doesn't like to be cooped up inside, as you know. I've told him we should get a conservatory built, but he says we can't afford it and in any case what he really wants is a veranda."

"Veranda." I repeated back. And in my head something shifted, settled solidly into place. A connection was made, a light went on, and I sat stunned with the revelation.

"Yes, dear, that's what I said. Veranda. Well, of course I told him not to be so silly, and that would probably cost more than a conservatory and wouldn't be as practical, I mean, you can use a conservatory in all weathers, can't you? Alison? Are you still there?"

I came back to the moment with a rush. "Yes. Yes I'm still here, but I've got to go now. Love to Dad, take care of yourself, bye."

I broke the connection, and sent a text to Sam.

"I know who it was!"

"VERANDA? THAT'S HER name?"

Sam stared at me with a raised eyebrow and an expression somewhere between perplexed and amused.

"Not exactly. Watch the road!"

"No problem," he said calmly, braking and taking the bend smoothly, if a bit faster than I would have done. He'd borrowed his Dad's car to take me out somewhere – which was nice. Wonderful, in fact, I couldn't remember the last time anything like that had happened, but the drawback was that I'm a terrible passenger. I forced myself to keep quiet as he pulled out to pass a cyclist and slipped back to the proper side of the road with a large van charging up the hill towards us. The clearances were less than I liked, but Sam had good reflexes and almost perfect distance judgement. It was just that he relied on them too much for my comfort.

"What does 'not exactly' mean, then?"

He'd wanted me to tell him when he rang me back, but by then I'd thought it through a bit more and had decided it was going to be easier to go over it all in person.

"Well, 'Veranda' was her nickname. She was a PCSO - 'Police and Community Support Officer' -"

Sam nodded. "I know what a PCSO is. I wasn't out of the country all that long, you know!" We'd turned onto the dual carriageway leading out of town, so I could relax a bit. And start wondering where we were going, and how far. Probably not somewhere I knew. I pushed the worry down again. I mustn't spoil the evening.

"Oh, right. Of course. So – this is going back a few years, now, but she was attached to our station when she finished training, and introduced herself to everyone as 'Vera Staysworth'. Of course, it didn't take long before someone discovered that she had a middle name – Miranda. And it was about ten seconds after that that she became 'Veranda'."

"Vera Miranda. Veranda." Sam chuckled. "I like it."

"She didn't. Got very uptight about it, even went and complained to her Sergeant. Who told her to lighten up and get over herself."

"She doesn't sound like a good fit for the police."

I turned that over in my mind. Hesitating, because I was well aware that I wasn't a great fit myself. Though it was maybe a little easier in CSI, where we spent a lot of time working on our own.

"She... wasn't a natural, let's say. She didn't have much sense of humour. I only met her a few times, but she always seemed very intense, and a bit on the edge, if you know what I mean?"

"Coiled spring sort of thing?"

"Yes. But not in a good way. And not the brightest of sparks. But she did work hard, put her time in and never complained about extra hours, with or without overtime pay. She got brownie points for that – with her boss, at least."

"And you think that it was her in the TV clip? Wearing the brown cagoule?"

I shook my head. "I don't know, Sam. Well, yes I do. I'm sure it was. And I'm sure it was her standing by the gate. But I don't know how I know, if you follow me. It might be something about the way she walked. She had this sort of stiff, upright gait, and always seemed to be in a hurry to be somewhere... but she's only in the shot for a few seconds, it's not really enough to be sure."

"But you are." He didn't say it in a challenging way, rather he was confirming, endorsing what I'd told him.

"Yes. Yes I am."

A sign came up – 'Anniston, 1 Mile' - and I realised where we were going.

"The Stag? That's where you're taking me?"

He nodded, and gave me a strange little sideways glance. It took me a moment, but then I realised that, for the first time, I'd seen Sam looking nervous.

"Is that all right?" he asked. "Only I thought it might be good. Since it was where we first met."

"Er – yes. Of course. That's fine." Somewhere I knew, after all. I'd been there before. I was able to release some of the worry I'd been trying to repress.

The Stag is on the outskirts of Anniston, just off a big roundabout. A large, sprawling place, with a kiddies' play area in the front, a motel at one end, and a semi-permanent marquee at the back for functions. Like wedding receptions. There wasn't one happening just then, but the place was busy enough, with at least two different birthday parties happening and several other families in as well.

"Ah. Not as quiet as I'd hoped." Sam admitted, as a shrieking child ran by with a balloon. A red-faced parent intercepted them and managed to persuade them back to the table. "Would you like to try somewhere else?"

I shook my head. "No, it's OK. A bit more upmarket than the Dreadnought anyway!"

Fortunately our table was round the corner from the main activity, and secluded enough to allow for a conversation.

"I hear they do a good starter," Sam suggested.

The menu had all the usual stuff. I had more I wanted to talk about, so I didn't spend too much time with it, just ordered the first thing that looked familiar. Soup.

"So, let's assume for a moment it was this PCSO Veranda – is there any reason why she would have been hanging around the Court that day?"

"That is just the problem, Sam. I can't think of any reason why she would have been involved in the bomb thing."

"So just chance, then? She happened to be walking by, glanced in the gate just as you and the Judge came out, stopped to take a look."

"Except that there must be more to it than that." I started giving Sam the full account of what I'd learned at the Dreadnought. "So she'd been there for a while before she walked past the gate. And she was still there when the TV crew arrived, after the bomb went off."

"If she'd been close enough to hear the explosion she'd probably have gone to see what was happening," Sam pointed out. "Half the town did, by the look of the pictures."

"Yes... but even so, what was she doing beforehand?"

"Waiting for someone to come out of court? Perhaps she'd been connected with a case?" He raised his eyebrows. "Ah, but I'm thinking that she's probably not on the Force any more, otherwise you'd already have gone to ask her?"

"Apparently she left a while ago. I did think I hadn't seen her around for a while – probably why it took me so long to recognise her – but I made a few enquiries this afternoon and it turns out she left about a year ago. Very discreetly, didn't say anything to anyone, just put in her notice, worked it out then left without so much as a goodbye."

"Not been seen around since?"

"Apparently not. I spoke to one of the other PCSOs, and nobody's heard anything from her. Granted, she didn't have a lot of friends, if any. But when you work closely with a group of people for a while then you do make some connections. You'd think that she'd have kept in touch with somebody."

"You're right, that is a bit unusual."

"And hanging round outside the court just before a bomb goes off?"

Sam dipped his head in acknowledgement. "Certainly something that should be investigated."

"Except that they won't. Because Special Branch won't know anything about her. She doesn't show on any CCTV, and they won't get much cooperation from the customers at the New Dreadnought. In any case, they're chasing down Muslim terrorists and far-Right extremists. I can't see her fitting into any of those categories."

"Well don't dismiss that altogether. We don't know enough about her."

I thought about it. "I suppose not. But that thing with the brown cagoule that she keeps taking off and putting on again. Doesn't that seem strange to you?"

"It does, but again, we've got very little to go on."

The Stag was quieting down a bit now, the birthday guests having taken their party bags and gone home. I found myself relaxing. Talking things over with Sam had that effect on me, I realised.

The conversation was interrupted by the arrival of our food. Steak, medium-rare for Sam. My soup was mulligatawny – not quite as good as the vegetable soup at The Nook, but tasty. And warm bread rolls with butter.

"So what now?" He asked.

"I suppose I could try and track her down. Some of her old colleagues might have kept in touch."

"Sounds like a plan. In the meantime – how's the soup?"

"Pretty good, actually. What about your steak?"

"OK, but not the best I've had."

"Oh? Where was that, then, and why didn't we go there instead?"

He laughed. "It was a little place I happened across down in Oz. Australia, that is."

The conversation turned to a pleasantly inconsequential discussion of what was good to eat where, broken only by ordering dessert. Ice cream sundaes for both of us.

It was a good thing that our conversation was flowing well, because the service wasn't as good as the food. It took twenty minutes for our sundaes to arrive.

"Do you want coffee?" Sam asked as I scraped the last traces of ice-cream off the bottom of my bowl.

"No thanks. Coffee straight after ice-cream doesn't work for me – and I don't want to spend another twenty minutes waiting for it. Unless you do?"

"No, you're right. I'll just get the bill."

That in itself took some doing. The waitress was only two tables away, but it took a while before she noticed Sam's raised hand, and then seemed reluctant to come over.

"You can choose to add a tip, if you want," she said as she passed Sam the card machine.

"I don't think so," I said firmly. "Tips are for good service, which doesn't mean waiting twenty minutes for ice-cream while you flirt with the lads on that table."

She flushed, and opened her mouth but then shut it again, and completed the transaction without another word.

I watched her stalk off with a sinking feeling in my stomach. There I went again. A perfect evening ruined because I couldn't stop my mouth running off. Not daring to look at Sam I grabbed my coat and headed for the door.

He caught up with me in the car park, but said nothing.

"Sam? I'm sorry."

He looked at me, and I felt compelled to return his gaze. His normal smile was overlaid with another expression that I couldn't quite interpret, but which I suspected was annoyance. It didn't show in his voice.

"What are you sorry for, Alison?"

"My little outburst back there. At the waitress. Wrecked the evening, didn't it."

"Hardly!"

"It did though. Making an issue like that and getting her angry over a tip."

"But you were right. She wasn't doing her job."

"I didn't have to point it out, though." I stared at him, wondering why he wasn't getting the point.

"You didn't have to. A lot of people wouldn't have. And she'd have gone right on thinking that it was OK to ignore customers if she felt like it – right up to the point where someone got really angry, maybe complained, and she lost her job."

He made as if to touch my shoulder, thought better of it and dropped his hand. "Alison, you weren't angry, or rude. You just told it as it was. And once she gets over that, she might benefit from it."

I shook my head. "You'd have said it better, though. You'd have found a way to tell her without causing an upset."

"Would I?" Sam raised an eyebrow. "Actually, I was about to add a tip. Because that would have been easier, and because I didn't want to risk upsetting you by making a bit of a scene."

"Really?" He was only trying to make me feel better, I told myself.

"Really. And actually – that's one of the things I like about you."

I had to make a physical effort to keep my jaw in place. "What – you like that I'm insensitive and awkward and upset everybody?"

"I like that you see things clearly, and speak clearly, and say it as it is. You don't upset people because you're spiteful or malicious, but because you're honest and open and brave enough to speak out."

I struggled to answer that. There was a lump in my throat. "Oh." I managed to gasp out. *Very eloquent,* said the critic in my head.

He held my gaze. "I thought that about you the first time we met." He nodded back in the direction of the building. "At the wedding. I've been wanting to tell you ever since, but it never seemed the right time. Until now."

We stood looking at each other in the car-park while time went on its way around us. Until I finally realised that the look I hadn't recognised was concern. Concern for me, or concern about me, that I might be upset with him.

Knowing that, and needing to put it right, finally moved me on. "Thank you." I said. "Thank you, Sam."

He nodded, and smiled properly. "You're very welcome. Um... shall we go? Only I just felt a spot of rain."

THE DRIVE BACK WAS very quiet. Both of us having too much to think about, I supposed. But as Sam parked up outside my place, I realised I hadn't thought the evening through.

Should I ask him in? Would he expect me to? Did I want to?

The answers, in each case were 'Not sure'.

Fortunately, Sam helped me out. Again.

"Well, this is a bit awkward, isn't it?" He laughed, and, as always, his laugh infected me as well, so we laughed together.

"I was just wondering..." I began. And wasn't sure then how to continue the sentence.

"Yes. I was as well! But the thing is..." he took a deep breath. "Time for me to learn from you and practise honest speaking. The thing is, Alison – I want things between us to go further. But I want them to go longer, as well. That is, I hope that us being together, isn't just for now, and not just occasional, but for a long time and quite often. So I don't want to rush anything now, because I hope we'll have plenty of time to do things properly and when we're both sure about what we want to do."

I looked at him. "Sam. I... like that idea very much."

He smiled, and leaned forward. But stopped.

"Sorry, I forget you don't like to be touched."

I considered that for a moment. "I don't usually like to be touched. But..."

Tentatively, I stepped forward and put my arms round him. He put his round me. It was frightening and thrilling and I wondered how ridiculous people would think it was, getting so worked up over a hug.

But when he left, I floated back into my flat.

Chapter 7

Police Cordons – Purpose: 1) To protect the scene, the public, and investigators attending the scene. 2) Control unauthorised access. 3) Prevent interference with the scene. 4) Facilitate emergency services operations. 5) Maintain scene integrity for investigative purposes.

Home for me is the top floor of a three-storey Georgian house. It's a very nice building in a nice area of a nice little village, which means that the rent is huge, even though I only have three rooms – bedroom, bathroom and combined kitchen / dining room / living room. It takes a hefty chunk of my CSI salary, and is the main reason why I have a moped instead of a car. But it has one significant advantage. It's a listed building – which means that it is unlikely to be demolished or extensively rebuilt. I like stability, continuity. I don't like change.

Sam was a threat to that. What he'd said implied change. Major change. Of course, I'd probably misunderstood him. After all, it was technically only our first date and what I thought I'd heard was, if not exactly a proposal, certainly a serious statement of intent. So I must have misheard.

Except that, first date or not, we'd known each other for a year or more. And what might have been a cheesy pick-up line if almost any other man had said it... just wasn't. Not coming from Sam.

So he was a definite threat. To my safe, comfortable, well-ordered and painstakingly constructed life.

In which case, what was this big bubble of happy that kept filling me up every time I thought about him?

I wandered around my flat – it didn't take long, there wasn't much wandering space – trying to suppress the random laughter that kept slipping out.

Oliver, who also dislikes change, was disturbed by my mood and did his best to shake me out of it. However, I was impervious to his hissing and yowling, so he scratched my hand and went out. I watched him go. His normal means of egress and ingress was through the bathroom window and out onto the rooftops of the main part of the house, which he rules as a personal kingdom. From there he can, if the mood takes him, descend to ground level via a fire-escape at the rear of the building.

I had to admit that his annoyance was justified. After all, it was now nearly ten in the morning and I'd been moving around in a daydream ever since I'd got up. I'd made three cups of coffee that morning and left them to go cold, and hadn't even gone through my morning check list yet.

"Pull yourself together," I growled at the mirror. "You had less trouble getting over the bomb than this!"

Perhaps that was part of the problem. The last few days had been an emotional roller-coaster: it wasn't surprising if I was a bit vulnerable.

I seized on that idea. It held out the promise of a return to stability. Safe, normal, slightly boring stability. In the meantime, I needed to get on with life. I turned away from the mirror with a renewed determination to stop acting like an emotional disaster area. Not before noting, as I had many times, that my face was too long and my mouth too wide.

Oliver had the right idea. I dressed, ran through my check list (but stopped at 'Are you OK', that was too complicated a question this morning) and went out.

My first thought had been to go into the station and talk to someone about Vera Miranda. But another idea occurred, and instead I took my moped down to the south side of town. There, not far from the Delford Mills project was the notorious Royal Oak public house.

I'd read somewhere that 'Royal Oak' was the third most popular pub name in Britain. If so, I hoped the others were doing better. A shabby looking building. Old whitewash peeling away from red brick walls, almost obscuring the giant crimson cross of St George that had been painted on the front and sides. A jumble of outhouses behind, and a few well-worn picnic benches in the yard to one side – which was advertised as a 'beer garden'.

As I'd hoped, there was still a scene on. Blue and white police tape over the front door and the carpark entrance. A police car was the only vehicle in there, with one occupant sitting in the front seat. He was wearing a blue PCSO uniform, and took no notice of me as I slowed down and stopped on the other side of the tape.

I knew him. Claydon or Haydon or something like that. We weren't friends. I'd once called him "lazy and unprofessional" for letting someone inside a secure scene that I was examining. He took offence. If I'd reported it as I should have done, he might have lost his job, but I'd taken the view that, since I'd almost finished anyway, no harm had been done and let it go. But I got no gratitude for it.

There was no point in asking him about Veranda. But was he the only one on the scene? Wasn't there a back way in to the Royal Oak?

I moved on, took the next right, and right again. A street of old terraced houses. Half-way down was the entrance to an alleyway that led to the Royal Oak. And of course, there was blue tape across it and a bored looking PCSO sitting on a low wall next to it.

Jenny Day. 'Happy' Day as she was – inevitably – known around the Station. One of the older PCSOs, who had been in the job almost since they created the role back in 2002. And one I knew well enough to talk to but who I hadn't yet managed to upset. As far as I knew.

Worth a try, at any rate. I pulled up in front of the alleyway.

As I did so, she stood up and shook her head at me.

"Sorry, can't go this way, there's a police scene on here."

I took my helmet off and smiled at her. "That's OK, Jen, it's not my sort of place anyway!" 'Happy' didn't seem to be the name to use, as she looked to be cold, bored and tired.

"Oh, Alison. Hi. Didn't recognise you without your van. Is this another budget cut, then?"

"Glad to see you've still got your sense of humour. How long have you been stuck out here?"

"Too long, and it's not humour, it's cynicism! But why are you here? I heard you'd been nearly killed by that bomb – unless you *were* killed and you've come to haunt me?" She poked me gingerly on the shoulder. I managed to control my usual over-the-top reaction to being touched, and put on a smile.

"No, I'm still solid. I wasn't even injured, really – just a few bruises."

"Well that's a relief. So are you back on duty? Only I thought that CSI were finished with this scene."

"We are, as far as I know. Actually, I'm officially off sick, but I wanted to ask a question or two – if you've got time?"

Jenny looked around at the empty street. "Hang on, I'll just consult my schedule... well, I am quite busy, as you see, but I might be able to squeeze you in for a moment or two! What's up?"

"Do you remember Veranda?"

She raised an eyebrow in surprise. "What, Vera? Vera Staysworth?"

"That's the one."

The surprise was replaced by a searching look. "And why on earth would you be wanting to know about Veranda of all people?"

I met her gaze. Jenny was a shrewd woman, and her years on the job had given her a lot of insight into human beings in all their aspects. She was not one to be fobbed off with a cock-and-bull story, and really there was no need to do so either.

"I saw her recently. Thought I saw her, that is."

"Uh-huh." Jenny nodded, and waited for the rest of the story.

"Actually, it was just before the bomb went off. She was standing at the gate as I came out into the car park with Ruth Darnley. I didn't recognise her at the time, but thinking back, I'm almost sure it was her."

"You don't think she had something to do with it, do you?" Jenny raised both eyebrows. "I mean – I know she was a bit of a weirdo, and she had a nasty streak as well, but – bombs? She wasn't linked to one of those far-right groups, was she?"

"Not as far as I know. I just wanted to try and track her down, that's all. To find out if she saw anything."

"Isn't that with Special Branch now? How come you're playing detective, Alison?"

"Ah, yes. Well, of course you're right, technically. Only, when I gave my statement I hadn't remembered who it was that I'd seen. So I left it out. And I have tried to let them know since, but they're not very interested at the moment. Too busy chasing down other leads."

Plus which I'd managed to seriously annoy the D.I, but there was no need to mention that.

"Of course, I'm not saying she actually set the bomb," I continued. "I doubt if she was bright enough to do something like that, even if she had any motive to kill the Judge."

"Ah. Well, you could be wrong on that." Jenny sat back down and patted the brickwork next to her. "Here, pull up a wall, take a seat and I'll tell you all about Vera Miranda."

I sat next to her. "What might I be wrong about, then?"

"For one thing, Veranda was a lot brighter than people gave her credit for. She had this rather old-fashioned name (not improved on by the nickname) and when she was in civvies she dressed a bit old-fashioned as well, sort of dowdy, if you know what I mean?"

I shook my head. "I only ever saw her in uniform."

"Well – long skirts, buttoned up blouses, sensible shoes, hair always kept very short. She was actually not bad-looking, but she never made much of herself. And she acted the part as well. Always had this slightly puzzled expression on her face, like she was struggling to keep up. Always asked for instructions to be repeated. People soon got the idea that she wasn't the sharpest knife in the drawer."

"But you thought otherwise?"

"Not at first. Actually, I had a lot of sympathy for her when she started. I thought she'd need some looking after – especially as we had some background in common: she was from Frayhampton, which is where I was born and brought up. I didn't know her then, we'd moved away before her family moved in, but I heard that there'd been a rather tragic incident. House fire, killed her entire family. Apparently she went to live with an uncle and his family down in London after that."

"Rough deal. I'm surprised she'd want to come back this way, with those sort of memories."

Jenny nodded agreement. "I know. But I never got close enough to ask about it. And then, after she'd been around for a while, I started to think that there was more to her than she let on. She kept a lot of things hidden."

"Like her intelligence?"

"Yes. She actually picked up on things really quickly, but made out otherwise. I couldn't understand why at first. Then after a while I began to suspect that she might have had good reason to hide things."

A car passed, slowing down opposite the alleyway to get a good look. The two young men in it gave us hostile stares before suddenly accelerating away at an unsuitable speed for a residential street.

Jenny frowned at the disappearing vehicle. "We're getting a lot of that. Some of the locals are really pissed off that we've closed their favourite boozer. They seem to think that acting aggressive towards us on the scene will get them back in quicker."

"So what was Veranda hiding?"

"Ah, yes... well, let me tell you a story about that. You remember a PC called Dave Carlin?"

"Vaguely."

"Dave was the one who came up with 'Veranda' for a nickname. Nice guy, good cop, but he liked to needle people, and never knew when to let something go. So he pushed this Veranda thing way too far. Changed her name on the duty board. Marked out a desk with her nickname on. Made feeble jokes about her having a brother called 'Balcony'. Stuff like that.

"It was obvious right from the start that she didn't like it. Got very huffy in fact, moaned to the Sergeant, but never came right out and told him to back off. Some of us tried to tell him to drop it, but Dave hated to let a good thing go.

"Then, a couple of months after all this had started, life suddenly went a bit pear-shaped for Dave. His wife kicked him out. Turns out that certain pictures had turned up on social media – pictures of him in a bar with some floozy draped all over him. He denied that it had been anything, he said he was just in there having a drink when the woman came on to him. But he had a hard time proving it. Took some compassionate leave to sort it out. I did hear that they'd got back together, eventually, but Dave left the force, found a job with more regular hours that kept him out of harm's way, as it were."

Jenny stopped and watched me think it over.

"You're saying that Veranda set that up?" I asked.

She shrugged. "I've no evidence. No one even thought it at the time. After all, Dave might have been trying it on a bit, couldn't put it past him. Or perhaps he was just unlucky. And no one ever did find out who'd put up the pictures, or who the woman was."

"But..." I frowned as I thought it through. "There are some who'd help set him up for a few quid. And social media isn't hard to find your way around."

"True. But that didn't occur to me for a while. Not till after the thing with Sergeant Muston."

"Bill Muston?"

"Yes. Him. Now Bill was a bit old-school, very strict on rules and regs. Tore a strip off Veranda one day. I can't remember what it was about, but he was pretty sharp with her.

"As you might recall, Bill liked his booze, perhaps a little too much for his health. Not that he'd ever drink on duty, far less be drunk. But one day the Station Commander did a locker inspection – all very routine, happened every now and then. And there in Bill's locker was a half-bottle of his favourite whiskey. Half bottle, half empty. Along with another one, completely empty.

"Of course, Bill absolutely denied that he had anything to do with it, but he couldn't explain how they came to be in his locker – which was secure. They checked the lock; it hadn't been tampered with. No keys unaccounted for. They even did forensics on the bottles - came back with Bill's fingerprints on the glass, Bill's DNA round the mouth.

"Of course, they couldn't let that go. Due to his long history of good conduct, they kept things as low-key as possible. Arranged for him to take early retirement. He was due in a few years anyway, they just moved things forward and encouraged him to take the opportunity. But it broke him, to have to finish his career that way."

"Veranda again? But that's a bit over the top, isn't it? To wreck a man's life because she got told off?"

"I've got no proof, Alison. All I'm saying is, if she did do it – then you have to think about what was involved. She must gone to his house and got the bottles from his bin, half-filled one of them with the right brand. Managed to steal a key to his locker then sneak it back without anyone knowing. Timed it perfectly – the bottles must have been put in just after the inspection was announced. Any sooner and Bill would have discovered them himself."

"It would have taken some planning."

"My point. Planning, intelligence – and a very nasty malicious streak."

"But still no proof that it was her."

"None at all. But it wasn't the only thing. There seemed to be a lot of bad luck going round about that time. People found their equipment missing or broken. Reports got misfiled, evidence bags not properly secured, rude emails were sent from people's accounts that they absolutely denied having anything to do with. I can tell you; it wasn't a good place to work in those days. The atmosphere got to be really strained."

"And all these things happened to people who had upset Vera?"

"Well, that was the thing. You couldn't ever pin it down to something as obvious as that. But I got very wary of her, very careful what I said and did when she was around."

The car came back again. A souped-up hatchback with all the trimmings – thin tyres, tinted glass, a massive spoiler that looked like it had come off an airliner. The exhaust sounded like it was blowing badly, but perhaps that was intentional.

The windows were down, and this time one of the occupants leaned out and made rude signs in our direction.

"Yes, love, that's all right, whatever makes you feel more manly." Jenny said it quietly, whilst smiling sweetly at the vehicle and fingering her radio.

"So what happened to Vera?" I prompted. "She left, didn't she? Was that because she got caught out?"

"No. No one ever caught her. Like I said, she was smarter than she seemed. Not just smart. Cunning. No, what happened was that Vera made the most basic mistake ever. She fell in love, and with the wrong man."

The conversation wasn't going the way I'd expected. "Who was the wrong man, then?" I asked.

"Micky Fayden," she said, and watched me closely for a reaction.

"What? DS Fayden?" Jenny got her reaction. I could almost feel my jaw hitting the ground. "Our local bent copper?"

"The very same. Of course, when Veranda fell for him he was still the golden boy of the Force, the rising star, the one everyone thought was on his way to the top."

"I thought he was a bit of a creep."

Jenny laughed. "You and me both. But Mickey was a bit like Marmite – either love it or hate it. And a lot of people loved it. He had no shortage of admirers and sycophants, male or female, and he lapped it up. Vera fell into line with the rest. Perhaps she saw him as her own way to the top, perhaps she recognised a kindred spirit. Heck, perhaps she just fell in love – it doesn't always need an explanation, does it?"

"I suppose not," I answered. Thinking for a moment about myself, not about Veranda.

"And maybe it was mutual. Hard to tell with a man like Mickey Fayden, who pretty much assumed that he was God's gift to women and acted accordingly. But he did start dropping into our office a lot – always when Vera was there. Of course, never came in without some sort of favour to ask, and she was always 'Yes, of course, Mickey, any time, Mickey,' and so on.

It was definitely something big for her, though. She started to change her image. Dressed better, looked happier, even relaxed a bit. Not so prickly."

"Did the other – er – incidents stop?"

"Hard to say, because things moved on pretty quick after that. First, Veranda got herself into trouble for being late on duty. She said it was because she'd been helping DS Fayden out on a surveillance job. Turns out that none of this had been authorised, and all sorts of unpleasant stuff hit numerous fans. But before that had been sorted out, things went really pear-shaped! There was a serious fire-arms incident over in Delford Mills, then they discovered a drugs factory underneath a pub – a pub which Mickey had actually raided, it turned out – then Mickey's done a runner and there's a warrant out for his arrest."

"I remember."

"It turned out that he had been working with this Spanish drug-dealer, Canoso, or something like that. They were flooding the country with some new sort of stuff, something really nasty that made people do all sorts of crazy things."

"Yes. Lappies was the street name. A sort of emotion inhibitor, apparently."

"Yes, that was it. I forget the details. But for Vera, it was a real shock. They asked her some questions, of course, but she didn't know anything about Mickey's dodgy dealing – or if she did, it never came out. She stayed in the job, but it was like she was just going through the motions. Not really caring. I think CID kept an eye on her, to see if there was any contact with Mickey, but that didn't seem to come to anything. At any rate, they lost interest after a while.

"Mickey was on the run for about six months or so. But it seems he'd been taking these Lappies himself, and when his supply ran out he had some nasty withdrawal symptoms. Ended up in hospital, where he was arrested. As soon as he'd recovered enough he went on trial and was sent down for eight years."

"Yes. I remember. I testified at the trial. Forensic evidence from his house." There was a memory there. Several memories, piling up in my head and shouting for attention. I put them aside for the moment.

"Veranda packed it in straight after the trial. Worked out her notice and slipped away."

"Where did she go?"

Jenny raised her hands, shook her head. "Who knows? Never heard anything more of her. Nobody did, as far as I know."

"Nothing?" I sat back and thought about it. "Where did she live?"

"She had a flat somewhere in town, but it was rented. I don't think she stayed there – some mail got redirected to the station as the only known contact address, so she must have moved on."

The car rolled up, but this time stopped in the middle of the road. The occupants leaned out and shouted some random abuse.

"They really need to get a life," Jenny said wearily. "If they keep this up I'm going to have to call it in... ah, hang on..."

She acknowledged a call on her radio. Her earpiece was in, so I couldn't hear the message, but the two lads in the car saw her talking and took off.

"Will do." Jenny said over the radio, and turned to me. "That's it then, scene's lifted – I'm off back to the station and the kiddies can have their play-pen back." She started wrapping up the police tape. "Nice chatting, Alison, sorry I can't be more help. I'll ask around, let you know if anyone's heard anything of her."

"Thanks, Jenny." I stood up and started putting my helmet back on. "Did she have anyone she was particularly close to? Apart from Mickey Fayden, that is."

"Not really. As I said, people began to keep their distance. But there was a bit of a crowd that used to hang round Mickey. Mostly CID, and they all scattered pretty quick when it came out what he'd been up to. But you could try them." She finished collecting the tape and bundled it under one arm. "I'll just find a bin for this lot... your best bet would be to talk to Cal. DC Carlo Cadenti, that is. He was Mickey's best mate and chief gofer, back in the day. If she kept in touch with anyone it might have been him."

"Good idea, thanks. But I thought he left as well."

"Yeah. Got out from under the convictions, but left the job anyway. Probably got asked to go, too much accumulated baggage if you know what I mean? I heard he went up north somewhere. See you around."

She headed up the alleyway towards the Royal Oak. I got back on my moped.

"Where to now, Alison?" I asked.

Chapter 8

Travel check list: Times, Tickets, Route, Alternatives. P.S. If in London, check Underground stations.

I was still thinking about it when I had a text from Sam.

"Lunch? The Nook?"

"There in ten." I sent back. Wondering if that seemed too keen, but not really caring.

"Sorry, need a bit longer," he replied. "30 mins, OK?"

"OK."

That gave me time for a little detour. Not far from The Nook, a bit further down the same road in fact, was the Prince William pub. Had been the Prince William. Now a coffee bar with flats above it. But a few years ago it had been the cover for a serious drug-manufacturing and distribution business. Mickey Fayden had been in it up to his neck, taking money to pass information and redirect police investigations. And taking the drugs as well, it seemed.

But had Vera been involved with that? Or just involved with Mickey?

I stopped and stared at the building for a while, but it brought no inspiration, so I carried on to The Nook.

Over lunch, I brought Sam up to speed.

"She does sound like a bit of a dangerous character." He frowned, thinking it over. "But even if she was responsible for all those other incidents, it's a big step up to murder."

"I know."

He met my gaze. "Possible though. That's what you're thinking, right?"

I shrugged. "I'd rather not think it. But the idea isn't going away." I took a deep breath, wondering where to take the conversation. "Sam, there's something about me you should know."

He put on an expression of exaggerated horror. "Alison – you're really an alien in disguise! I thought there was something!"

I laughed. "No, not as dramatic as that... wait a minute, what did you mean 'you thought there was something?'"

He waved that away. "Just added for effect. Honestly, I didn't have a clue. So, what are you inside that cute human-woman suit? Insectioid? Bug-eyed and slimy? A cloud of intelligent gas?"

I laughed again. "You say the nicest things to a girl... can we get back on topic please? I was trying to tell you; I have a habit of seeing patterns. Seeing connections. Trouble is, I'm not always sure that they are real. So, yes, I am seeing, or feeling, that Vera's vengefulness might have taken her as far as murder. But I need some grounding, Sam. I need you to give me some outside perspective, to tell me what's realistic and what's just my fevered imagination."

"Fair enough. I'll stay serious, O Empress of the Galaxy."

I spent several seconds giving him a severe look, until he raised his hands in surrender and I managed to suppress my laughter.

"I've remembered a few things," I continued. "First of which is, the Judge who tried Mickey Fayden's case was Ruth Darnley."

"Ah. So if Veranda was in love with Mickey, then she could have a grudge against Darnley. That does fit. If you factor in the thing about her getting her own back in devious ways."

"Yes. So you see what I mean about patterns?"

"I'm afraid I do. And... maybe something you missed."

I raised an eyebrow. "What's that then?"

"You were involved in this Mickey Fayden thing, right?"

"Yes. When he did a runner, his house obviously became a crime scene. I did most of the work on it, and found some incriminating stuff. Like, some of those drugs I was telling you about – the Lappies? - he'd had a little hiding place for them in his bathroom. He took most of them with him, but I found a few that had slipped out."

"And you gave evidence about that? In court?"

"Of course. Not that I had to do much apart from confirm the details of my statement, but with a serving police officer involved, they went overboard in covering all the details."

"So Vera would have known that it was you."

"Oh yes. In fact, I saw her in court, sitting in the public area. Which was packed – there was a lot of interest – and I was wondering why she was bothering to be there at all. Of course, I didn't know about her and Mickey then, but in hindsight I suppose..." my voice trailed off as a I made a connection. Suddenly, I felt cold. "You're thinking that I might have been the target."

He gave me a concerned look, and reached out to touch my hand, but stopped half-way. "I don't know that. Sorry, perhaps I shouldn't have mentioned it."

"No, that's all right. I'm glad you did. I would have thought it sooner or later anyway. The whole idea's probably a bit far out anyway. After all, if it hadn't been Darnley, it would have been another judge, and the result would probably have been the same. There was never any doubt that Mickey was going down for a long stretch. And it could easily have been another CSI who did that scene. I just happened to be on call when it hit the fan."

He nodded, and gave me a reassuring look. "Of course. That's absolutely right."

I held his gaze. "Really, the whole idea of a revenge killing is nonsense. Someone would have to be really twisted to do that. Much more likely to a be a terrorist thing."

"Yes. Just what I was thinking."

"And in any case, it must have been the Judge who was the target. The van – the bomb! - was parked right in front of her car, the note with the trigger number was on her windscreen. There was no way it could have been aimed at me. If I'd been killed, that would just have been collateral." "Good thinking!" Sam smiled. "It wasn't about you. Couldn't have been."

"Right."

I looked at my plate. Soup. I'd really gone wild and taken a risk today, though. Tomato and coriander. I wasn't sure if I liked it. I broke off a bit of crusty roll and dipped it in, tentatively.

"What are you thinking now?" Sam asked gently.

"I'm thinking that..." I ate the bread slowly. "I'm thinking that this still doesn't explain why Vera was at the gate just before the bomb went off. When she's not been seen around here in such a long time. Bit of a coincidence, isn't it. Or am I out of touch with reality here?"

There was a long silence. Sam had chosen a panini, with salad. There wasn't much left now, since he'd been eating whilst I did most of the talking. But he was taking a long time over the last bit of crust.

Eventually he finished. "You're not wrong, Alison. There is something strange here. Nothing clear, nothing you can put your finger on, but I'm getting a nasty feeling about it."

"Thank you. I'm glad to know it's not just me with a wild imagination."

"Of course, it could be both of us!" he said with a flash of his usual smile. But he turned serious again at once. "The question is, what do we do about it? I take it that you don't feel ready to go back to Special Branch with it?"

I shook my head. "There's nothing concrete. And perhaps they would follow it up, but the mood music suggests that they are fully invested in the terrorist theory. I need something better to get their attention. Better than old stories and bad feelings."

"So. Next step. Find out more about Vera, I'd suggest. And about her relationship with Mickey Fayden. This bloke Cadenti – sounds Italian?"

"Italian parents, I think. Or father, at any rate."

"OK. So all we know about him is that he moved up north. We need to dig around, see if we can track him down."

"There might be someone at the Station who's still in touch. I'll see."

"Actually, I was thinking of starting with an internet search, see if his name comes up anywhere. I can have a go at that if you like."

"Right. We can do both. I'll ask around this afternoon. And while I'm at it, I'll see if anyone knew where she lived down in London. If I can contact her family there, they might know where she is now."

We paid the bill and began getting ready to leave. As we stood up, I hesitantly touched Sam's sleeve.

"Thanks. For being with me on this."

"Thanks for letting me be."

We smiled at each other, then hugged. Quite naturally. As if we'd been doing it for years. Except that I wouldn't expect my heart to pound quite so much after years.

"I need to get back to work," Sam said. "I have to set up the studio for a big shoot this afternoon.

And probably into the evening as well, so I might not see you again today. I'll call later, OK?"

"OK," I agreed. Very OK, I thought. Very, very very...

"You know, I'm wondering if there isn't something we've missed," he added. "It just occurred to me – wouldn't talking to Mickey Fayden be the obvious thing to do? I mean, if we can get in to see him?"

"Oh. I didn't tell you that, did I?"

"Tell me what?"

"Mickey... the drugs he'd taken did some permanent damage. They got him through the withdrawal, enough so he could stand trial, but he never really recovered. He had several strokes, then his heart gave out. Died in prison just over a year ago. He was only six months into his sentence."

TRAINS ARE LIKE BUSES. You can stare out of the window, or keep your eyes on your phone, or just pretend to go to sleep, and no one will bother you.

It helps when you travel off-peak. The 9.50 to London St Pancras was moderately busy, but I had no trouble finding two empty seats together. I sat by the window and dumped my bag next to me, to discourage any visitors.

Not having to concentrate on people-avoidance gave me chance to think – but that wasn't a totally positive thing. Thinking reminded me that I was going to a place I'd never been before, to talk to a person I'd never met before, about something they might not want to talk about. And to do it without the protection or justification of being on official police business.

The idea alone knotted my stomach, and no amount of telling myself that I was over-reacting would ease that. I just hoped I'd be able to go through with it.

My attempts to track down Carlo Cadenti had been a complete failure. I'd phoned everyone I knew, but nobody knew anything more than I'd already learned. And nobody wanted to talk about him, either. Nothing more toxic than a bent copper, even if only bent by association.

I didn't have much more success talking about Vera. Most people barely remembered her. Those who did, hadn't liked her, confirming Jenny's opinion.

It was Jenny herself who provided the only information of value. I hadn't intended to bother her again, but after I'd gone through all the possible contacts in my phone, I was left with phoning round different offices at the station, and she answered.

"Not off yet?" I'd asked.

"Catching up on admin stuff. They tell us that putting everything on computers will save so much time, then make us add the same information to three different databases!"

I made appropriate sympathy noises. It was a moan we'd all had many times. "OK, I won't keep you, then. I was just wondering, you don't happen to know where Veranda lived when she was in London?" No point in asking about Cadenti, and probably none in asking about Vera.

To my surprise she came straight back with an answer.

"Eel Pie Island." "What?"

"Eel Pie Island. We were having a general conversation in the office once about weird place names. Someone had been to a job on Quondam Road – it's gone now, burned down in that big fire – and they were wondering aloud about where these weird names came from. So we were all chipping in with strange roads and funny villages. Vera's just sitting there saying nothing, as usual. But this must have been in her happy period, after she'd started whatever it was with Mickey, because she suddenly put in that she'd once lived on Eel Pie Island. Unusual name, and even more unusual for her to tell us something like that, which is why it stuck in my head."

"Eel Pie Island," I repeated back. "It's certainly unusual enough to remember. She didn't say where it is, exactly?"

"Sorry, not a clue about that."

"Right. Well, I'll do a bit of research then. That's another one I owe you, Jenny."

"Don't worry, a claim will be made in due course! See you around, Alison."

She hung up. I got on my laptop and started researching Eel Pie Island.

Which, as it turned out was in Twickenham, which I'd only previously heard about in connection with rugby. But Eel Pie Island was its own little community, with no vehicular access to the mainland. Just by boat or a footbridge. The name came – not surprisingly – from the brisk business in eel pies that was once done on the island (the Thames having had a good population of eels at the time). Since then it had had a surprisingly colourful history. At one time the island's hotel had been the go-to place in London for jazz: later on, it had hosted some of the great names of rock. The hotel was abandoned and eventually burned down, but the island still had several boatyards, some artists' studios and about fifty homes.

But did any of them belong to Vera's family?

I'd had no success at all in tracking down any Staysworths in London. Which didn't mean there weren't any. It might be down to my lack of search skills. But it meant that Eel Pie Island was the only clue I had.

Still, at least it was a small island. Only fifty homes. And probably everyone on the island knew everyone else. I just had to knock on a door or two, ask a few people. Simple stuff.

My stomach knotted again.

The vast glass ceiling of St Pancras should have produced a feeling of space and light. But there was precious little space down on the platform. Being caught up in the torrent of passengers surging towards the exit was a nightmare experience. Literally. It brought back half-remembered dreams from childhood, formless impressions of crowding, touching, and an imminent danger of being crushed.

I hung back, moved aside, stayed away from the worst of it, but couldn't avoid the narrowing space at the end of the platform. Funnelling me into an even larger crowd, and these people not even going in the same direction. Wandering backwards and forwards, standing still, clumped together, eating, talking, staring. With bags and cases ready to bump, elbows ready to jab, mouths ready to snap and shout.

I reverted to basic survival mechanisms. Look down, watch your feet. Focus on where you're going – just quick glances up to check, looking down again to avoid eye-contact. Make lists.

Keys, wallet, mobile, in their pockets. Tickets, cash, card, in the wallet. Bag, on shoulder. Contents of bag... item, item, item...

Everything there that I needed. Every possibility covered.

"You're OK, Alison," I whispered. "You're OK."

It was more desperate than confident, but it got me down to the underground, where I spent ten minutes frantically scanning the underground map before realising that there was no Twickenham station anywhere on the system. Something I hadn't planned on. You can get anywhere in London by Tube, can't you. So I'd assumed.

Never assume, I'd been told in training. I never did, when examining a scene. But that bit of basic common sense had deserted me in this case.

Fortunately, there was still an office manned by a human being who could answer random enquiries. "Closest station to Twickenham? You want Richmond." A short pause, then the tired looking lady behind the window took note of my frantic expression and explained further as she produced the ticket. "Victoria line to Victoria, change to the District line. Westbound. Make sure it's the service to Richmond. Otherwise you'll end up in Wimbledon or Ealing Broadway."

Back into the crush of people, pouring onto the monstrously steep escalators that carried the flow down to the platforms. And, of course, back up again, which spoiled the analogy. But I had no head-space to think of anything better. Six different Underground lines intersect at Kings Cross / St Pancras, more than at any other point on the system, which explained the huge volume of bodies passing through, and also meant that navigating through them to the right platform was essential. A wrong turn or a misread sign could have taken me off to almost anywhere in London. Except Twickenham, of course.

I was finally swept into a packed carriage, and stood clinging to a post with my eyes tight shut against the information overload. I would have put my earplugs in as well and played familiar music as loudly as possible, but for the fear of missing the station announcements. So I stood and listened to the whine of electric motors, rising as the train pulled away from the station, falling again as it decelerated into the next one. The hiss of air passing, the rattle of wheels and squeal of metal-on-metal at bends. The low mutter of conversation – but very little of that, most people seemed stunned into silence, as if as traumatised by the experience as I was. I carefully listed everything I heard.

Victoria was only five stations away from St Pancras, and significantly quieter. I found my way to the correct platform for the District line, westbound, and noted that the Richmond train would be the second one to arrive. Time to catch my breath, then. I wandered along to the quiet end of the platform and stood taking deep breaths of the muggy underground air.

"You can do this," I told myself firmly. "You are doing it. That's the worst bit over."

Of course, I still had to come back. To take my mind off that thought, I started looking at the posters, advertising shows and events, tourist attractions and blockbuster novels.

One stood out from the others, by virtue of being rather bland. Just plain black text on white, with a police logo.

'A fatal incident occurred here on...' Standard appeal for witnesses. Someone had died here. 'Incident' could mean anything. An accident or a murder. A mugging gone too far, or someone jostled off the platform into the path of a train. Professional instinct had me considering possible scenarios, and looking round for CCTV cameras. Not many of those, plenty of blind spots.

The first train came in. Doors opened with a hydraulic hiss, and I shrank back against the wall for fear of being carried off to Wimbledon, They closed again, leaving the platform emptier than ever as the train whined its way onward.

The poster itself looked forlorn and shabby. It had long outlived its usefulness: it referred to an incident months past. Little chance of getting any useful response now, I thought. Probably should have been taken down, but someone had overlooked it.

My train arrived, sooner than I'd expected, and I scurried aboard.

With decreasing crowds and the sense of having got through the worst, my stress levels dropped as we left the centre of London, and were almost back to normal when I left the train at Richmond. I did have some trepidation as I considered how to complete my journey to Eel Pie Island. There would be buses, of course, but the prospect wasn't encouraging. There were taxis as well. But consulting the map app on my phone I realised it was only about two miles away. An easy walk. I'm good at walking.

The route took me through some busy streets – but nowhere near as busy as the centre of London. I crossed the Thames at Richmond Bridge, then took a slight detour from the direct route to go through Marble Hill Park. Walking, especially with a bit of nature around, calmed me further, and by the time I reached the footbridge across to the Island I felt ready for the real business of the day. Even the forbidding notice at the end of the bridge – warning in large letters that this was a Private Island, with No Thoroughfare or Access To The River – failed to put me off.

Instead I wandered along concrete paths, slightly bewildered by the eclectic collection of architectural styles and the obvious eccentricity of some inhabitants. One garden was entirely filled with plastic dolls of various size. Perhaps not essentially different from the more popular garden gnomes, but it felt decidedly creepy. I'd been wondering which house to stop at to make enquiries, but decided it wouldn't be that one.

An elderly man came along the path towards me, pushing a shopping bag on wheels. Probably a local, I thought. Worth a try.

"Ah... excuse me? I'm looking for the Staysworths?"

He stopped and surveyed me from under bushy eyebrows. "Friends of yours, are they?"

"I used to work with one of the family." Stretching a point, perhaps, but essentially true. "We've lost touch, but I understood they lived on the Island?"

"Hmm. Staysworths, eh?" He nodded sagely and continued to inspect me closely. "Rum lot, them."

"Rum lot?" Archaic turn of phrase. Appropriate to the speaker, though.

"Aye. A bit strange." His expression suggested that anyone acquainted with the Staysworths must be a bit strange themselves.

"Oh. Well, I didn't really know the family. Just my colleague." Who I suspected of having planted a bomb, which could be considered a strange thing to do – but no point in mentioning that.

"Aye." He said again. "Well, they had a place here, right enough."

"Oh, good. If you could direct me..."

"Haven't lived there in years." He watched carefully to see if the disappointment had sunk in before he continued. "They still own the old place though. Rent it out to holidaymakers."

"Really? Well, perhaps they might have a contact number..."

"No holidaymakers in at the moment."

He was still watching me, but I was catching on to his game, and merely nodded. He looked disappointed, but continued. "That girl's living there now. Daughter, I think. Her with the baby. No husband around, though."

"I'll talk to her then."

"You can try. Not a friendly sort."

I wondered why that might be, but kept the thought to myself. "And which place is it?"

"Back the way you came. Past the footbridge, other end of the Island. Old wooden building. Painted blue. Big trampoline in the garden."

"Thank you so much. You've been a great help."

He sighed at the thought, but perked up as another thought struck him. "She's probably out!"

"I'll leave a note!" I called back over my shoulder as I headed back down the path, and left him looking disgruntled.

I was relieved find that the blue wooden building actually existed. I wouldn't have put it past my informant to have made it up, but it was as stated, complete with trampoline. There was also washing hanging out to dry, a promising sign of occupancy.

No answer to my initial knock, however, which was worrying. In spite of my parting words, I really didn't want to have to leave a note and possibly come back again. I knocked again, a bit louder this time.

"All right! I'm coming!" The voice from inside sounded half awake and not happy about it. I braced myself for a difficult confrontation – exactly what I'd been dreading.

The door was opened by a round-faced young woman. She looked tired, and what might have been a naturally pleasant expression was more like fearful. She was wearing a stained and crumpled grey tracksuit and was making half-hearted attempts to brush her tangle of light brown hair out of her eyes.

"What?" she asked. Clearly she had no energy for long conversations.

I put on my best smile. "So sorry to bother you. Is your name Staysworth?"

"Mmm. Yes. Laura Staysworth. Who are you?"

"My names Kepple. Alison Kepple."

"Right."

"You don't know me, but I used to work with Vera Staysworth - that's your cousin, right?"

At the mention of Vera, a look of alarm, even panic flashed across Laura Staysworth's face.

"Vera?" Her voice was somewhere between a gasp and a whisper. "You're from Vera? Is she here?"

She leaned forward, peering round me, as if expecting her cousin to be hiding round the corner of the house.

"No, she's not here," I hastily assured her. "I'm trying to get in touch with her, that's all. I wondered if you knew where she was? Do you have a forwarding address, or a contact number that I might be able to reach her on?"

She turned her attention back to me. "What do you want Vera for?"

"I'm a colleague of hers. Well, used to be." I wondered if I should indicate that it was a police matter, but Laura already looked scared, and mentioning the police might make that worse. "I was just hoping to re-connect with her."

"Connect with Vera? Hah!" Her laugh was more cynical than humorous. "You really don't know her at all, do you?"

Clearly, Laura did know her, and wasn't a fan. "Not well," I admitted, "But I do need to speak to her, so..."

"I don't know where she is."

Inside the house, a baby started crying. Not a quiet little whimper, but a full-on demand for attention.

Laura closed her eyes for a moment. The exhaustion showed clearly in her face, but I thought I saw more than that. For a moment it looked like anger. Or resentment.

I recalled the old man's words - 'No husband around'. Laura was doing this by herself, and it was breaking her.

"I'm sorry, this obviously isn't a good time." I hoped that my sympathy sounded as genuine as it felt. "I wouldn't be bothering you, except that it really is important that I find Vera. Any information you might have about her would be helpful."

"Vera doesn't give information. Just orders. I haven't seen her in months. Don't know where she is, or what she's doing."

The baby's crying went up a notch. Laura turned away, began to close the door.

"When did you see her?" I asked quickly. "Did she say when she'd be back? Did she give you any idea what she might be doing?"

"Months ago!" she repeated. "She said she had some business to take care of. That's all I know!"

The door slammed shut. I could still hear the baby crying.

The return journey was less stressful than the outward trip. Mostly because, having abandoned my fixation on the using the underground, I realised I could get a train – above ground – from Twickenham direct to Euston. From there it was a short walk back to St Pancras, and a short wait for the train home.

I spent most of that journey trying to convince myself that the day hadn't been a complete waste. OK, so I still had no clue about where Vera was now, but I knew she'd visited her cousin a few months ago, and that meant something, didn't it?

The trouble was, I couldn't see any way in which that vague piece of information was in any way significant.

Perhaps what was more important wasn't what Laura Staysworth had said, but how she had acted.

The more I thought it over, the more it seemed that she had been frightened by the mere mention of Vera's name. The rest of the conversation had hardly been a great testimonial to Vera's character, either. Someone who gave orders, but not information. Someone it was hard to connect with – even if you were a member of her family and had grown up with her.

Contemplating that, I felt considerable sympathy for Laura. With all I was learning about Vera, having to share a house with her sounded like a small slice of hell. And then to find herself a single mother, apparently abandoned by the baby's father and possibly hidden away on Eel Pie Island to avoid family embarrassment? I forgave her the abruptness and lack of helpful information.

Which brought me back, again, to the sad fact that, no matter how I looked at it, I had nothing worthwhile to show for a long and stressful day.

Settled into my seat for the last leg of the journey, I watched fields flicker by under evening sunlight, and wondered if I was missing something. I felt like I was missing something. But perhaps that was just wishful thinking. I'd been over the conversation with Laura umpteen times by now, and there was nothing there.

Talking it over with Sam might help. I tried to call him, but it just went to voicemail. I tried a couple of times, in case he just hadn't noticed, but then gave up. He was probably busy. I sent a text instead.

'On the way back from London. Not a great day! Hope yours was better. Talk to you later.'

With only my own thoughts for company, I kept coming back to the fact that Laura had seen Vera few months ago. I still couldn't understand why that could be important. Was there a connection? Had something else happened a few months ago? The trouble was, my mind often imagined connections that didn't actually exist.

I started making another list. This time, a list of everything I'd seen and done that day. It was a way of clearing my head, of organising information in a way I could deal with it.

1. Train journey down.

1. Arrival at St Pancras, walk to the Underground. (Crowds, crush and claustrophobia). Discover that I couldn't get to Twickenham on the Underground. Panic averted by helpful

advice at the ticket office.
2.   Underground to Richmond via Victoria.

I thought about that for a moment. My nerves were tingling. Something about that part of the journey.

I'd changed trains at Victoria.

There'd been a poster. An incident that had taken place there. Months ago.

I swore. Not loudly, but the lady across the aisle from me gave me a worried look. I ignored her.

That's all it was. My subconscious had linked two completely separate things. Laura had last seen Vera 'months ago'. There had been an incident at Victoria Underground 'months ago'. No possible connection between the two things except that they had happened in roughly the same time-frame.

My mind works like that. Sees patterns that aren't really there. It's frustrating sometimes. I keep thinking I'm on the verge of something amazing, but then it turns out to be nothing.

Still, my professional curiosity was aroused. What had that incident been? A fatality. I was wondering about the details. How and who?

It took a while searching the internet on my phone, but eventually found the story. A man fell in front of an oncoming train and was killed instantly. Some witnesses thought he'd been pushed. But there was no clear description of the possible assailant.

"He just staggered forward and fell off the platform," said one. "It might have been an accident, but I'm sure he didn't jump."

It had been a busy time of day. A crowded platform. Everybody's attention on the arriving train. Easy to give someone a shove, and disappear.

The name of the deceased was withheld, probably to allow contact to be made with family. I searched a bit further, to see if there'd been any follow up, but it didn't appear that the investigation had gone anywhere. I wouldn't have expected it to, under those circumstances.

The only other thing I could find about it was a brief mention of the inquest, where the Coroner had given a verdict of 'Accidental Death'. I would have expected an open verdict, but the suggestion of possible murder had been dismissed, presumably because there was absolutely no evidence to back it up.

There was a name. The deceased was Jonathan Martin Aberson.

I read that several times. My internal alarm was sounding again. I knew that name.

The article said he was a lawyer. So perhaps I'd seen him in court?

I googled the name. Not just a lawyer, a barrister. And I *had* seen him in court.

He'd defended Mickey Fayden.

IT WAS LATE WHEN SAM finally got back to me. I'd sent him several messages, but the only reply was 'Sorry, busy, catch you later.' When he finally rang I was already in bed, feeling emotionally and physically drained from the day, and starting to drift into half-dreaming, half-imagining speculation about what had actually happened on the platform at Victoria Underground station.

"Sorry, did I wake you?" he said, probably because my initial attempt at answering had been something between a grunt and a mutter.

"No. Yes. 's OK. I had to answer the phone anyway."

He laughed. "I suppose we're even then!"

"Yeah. All good." I was surprised at how quickly the sound of Sam's voice woke me up. "You had a busy day?"

"Rush rush rush. The boss had double booked – two weddings to do within half an hour of each other and twenty miles between them. So he rushed off to the first, sent me to cover the other and finally turned up there, hot and sweaty, to find that the bride and groom had already left. Also that the buffet had finished, the bar had closed and that the bride's father was threatening to demand his money back if the photos – my photos! - weren't good enough."

"I bet they were, though."

"Well, yes, they were OK. At least, we managed to convince him that I had done everything that the boss would have done if he'd been there, and with a bit of a discount on extra copies that left him happy. Mind you, I still had to spend several hours in de-briefing afterwards, with the boss going over every image in fine detail! Overall, though, it counts as a win, I think. Better than your day, if I caught the drift of your messages?"

"I didn't get what I'd hoped for," I admitted. "No clue as to where Vera might be or how to contact her. But there was something interesting..." I filled him in on events at Victoria.

"That is interesting," he said when I'd finished. "And to be honest, scary. Vera is starting to look like a total psychopath. Which means chasing after her is dangerous. I'm not sure you should be taking this any further."

Instead of worrying me, his words warmed me. "I know, Sam. I thought that as well. But there's still not enough to go back to Special Branch with. No solid evidence, just coincidence and conjecture. Unless you've turned up something about Cadenti?"

"Sorry, haven't had chance yet. I'll get on it tomorrow, promise."

"Right, well in that case I think I'll take a look round Frayhampton. There might still be links I can pick up on. Perhaps there are some people around who who knew the family."

"Alison..."

"I'll be careful," I promised, loving the concern in his voice.

Chapter 9

Moped check list: Numberplate (clean), Fluids (oil, water, fuel),
Throttle, Brake, Clutch, Chain, Tyres, Lights and battery, Mirrors.

I'd been in Frayhampton many times, but mostly just to get off the
bus and start my walk. I'd also been here a couple of times in a
professional capacity, but the last had been over a year ago, for a
burglary. The 'walk-in' sort, where someone steps through an open
door, picks up a handbag or something else of value, and nips out
again. Nothing damaged, nothing touched, in the words of many
scene reports, 'Nothing of forensic value'. Total examination time,
ten minutes. It's not a high-crime area.

I parked my moped in the little square by the church. The bus
stop was on one side, the river ran down the other. Usually I got off
the bus, went over to the river and walked up or down the path along
its bank. Barely even acknowledging the village itself.

I took a bit more time over it today. Behind the bus stop was
a little shop and post office, which sold small amounts of nearly
everything. I'd been in a couple of times for essential walking
supplies, i.e. chocolate. Next to it was a hairdressers, a Chinese
takeaway, and a hardware shop which I'd never seen open and wasn't
now.

Opposite the church was the pub. One of the pubs. There was
another one out at the end of the village. This one was 'The Unicorn'.
The question was, where would I have the best chance of getting
some information about Vera?

Well, it wasn't an either / or thing. I decided to start with the shop.

The shop was being looked after by a girl in her early twenties, who looked as if she was trying to go Goth but hadn't fully committed. Unnaturally dark hair and black lipstick, but no matching jewellery and wearing a bright pink fleece. Her age was a little disappointing. I'd hoped for someone old enough to know some local history. But I would have to go with it anyway.

I'd rehearsed my opening line multiple times on the way, trying to find the right tone and words that would elicit information and wouldn't cause offence.

I couldn't remember any of it.

To give myself a moment's respite, I pretended to study the magazines on the rack, and appeared to be taking a long time choosing between 'Knitting World' and 'Modern Angler'. I can't knit and I've never fished, so I took them both to the counter and added a bar of chocolate, which at least I could eat.

"Just those, thanks." If she thought my choice was weird, she didn't show it, just passed over the card machine. "Um... have you lived here long?"

"Oh, I don't live here. I'm from over in Oaklea."

One sentence in and my plan was already down the tube. I'd have to improvise.

"Alright. Well, I was just wondering about someone I know who used to live here. Vera Staysworth. I don't suppose you know her? Or any of her family?"

The girl's reaction was unexpected. Her head snapped up, her eyes narrowed, and her mouth tightened.

"Why do you want to know about Vera Staysworth?"

Obviously I had offended. Again. But this time I had no idea how or why. "She's a colleague. Used to be. I'm trying to track her down. Or her family."

I got a long, hard stare. Then a very slow and deliberate shake of her head.

"I can't help you."

"Oh. Well, do you know if anyone else might.."

"No."

"Right. Only, I was thinking that she might have gone to school here, and perhaps someone would remember her?"

"The village school closed years ago. Was there anything else?"

I met her gaze, but there was no indication that she was going to change her mind. "No. That's all, thank you."

Outside, I took several deep breaths. Her sudden hostility had taken me by surprise. Either my natural talent for causing offence had gone turbo, or there was something else going on. And the more I thought about it, the more I was inclined towards 'something else'.

She'd known the name. I was certain of that. And if I'd been a real detective, with the proper skills and actual police powers, I would have quickly got the truth out of her. But I wasn't, hadn't and couldn't.

Frustrated, I glanced back into the shop. The proto-goth stared back at me. She was talking to someone on a mobile.

I could imagine the conversation. *"There's a woman here asking about Vera."*

Or was I getting paranoid? But then, if Vera was living back in Frayhampton, she might well have made some contacts, set out some trip-wires. *"Let me know if anyone comes looking for me."*

My instinct was to get on my moped and get out. But that was ridiculous. Even if Vera had been warned of my presence, what was she going to do? Send round a couple of heavies and have me dumped in a lake?

No, more likely she'd scurry off somewhere else. So all the more reason to try and find her before that could happen.

The pub seemed the next best place to try. All local gossip goes through the pub, after all. Plus which, I could use a drink.

I'd been in the Unicorn a couple of times, when I'd done my usual walk in reverse and finished at Frayhampton. Scary, the first time – a new place always is – but there had a been a group of walkers going in, so I'd just followed along. It turned out to be a good place for a pint of cider.

No walkers here today, though, and the bar – a typical village pub interior, well decorated with horse brasses and old photographs – had only a few people scattered around. I took a deep breath, forced myself to relax, dumped my magazines on an empty table, and, since I was on the moped, ordered a fruit juice.

"I'm trying to track down a colleague who came from here," I said as I paid for the drink. "You don't happen to know a Vera Staysworth, do you?" I braced myself for another hostile response.

However, the barman just shrugged. I remembered him from previous visits, a portly middle aged man who I thought was probably also the landlord.

"There was a Staysworth family around here, I think. But that was before my time. I've only had the place for the last six or seven years. The names been mentioned though. Hey – John?"

He called over to a pair of locals chattering over pints, one of them looked up, then came over.

"Young lady's asking about a Vera Staysworth. You knew the family, didn't you?"

"Can't say as I knew them, exactly. Knew of them, but they kept themselves very much to themselves. Lived up the hill beyond the church, as I recall."

"Oh, so they're not there now, then?"

He fumbled through a luxuriant growth of white whiskers to scratch at his chin. "Nobody's there now. Place burned down, must be about ten years ago. Tragic thing, the Staysworths were inside. Only the daughter made it out."

"The daughter – that would be Vera, then?"

"I suppose. I don't think I ever knew her name. Quite a story at the time, it was, worst thing ever happened in this place."

I nodded in agreement. I'd been to a lot of arsons and suspected arsons in my time, and the results of a fire are never pretty. But a death in a fire was the worst in my opinion. The chain of thought brought back a sudden vivid picture. Ruth Darnley, embedded in her car's windscreen, nearly obscured by the flames.

I pushed the image away. "What happened to Vera, then?"

He shrugged. "Dunno. Went to some relatives, I think. Terrible thing it was. They never did find out how it started."

I carried on talking to him for several minutes, but he couldn't tell me anything else. The Staysworths had been in Frayhampton for over twenty years before their deaths but had never really integrated. There was certainly no indication that Vera had ever been back.

Sitting down with my fruit juice, I pretended to read through the magazines but thought about the fire. Multiple fatalities would have meant a full investigation. And Fire Investigators were very good at finding causes. If my informant was correct, and no cause had been found, that would have been unusual. But it happened.

Of course, there always *was* a cause. Fires didn't start themselves. Even so-called 'spontaneous combustion' had its origin in a combination of factors. Materials, conditions, sources of heat. However, the cause could be difficult to find – or it could be deliberately concealed.

Most arsonists gave themselves away. Too much accelerant used, for example. Slosh a lot of petrol over a carpet and you'd expect it to all burn away, but in fact traces soaked through and could still be detected in the debris even if the entire building had burned down.

Multiple points of ignition were another tell-tale sign. Accidental fires didn't start simultaneously in more than one place.

But a clever arsonist could avoid these things. You didn't need to use detectable liquid accelerants; you didn't need multiple ignition points. There were ways of starting fires that left no trace, or none that would survive.

I suddenly realised the implications of this train of thought. Was I really thinking that Vera had deliberately started a fire that had killed her own parents?

The shocking thing was that I wasn't shocked at all. Somewhere in the back of my mind, I'd already come to that conclusion. My habit of seeing patterns and jumping to conclusions had taken me to a dark place, and I tried, frantically, to pull back again.

"There's no proof," I told myself. "And she must have been around sixteen or seventeen when that happened."

So how many sixteen and seventeen year old murderers had there been, I wondered?

Bad question, because the answer was 'quite a few.' Not a huge number – but it definitely happened, and family members were often the victims.

I'd seen a documentary recently – not on murders, on the inspiration behind hit songs. Apparently, 'I Don't Like Mondays' by the Boomtown Rats had been inspired by one Brenda Ann Spencer, who on a Monday morning decided to start shooting at children as they waited for their school to open. She killed two people, injured several others, and gave as her reason "I don't like Mondays, this livens up the day." She had been sixteen years and nine months old.

But Spencer had been mentally disturbed, hadn't she? Psychotic, even?

And did I know that Vera wasn't?

I sighed and shook my head. What it all came back to was that I needed more information. I finished my drink and left, leaving the magazines behind for some lucky reader.

The sun had been trying to push through the low cloud all day: it had finally succeeded and a swathe of bright light lay across the old parish church, making it look very picturesque. I wondered if Vera or her parents had ever attended. Vicars often stayed quite long in one place, didn't they? Or if not the Vicar, then one of his parishioners. Someone must remember a bit more about the Staysworths.

But how to track them down? The Chinese takeaway was shut until the evening, the hardware shop was always closed. I could try in the hairdressers, and if that didn't help, I could drop into the other village pub on my way home. First thing, though, would be to have a look at the Church noticeboard, and see if that generated any contacts.

I was halfway across the square when a man came out of the shop and headed towards me.

My paranoia returned with a rush. He was definitely coming towards me, looking straight at me. A beefy young man in jeans and a sleeveless hoodie. Taller than me and a lot heavier. Probably a lot stronger as well.

Police self-defence training emphasised that the best form of defence was often to run away. I had no problem with that, but *which* way? Back to the pub? Into the church? Get on my moped? Could I get it going before he had time to catch up with me?

As I dithered, he got closer, and as he got closer, my alarm subsided. He might be big, but he didn't look dangerous. In fact, he looked even more nervous than I felt, and as he got closer, he slowed down as if reluctant to actually reach me. Emboldened, and already too late to make a run for it, I stood my ground and tried to appear relaxed about it.

He stopped several feet away from me.

"Um... are you the lady who's been asking about Vera Staysworth?" he asked.

Here it comes, I thought. The warning-off. But it wasn't going to be very impressive coming from this scared young man. Youth, even. I doubted if he was twenty.

Unless he was just a distraction? I glanced round, half expecting to see a couple of serious hard men coming up from the river path behind me. But there was nothing there but some ducks. I turned back to him.

"Who wants to know?"

"Jackie in the shop, she said you'd been asking about Vera Staysworth." I got the impression that he'd be happy if I denied it so he could go away again.

Instead, I nodded slowly. "Yes, I have. Can you tell me anything about her?"

He looked startled, as if he hadn't expected that question. "Me? No. But – you need to come with me." He tried his best to put some authority behind that. It didn't work.

"Why?"

"Because – because you do. There's someone who wants to talk to you."

"Who's that, then?"

He shook his head vigorously. "I can't tell you that. But you need to come with me." He nodded to a battered looking saloon parked nearby. "Get in the car, I'll take you."

There was no way I was getting into any car. "Just tell me who we're going to see and where they are."

"I can't!" he repeated, a note of desperation coming into his voice. "I have to take you. And you need to put this on." He pulled a small sack out of his pocket. "Over your head."

This was turning into a farce. "What? Seriously? No, I don't think so."

His nervousness was increasing, but so was his desperation. I started to wonder if this could get dangerous after all. "Yes! You have to! Or I'll..." he reached out a tentative hand as if to grab my shoulder.

"You touch me and I'll call the police and have you arrested for assault," I said firmly, and he dropped his hand at once. "Look, there's no need for this. I want to find out about Vera Staysworth, and you know someone who wants to talk to me about her – right?" He gave a tentative nod to that, so I continued. "So why don't you get in your car. I'll follow you on my moped. That'll work OK, won't it – and no need for any hoods or threats."

"But that's not..." he was getting agitated now. "You're not supposed to know where we're going!"

"Why not?"

"In case she finds out!" He caught himself, and stopped, worried that he'd said more then he should. Then realised it was too late and carried on. "In case you're a friend of hers."

"A friend of Vera's, you mean?"

"Yeah. That's right."

I shook my head, emphatically. "I'm not. Not at all. Far from it. I'm just trying to find out more about her, that's all. I think she might have been involved in – something." I nearly said too much myself, then. I was already sure that this lad was OK, but I still didn't know what his connection was, so the less said the better.

He was chewing on his lip, nervously. "Right. Just – just wait there a moment, will you?" He walked away again, pulling a phone out of his pocket as he did so.

The conversation lasted several minutes. When it started, he was talking quietly, but as it progressed he became louder.

"How am I supposed to make her?" I heard. "I can't..." He stopped and listened for a while. "She said she'd call the police."

Another pause. "I think she does mean it!" And finally "OK, I'll tell her, but she might not go for it."

He came back over to me. "The person who wants to speak to you – she used to know Vera

Staysworth. Here, in the village. They went to school together. She can tell you lots about her. But you'd have to come with me. I'll bring you back here, I promise."

I considered it. It sounded like the best source of information I could hope for. I couldn't let that go.

"Right then. But no hood."

We began walking across to the car, a blue Honda.

"Ah – about the hood...'

"No."

"Yes. Well, the thing is, without the hood, you'll see where we are. And my sister..."

"It's your sister that we're going to see? The one who knows about Vera?"

He frowned. "OK. Yes. My sister – look, I know it sounds daft, wearing the hood an' all. But she's really worried that Vera might find out where she lives now."

"I wouldn't tell her."

"Yeah. Sure." We'd reached the car, and he fumbled with his keys. "But we don't know you. And we're taking a risk. Because Vera – Vera's nasty. Dangerous. Kay can't risk her finding out."

"Kay – is that your sister, then?"

He closed his eyes and shook his head. "I didn't mean to say that. Yes. Kay. Look, she's really scared. She's got reason to be. So – please?" He held out the hood.

I looked at him, looked at the hood. Then took it, and got in the back of the Honda.

"I really can't believe that I'm doing this," I muttered, and put the hood over my head.

Chapter 10

Investigative Interviews should follow the PEACE model. The first element of this – Planning and Preparation – is one of the most important, and operational circumstances should not allow this to be minimised.

The hood was an old hessian sack. It smelled very strongly of onions, and was so loosely woven that I could actually see quite a lot through it. Enough to realise that my driver wasn't going the direct way. He drove right round the village twice before finally getting onto a narrow lane that paralleled the river valley. The same one I'd often crossed on my walks.

Either he had got lost, or else this was an attempt to hide how long it took to get to our destination. Obviously, he'd seen a few films.

The delay was useful, though. It gave me chance to calm myself. There was a loud voice in my head asking what I thought I was doing, getting into a strange car with a strange man going to a strange place to meet with another stranger. There was a growing tension, a desire to hit the panic button, have a meltdown, tear the hood off and jump out of the car.

I took deep breaths, thought calm thoughts, told myself to be professional, it was an investigation, I was just going to talk to someone about a crime, The same as I did every working day. I listed what I had already learned: I was going to see a woman called Kay,

she was my driver's sister, she had been at school with Vera, she had
reasons to be scared of Vera. Reasons which I wanted to know about.

It was all progress. The tension eased a little and I put aside the
panic button.

After about half-an-hour, only ten minutes of which was spent
actually going somewhere, he pulled over and switched off the
engine. I took the sack off, and looked round.

"No! You're supposed to keep it on till we've gone inside!" he
protested.

"That's not happening," I assured him. "I am not getting out into
the street with a bag on my head. Do you want the neighbours to
think you're smuggling home an exceptionally ugly girlfriend?"

"You're not at all ugly!" he said, and blushed.

"Well thank you, Kay's brother! You do say the nicest things." I
got out of the car, reflecting that, taking into account Sam's remark
about a cute human-woman suit, I'd had two near-compliments in
one day. A personal best.

We were standing outside a row of terraced houses, half-a-dozen
of them, near the bottom of a narrow valley. The lane ran past them
and finished a little further up in a jumble of ruins. A remote little
spot with no other buildings visible.

Remote, but I knew where we were. I'd been through here once
or twice before on some of my longer walks. It was one route up onto
the high moorland, though not the best known one.

"There aren't many neighbours anyway. The end two houses are
empty." He nodded up the street.

"Nobody in them for a while. You can see they're all boarded up.
The two in the middle – one belongs to some sort of sales rep, spends
more time away than here. Old Mrs Derry is next to us – or she was,
till she got taken into hospital. Probably going to put her in a home,
she's past looking after herself. Me and Kay have been taking care of
the place for her. The end house, other side of us, that's someone who

lives down in London. Comes up here now and then, likes to do a bit of walking in the hills. Rents it out in summer, but hardly anyone uses it otherwise. So no one's around to see us." He nodded at the second house up. "We're that one. Number 2. I'll just go in and tell Kay we're here."

I stood by the car and looked round as he went inside, through a door with peeling varnish. The house in general had a sad, slightly neglected look. Actually, none of the properties were in the best shape. As I recalled, they'd been built well over a hundred years ago to house workers for the mill at the top of the valley. The mill had closed and fallen into ruin, but the houses were still hanging on.

The door opened again. "OK, you can come in now."

He ushered me into what I supposed was the front room, but I couldn't see much of it. The curtains had been pulled and until my eyes adjusted it was pitch black. I banged my leg on something, felt around and found it was a chair.

"Sit down." A woman's voice, coming out of the shadows. Kay, presumably. She sounded harsh, but from what I'd learned, that was perhaps to cover her fear.

I felt my way into the chair.

"Why are you asking about Vera Staysworth?"

"The girl at the shop told you that? Is she a relative of yours?"

"That's no business of yours! Just tell me what your interest in Staysworth is!"

"I will tell you. But you can stop all this cloak and dagger stuff, Kay. I'm not a threat to you."

"What? You told her my name? You idiot, Liam!"

"Sorry, I let it slip," Liam muttered from behind me.

"Just like you let his name slip," I pointed out. "Pleased to meet you, Kay, Liam. I'm Alison. So now we're properly introduced, can we have a bit of light here and talk properly?"

There was a moment of silence. "Kay, I could just put the little light on?" Liam suggested.

"If you must."

A small table lamp clicked on behind me. It wasn't very powerful, but between that and the adjustment of my eyes I could now see Kay, sitting in an armchair on the other side of the room. Only just, though. The chair was some dark material, leather perhaps, and she was wearing dark clothes. Shadow on shadow in shadow. It was worse than just a voice in the darkness.

"I'm looking for Vera Staysworth because I think she might have some connection with the bomb that went off at the court a few days ago."

"The one that killed the judge woman?"

"Yes. And it very nearly killed me as well, so you can be assured that I am not Vera Staysworth's friend. Certainly not if she did have something to do with it. And I saw her there, just before the explosion."

"Are you with the police?"

"I'm a CSI. But I'm not here officially. I can't prove that she was there, you see. So I'm trying to find out more about her, and perhaps get a clue as to where she might be."

"So. She's moved up to bombs now."

"If it was her. I don't know that. But you don't sound surprised."

"Nothing Vera Staysworth did would surprise me."

"You knew her well, then?"

Kay laughed. It had more bitterness than humour in it. "Oh, I knew her better than anyone. I was her best friend. Her only friend, really."

Vera's best friend?

I thought about that for a moment, then glanced casually over my shoulder to where Liam was standing in front of the closed door, well-muscled arms folded across his chest. In the darkened room, he looked a lot more menacing than he had out in the daylight.

I still couldn't see Kay properly. Dark clothing, a pale skin framed by dark hair. Not a small woman, though. As surreptitiously as possible I reached into my pocket for my phone.

Her eyes were better in the dark. "What are you reaching for? Liam – has she still got her mobile?"

"I couldn't very well take it off her out in public, could I?" He sounded surly.

"Well take it now!"

"You're taking nothing!" I said, standing up quickly. "I've got this on speed-dial to the police control room: even if you get it off me before I said anything they'd have the location and they always respond to interrupted calls. Especially from police officers – or CSI's!"

The entire sentence was made up of hope, lies and speculation, but it sounded plausible – at least it stopped Liam, who had taken a hesitant step away from the door. Which confirmed my first impression of him – he wasn't a hardened villain, just a big lad with a slightly paranoid sister.

"How do we know you're a CSI," she asked. Which served to confirm my opinion of her.

"I'll show you my I.D. It's inside my coat. I'll take it out and you can check it."

I kept the phone in my right hand, fumbled out my ID with the left, and tossed it into Kay's lap.

"There. Now, what's this about being Vera's friend. Do you know where she is?" A frightening possibility occurred to me. "She's not here, is she?"

"What?" Kay sounded shocked at the idea. And even more scared by it than I had been. "No, of course not. Not unless you brought her! Liam, were you followed?"

"No, we weren't. Sure of it, Sis."

Kay relaxed. Only a little bit. She looked at my card again, and tossed it back to me.

"Satisfied?"

She nodded slowly. "For now."

"So what can you tell me about her? When were you friends?"

"At school. Friends isn't perhaps the right word for it. I was more like her slave."

There was a long pause. I didn't break it, and after a while, Kay began speaking again.

"We were neighbours to start with. Lived down in the village, in Frayhampton. On Hill Street, behind the church. Our whole family was there. We had one side of a semi; my uncle and his family had the other. Grandma and Grandad were a few houses down, until he died, then Uncle John had an extension built for Granny.

"There was a big detached house right at the end of the street, next to us. The Grange. That's what everyone called it. Used to belong to some retired Colonel, but when he died the Staysworths brought it. I must have been eight or nine when they moved in."

"So you and Vera grew up together?"

She shook her head. "We didn't even know about her at first. They were a strange family. Reclusive. Never made any contact with anyone else. Mr Staysworth – no one ever found out his first name – worked away somewhere. Drove off in the morning, came back at night. Mrs Staysworth stayed in the house.

"When they first moved in, my Mum went over with a little basket of things – some cakes she'd baked, a bit of fruit, eggs from the chickens we used to keep in the back. It was what we used to do in the village, make people welcome. Except that the Staysworths didn't want to be made welcome. Wouldn't even let my Mum through the door. Spoke to her through the letterbox, said 'No thank you, now please leave.' My Mum was a bit put out."

"I can imagine."

"She said 'Well, she must be very shy. I expect we'll see more of her when she's settled in. She'll have to come down to the shops sometime.' But she never did. Mr Staysworth did all the shopping somewhere in town. She never left the house, as far as we could tell."

I shook my head. "That's bizarre."

"Yes. The whole village thought so. A lot of gossip about what might be going on. Someone went so far as to go to the police about it, but they said they couldn't intervene since no actual crime had occurred."

I thought that over. Some coppers I knew would have found an excuse to go round there, try and find out what was going on. They should at least have done some background checks. But there were others who wouldn't, and in this case, didn't.

"And what about Vera?"

"It was months before we even knew she existed. They'd moved in around October or November time, and it was a cold, wet winter that year. But when it started getting a bit warmer, I was out playing in the garden. There was a hedge between our property and theirs, but there were gaps in it, and one day when I looked through I saw this little girl. I say little – my age, but smaller than me.

So I called her. 'Hello?' I said. 'Do you live there? My name's Kay. Who are you?'

"She looked and saw me peering through the hedge. And then turned and ran back into their house.

"I told my Mum about it, and it was all over the village by evening. Next day I was looking through the hedge again, but she didn't appear. The day after that some workman came and put up a fence. Ten feet high and solid wood. No gaps at all. All round the Grange.

"Of course, that all sparked a frenzy of gossip in the village. It was obvious that this child wasn't going to school – not the village school anyway – so of course someone reported it somewhere, and somebody official had to look into it.

"But nothing came of that either. The rumour was that this girl was being home-schooled."

"How long did that go on for?"

"Years. We hardly ever saw Vera or her mother in all that time. Occasionally we saw her out for a walk with her father – but never her mother. Sometimes we saw them in the car together. Once or twice the entire family came down to the church on Christmas morning, but apart from that the only person anyone saw was Mr. Staysworth, driving through on his way to work, we presumed."

"That's appalling. Keeping a woman and a child prisoners like that is criminal."

It was hard to see in the darkness, but I thought that Kay shrugged. "Everybody said it. No one did anything. No one could. I know some tried – my Dad was a Churchwarden, and he said that the Vicar had gone to visit on several occasions, but never got past the gate. The authorities wouldn't get involved. Apparently Staysworth had money and was well connected, so he was able to keep any official investigations at a distance. Eventually the Vicar got a letter from some legal firm, telling him to desist from any attempt to contact the Staysworths or a court order would be obtained against him. Or some such legal jargon. I only heard that by eavesdropping on my Dad telling my Mum. They stopped coming on Christmas morning after that."

"But you said you were friends with Vera? What happened?"

Kay sighed and shifted in her chair. "I think maybe they'd had enough of home-schooling her. Or perhaps the authorities finally did something. Whatever. But when I was eleven, I started secondary school. In town. Monument Hill."

"I know it."

"Just a few days before I was due to start there, we had a letter. From the Staysworths. Hand delivered. It said that Vera – first time we'd heard her name! - was going to start at Monument Hill, and since she wasn't used to socialising, they hoped that she would be able to accompany me on the bus.

"I was in two minds about that. Curious about actually meeting her for the first time, but not keen on having to look after her at school. Truth to tell, I was more than a bit nervous about moving up to 'Big School' anyway. I didn't need to have her to worry about.

"But Mum didn't give me a choice. 'Of course you can look after her! Just think how scared and lonely she'll be, after being on her own in that big house all these years!' And of course it would give Mum the inside track on all the gossip that would come out, but neither of us mentioned that.

"Morning of the first day, I came out of our house and Vera was standing next to our door waiting for me. No sign of her parents. Just her in a brand new uniform, brand new bag. She was smaller than me, dark hair cut very short, little white face and dark eyes. She just stared at me, no expression at all, then said 'I am Vera. Mother and Father say we must be friends.'

"And that was it. End of discussion."

Kay was silent for a moment. "Must have been weird,' I prompted.

"Yeah. Weird is definitely one word for it. You know that first day, I don't think she spoke after that first couple of sentences. I did my best. Talked and talked all day. She looked at me whenever I talked, but didn't say a word. Not even to answer questions. Stuck to me like glue – I couldn't even go to the loo on my own – but didn't speak. Not to me, not to anyone. Even when the teacher asked her name, she just looked at her, and I had speak for her.

"It would have been difficult enough starting at that school anyway. New kids get picked on everywhere, and there was a bit of a tradition at Monument Hill – kids from Frayhampton got picked on most. But Vera, with her strange manner and her old-fashioned name, she was a magnet for all the school bullies."

"You kept them off her!" Liam put in. Loyal to his big sister.

"True, I tried to protect her, but some of them were bigger than me, and there was more of them. So the first few weeks were rough on both of us. OK, to keep it in perspective, it wasn't one of those schools where the kids carry knives for protection. It never got that bad. But we got jostled and pushed and our school bags got emptied and at lunchtime our sandwiches were liable to get knocked on the floor. One or two real fights as well, and a few times I came home with bruises or torn clothes.

"Vera started to talk a bit more – at least to me. She stayed quiet in the classroom, didn't mix with the others at break. Which meant I couldn't either. Other kids, and even the teachers, started to think she was a bit dim – and by association, so was I. So it ended up that we were together nearly all the time. And I found myself stuck with that.

"One day, after we'd been there about a month I suppose, we had a particularly bad time. Some kids from the next year up had grabbed Vera's bag and emptied it all over the playground. When I tried to intervene I'd been pushed down and kicked."

"Weren't there any teachers around?"

"This was round the side of the playground, out of sight from the main part. We usually avoided that end, but our last lesson had been in the end classroom, and they were waiting for us when we came out.

"So after they'd had their fun and left us alone, I helped Vera pick up her stuff, but I was hurt and angry and humiliated. Especially as I'd started crying. And I said 'It's not fair, they shouldn't be doing this. I wish we could hurt them for a change, make them scared of us!'

"Vera looked at me, and nodded. 'Yes, that's a good idea.'"

Kay paused again. "I wish I hadn't said that" she added. Almost to herself. "I never should have said that."

"What did she do?" I asked.

"Next day, she brought a hammer to school. Two hammers, actually. One for each of us."

"Oh, heck!" I hadn't seen that coming. "She really planned to use them on the bullies?"

My eyes were fully adjusted to the shadows now, so I could see that Kay was nodding – though with the long dark hair that fell across most of her face, I couldn't properly make out her features.

"She told me, 'With these we will hurt them very badly, then they will be too scared to hurt us again.' When I started to tell her that we shouldn't do that, she started to get angry. The first time I'd ever seen her show that much emotion. I think that she usually kept it bottled up. She kept insisting that we must hurt them, make them afraid. It was obvious that she wasn't interested in hearing that it was too much. Over the top just wasn't in her vocabulary. So I told her that they would tell on us, that there was no way we could hide that sort of thing, and that then the school would call the police and we'd be taken away and sent to prison – and so on. I didn't know for sure exactly what would happen, but I was pretty sure that it was nothing good.

"Eventually, I managed to persuade her. She was very reluctant. She liked her plan. I think she'd been quite looking forward to instilling our enemies with absolute terror. But in the end, she gave me the hammers and I kept them in my bag. They were there all day and I was terrified that someone might look and find them. I had no idea how I would explain it if they did.

"Next day, there was another incident with the bullies. There was one group in particular. A girl called Izzy was the ringleader. Isobel Black. Her and her mates. It wasn't just us they went after, but we were their favourite targets. They had a game where they surrounded us and started pushing, keeping us off balance. The idea was to see how long they could keep us bouncing round until we fell over. Then they'd give us a few kicks when we were down.

"All the other times they'd done this, Vera had stayed silent. I shouted and screamed at them, and they laughed back, but Vera – not a word, not a cry. Until today, when she suddenly grabbed Izzy by the shirt and shouted in her face, 'You are going to be afraid! You will be so afraid!'"

"There was absolute shock, and I took the opportunity to grab Vera, push our way out of the circle and run. Behind us, I could hear them suddenly start laughing, as if it was a big joke. Then they came after us, but we managed to make it into the library, which was safe because there was someone on duty in there.

"I asked Vera 'What did you mean, they're going to be afraid? You know we can't do anything that will get us into trouble."

"She just nodded. 'I've thought about it. We just have to make sure no one knows that it's us. You'll help me.'"

"Of course, that wasn't a request."

"Two days later, one of Izzy's gang had an accident. Her name was... Georgina, I think. Orange hair and freckles. Always late, always last in to registration. Always being told not to run in the corridors – there were some short flights of steps which made it dangerous. But she must have been running that day, and fell down the stairs. Landed badly, broke her nose and knocked some teeth out. Terrible thing. Blood everywhere."

"Vera did that?"

"We did that. There was an alcove, with cupboards in it, just near the stairs. I tied the string one side; Vera was on the other and pulled it tight. By the time anyone came out to look, the string was gone and so were we.

"Next was Sue Sharp. She used to lean back on her chair to talk to Izzy who was at the desk behind her. But her chair suddenly collapsed and she cracked her head on the edge of the desk. Had to go to hospital and have stitches put in."

"Just a minute. If you sabotaged the chair – sawed through the leg, or something – that must have been obvious afterwards, even if it wasn't noticed before?"

"Ah, but that was the clever part. We didn't do anything to the chair. Just switched it for an old one that the caretaker had put aside to mend or throw out. I say we. I did the switching, but it was Vera's plan."

"She had a talent," I observed.

"Oh, yes. People still thought she was a bit slow, but she was so cunning. And once she'd discovered what she could do... I think it was something new to her. To have power. To be able to make things happen.

"In the next few weeks, several of the bullies had accidents. Not all so serious. One girl had a door slam in her face when she was walking through it. Nasty bruise. Someone else burnt their fingers in Domestic Science because they hadn't realised how hot a plate was."

"Didn't anyone realise what was happening?"

"Yes, of course. And rumours started going round the school. Izzy was furious, of course. She was really out to get us, but we'd learned how to avoid her. She wasn't that bright, and we made sure she never caught us on our own.

"I'm not sure how it would have ended, but then Izzy got sick. Seriously ill – hepatitis, I think. Not our fault, of course. Even Vera couldn't arrange that. But by then anything bad that happened to anyone was put down to us.

"With her out of the way, and with the reputation we'd got, the bullying was over. I thought that was the end of it. But Vera – she'd developed a taste; I suppose you could say.

"Things kept on happening. Smaller things. Pens broke and drenched people in ink. Schoolbooks got shredded. Unpleasant things turned up in desks. And it always happened to people who had upset Vera in some way. It didn't have to be much. Just make a joke about her, or call her a name, or make her look bad in front of the teacher.

"Nobody could prove anything. But the whole school was afraid of us. Vera and me."

"But the teachers..."

"Couldn't do much. Oh, they knew something was going on. And they heard the rumours, of course. They had us both in for a talking to. But we were never caught actually doing anything. On the surface we were model students."

"You could have stopped it," I pointed out.

She didn't answer that for a while. "Perhaps." She sighed. "I never tried though. I was scared of her as well, you see. More than anyone else, because no one else really knew what she was capable of. But I knew. I knew about the acid that she'd taken from the Chemistry lab. The razor blades she hid in the lining of her bag. The box of matches and the lighter fluid she had in a safe place. And I knew all the ways she'd thought of using them. It was all I could do to keep her from doing more. I managed to persuade her it wasn't a good idea to target the teachers directly, but she hated having any restrictions put on her. She had this way of looking at me if I disagreed with her – and I knew that it wouldn't take much to turn me from an ally into a victim.

"So I kept on helping her. Getting things that she asked for. Creating distractions. Being her lookout, watching her back.

"And, to be honest, being Vera's friend had its benefits. I was scared of her, but everyone was scared of me. Because it wasn't just the people who upset Vera who got hurt. Anyone who crossed me was in trouble as well. I heard them talking – heard them whispering.

'Don't make Kay angry with you.' In that school, we were the rulers, the Royal Family... and it felt good. Having power felt good."

"Sis... it's all right. You didn't mean to be like that. She made you that way." Liam moved from the door and went round to his sister, leaning over her and giving her a hug. She let out a small sob, and it was only then that I realised that she was crying.

"I just don't like to think of what I was then. I look back and I can't believe what sort of a person I'd become. And it all began because I was trying to do the right thing, to be her friend... instead, I lost all my friends. You can't be friends with people who are scared of you. And everyone was, except Vera."

Chapter 11

PEACE interview model checklist:
Plan and Prepare, Engage with interviewee, Account clarification and
challenge, Closure, Evaluation.

I thought, briefly, of my own school days. Not the happiest time of my life. I'd always been a loner, an outsider. But listening to Kay's story, it now seemed idyllic.

"Well, that's how I knew Vera." Kay shook her head. "Now you know what she was like. Now you know why I wouldn't be surprised if she had something to do with that bomb. If that judge had upset her, somehow... I hope you catch her. She needs putting away."

It was sounding like Kay wanted to finish at that. But there was more. The story didn't feel complete. There was a reason she was hiding in the dark, and it wasn't just school bullying, no matter how vicious.

"Tell me the rest, Kay," I prompted.

There was a long silence.

"If she doesn't want to say more, you can't make her!" Liam put in. "Come on, I'll take you back."

I ignored him. Perhaps a less direct approach would get Kay talking again?

"How long did it go on like that?" I wondered aloud. "You and Vera?"

"Over a year," Kay said. Reluctantly, but once she'd started talking again, she didn't want to stop. "We'd moved up a form. But then Izzy came back. We didn't expect it, she'd been off for so long we'd forgotten about her. But she hadn't forgotten us. She didn't like what she found, that's for sure, with us being in charge. So she got some of her old friends together. And some new ones. She had a boyfriend, a bit of a thug himself, from a couple of forms up. And he had mates too.

"We'd forgotten to be cautious, and one day, after school, Izzy and her new gang grabbed us, hustled us off to the sports field behind the school. There was an old pavilion there – only used for storing equipment, supposed to be kept locked, but everyone knew that there was a way in, and the older kids used to sneak in there to smoke and sniff glue and whatever else. They got us in there and... well, seemed to go on for hours. We were tied up, they slapped and punched and kicked and used cigarettes. And Izzy presided over the whole thing. She kept asking 'Are you scared yet?' I was, of course. I was a sobbing wreck. I said I was sorry, I begged them to stop. But not Vera.

She cried, she screamed when they burnt her, but she didn't say a word. Just kept staring at Izzy. Which made her really mad.

"Eventually, they let us go. We were very late home, of course. But Vera made up a story. 'Don't tell anyone what happened,' she said. 'We'll deal with it.'

"So I cleaned myself up as best I could, and hid the cigarette burns on my legs, and told the story of the detention we'd been given because of something we hadn't done, and how we'd missed the bus... just what Vera had told me to say.

"Back at school next day, and Izzy was ruling the playground again. Her old mates were all round her. But the rest – the sensible ones – were hanging back, staying quiet and waiting to see what would happen next.

"First, there was a rumour that went round the school. Vera was good at rumours. She knew how to drop a word in here and there, so that soon everyone was talking about it but no one knew how it had started.

"This rumour was that if you mixed certain things together, you'd get a buzz. A bit of a high. And then kids were saying that ammonia and bleach were the best."

"What?" I was aghast. "Ammonia and bleach – that makes chlorine! Poison!"

"Yes. Vera knew that, of course. So did most people, anyone who knew anything about chemistry. And when it got back to the teachers, they were quick to put a stop to it. The Head made a big thing about it in assembly, so everyone knew that it was really dangerous and really stupid to mess around with chemicals like that.

"It didn't matter. The point is, the idea was out there. It didn't matter to Vera if anyone believed it or not, just that everyone knew it had been talked about."

"Just a minute – do you mean she was planning to actually use this? To kill someone?"

"I asked that. I was really afraid. But she denied intending any harm. 'I'm just going to make a bad smell,' she told me. 'But if they think it's chlorine – that'll scare them! That's what we want to do, scare them.'

"And I believed her. I didn't dare do anything else."

Kay's voice sounded strained. As if she was fighting to get the words out. Her brother was sitting on the arm of the chair now, his arm round her. "You don't have to talk about it," he said. "She's got the idea now. You don't have to go into details."

She grabbed his hand. "I think I do. Someone has to know the truth. If she's back – if she's out there – someone else has to know the truth about Vera."

She turned back to me. "I believed her, because I didn't really think that she would go that far. Or I maybe I just didn't want to think it.

"I told you about the old pavilion. Izzy and her boyfriend – I can't even remember his name – they used to go down there a lot, to smoke and – well, I don't know how far things went, but I think they did more than just smoke! Since she'd re-established her rule, they had exclusive use of it. No one else dared go near.

"They usually went there at lunch break. But one day Vera got there first and set things up. The door was supposed to be padlocked, but everyone knew that the hasp could be pulled out without any problem. The place was full of junk – old sports kit and the groundsman's tools. Who was going to notice one bucket shoved up next to a bench? Or the plastic bottle on the bench just above it?

"I was keeping a lookout, as usual. Vera just crept up to the pavilion. She waited until they'd lit up. She wedged the door shut, and pushed a stick through a hole in the wall – plenty of those, it was an old wooden building, the planks were rotten in some places – tipped the bottle over so it emptied into the bucket. Which already had the bleach in it.

"We'd got the stuff from the school kitchens. Oven cleaner had ammonia in it. That was in the bottle. They used bleach for the drains and for soaking the dishcloths."

Kay was silent again for a moment. When she continued, she was speaking very slowly.

"I didn't actually see inside. But it was very quick. It worked much faster than we'd expected. Vera didn't need to wedge the door; they didn't even get to it. She'd made a little notice that she was going to hold up at the window. It said, 'Now you're scared!' But they didn't have time to read it. She was disappointed about that.

"She took away the wedge and the stick and the notice, got rid of them. I expected Izzy and her boyfriend to come out gasping and spluttering and furious. I was ready to run. But nobody came out.

"We went back to school, went to afternoon lessons just as normal. I wasn't concentrating. Because I knew what had happened. What Vera had really done.

"Izzy and her boyfriend were marked up as absent, of course. But no one thought much of that.

Wasn't the first time. No one went near the pavilion all day. We went home on the bus, as usual. But that night I couldn't sleep.

"I didn't want to go to school in the morning. I told my Mum I felt sick, but she told me to go anyway and come home if it got worse.

"When we got there – the police were there, the sports field was taped off. They wouldn't let us into the school. Eventually the Head came out. He looked wretched. That's when I actually realised what we'd done. When it finally sunk in. It hadn't occurred to me to think of the effects it would have on other people.

"He sent everyone home. The school was closed all that day. They didn't tell us why at the time, but eventually the news leaked out. That two pupils had died. They didn't say how, but the groundsman had found them that morning when he noticed the pavilion door was open."

"Did they investigate it as a murder?"

Kay shook her head. "Vera's preparation worked. Everyone knew what Izzy was like. They thought she'd just decided to see for herself if you could get a buzz from ammonia and bleach. And of course, who'd have expected a couple of school kids to plan and carry out a cold-blooded murder? I didn't, and I was one of them!"

She made a noise that might have been a laugh, and Liam pulled her close to him. "You didn't know, sis. You didn't know." He was crying himself.

After a few moments I asked, "What happened when you went back to school?"

"When they opened the school again – there was a special assembly. The Head told us what had happened. Not the details, of course. Poor man. He was so shaken; he could barely get the words out. He mentioned their families. I hadn't thought about them before.

"I don't know how I got through that day. I felt sick the whole time. I can't remember anything after the assembly, but I know I was thinking the whole time that I had to tell someone.

"But Vera was there, of course. Sitting next to me, as she always did. Sitting quietly and looking a bit dumb. But I knew better. I knew she was watching everything. I knew she was watching me.

"After school, we went to get on the bus, as usual. Vera went on ahead of me, and suddenly I saw a chance.

'Oh,' I said. 'I've forgotten something. You go ahead – I'll see you tomorrow.' And I slipped out of the queue. She turned round to follow me, but the other kids were pushing their way on. She couldn't get past them. I turned and ran up to school.

"I went to the toilets first. To think about what I wanted to say. I had to get it clear in my mind. Then I went to see Mrs Clarkson. She was the Deputy Head. Everyone's favourite teacher. Firm, but fair, very approachable.

"There was already someone in with her. I think she'd been seeing pupils all day, trying to help them through the shock of it. So I waited outside, in the corridor. And as I was waiting..."

Kay put her head in her hands. She was trembling.

"She came up behind me. I didn't see her. Not until she put her hand on my shoulder. 'Hello Kay,' she said. 'Surprised to see me? Don't ever do that again, Kay. We're friends. We stick together, don't we.'"

"Vera?" I asked, though it was obvious really.

"Yes." Kay's voice had gone so quiet that I could hardly hear her. "She slipped off the bus at the next stop, ran back to school. 'Good thing I caught you in time,' she said. 'I think you might have done something really silly, Kay'.

"I tried to stand up to her. I did. I told her that what she had done was so wrong, that I had to tell someone.

"She just looked at me with a little smile. 'What I did? But Kay – it was all you. I didn't know what you were doing with those chemicals. You were the one who took them out of the kitchen, weren't you? And you were the one who put them in the pavilion. Well, that's what everyone will believe, isn't it. Because you're big Kay, the smart one, the bully. I'm just dumb little Vera who follows you around and does what you tell her. That's what people see, Kay.'

"And of course it was true. Oh, she was so, so cunning... I realised then why she wanted me as a friend. I was her cover, her front-person, her dupe. She hid in my shadow.

'Think about it,' she whispered. 'Everyone will know you're a murderer. The whole school will know. Your family will know. The village will know. They'll look at you and think - 'She killed those people! Her own schoolmates! She poisoned them!' And you'll go away to prison for a long time. Perhaps for the rest of your life. Perhaps they'll put you in the nuthouse, because you must be crazy to do such things! But me – they'll think, 'Poor, dumb little Vera, she didn't know what she was doing, she was bullied into helping, she was a victim as well.' But you – you'll be the monster,

the killer.'

'No, you did it!' I said. 'It was your idea!'

'My idea?' said Vera. 'Wasn't it you who told me that we had to make people scared of us? Wasn't it you who said we had to hurt them? Because that's what I'll say happened.'

"Everything I'd said she twisted. Everything that we'd done or she'd done was my fault. I didn't know how to deal with it.

"I let her take me away from school. We got the next bus home, got off in the square and walked up the hill together. Just two normal schoolgirls, on their way home as normal. Living normal lives. No one knew any different. No one ever would.

"She whispered that to me, all the way. Told me again and again, that everything was all right, just normal. Until we got to my house, then she looked at me very closely.

'Kay. Don't ever think of betraying me. Never again, Kay.'

"That was it. No actual threats. But I knew what she meant. And after that I never even considered telling anyone."

"So you just went back to school?" I asked. "As if nothing had happened?"

"Yes. Just like nothing had happened. Except that it had, of course. A lot of things happened. The Headmaster left. They said he had a nervous breakdown. The groundsman and the caretaker both lost their jobs. And the school – the school was a terrible place. For the next two years.

"There was no one else to challenge Vera. To challenge me and Vera, that is, because I was still her cover, the one out in front.

"She was more careful after that, though. She didn't kill or even injure anyone else. Just did a few little things, now and then. But the fear was still there, all through the school. I wasn't enjoying it any more, though.

"I didn't do very well at school. My reports were all bad. Vera did quite well, especially considering she was supposed to be the dumb one. But I could never concentrate well in lessons.

"Vera started talking to me a lot more than she had before. Now she knew I was completely under her control, she told me things about her family. About how her Dad dictated everything that happened in the house. What time they ate, what time they went to bed or got up, even when they went to the bathroom. Total control freak. But when I said that to her once, she was quite annoyed with me, and I came to realise that she actually quite admired him. Or at least respected him."

"What about her Mum?"

"A nonentity. Vera despised her, because she had no power at all. I felt sorry for her, trapped between her husband and her daughter. Her life must have been hell.

"As time went by, I began to realise from what Vera was saying that there was a bit of a power struggle developing between her and her father. She found little ways to push at him, to test the limits of his control, to see how far he would go. And eventually, he would react. Once she was off school for a week. 'Bad cold' she said when she got back, but I think she'd pushed too far and got the beating of her life. I wasn't sorry for her.

"But after that I felt a change in her attitude towards her Dad. She didn't talk about him as much, but when she did it was with an edge to it. I recognised the signs. It was how she got if she thought someone was threatening her. She was planning something.

"It was near the end of the summer term; we were all getting ready for summer holidays. I was looking forward to it. It was the time of the year when I could get out from under Vera's control. Even then, she was still mostly confined to her house outside of school.

"Monday afternoons, we had double chemistry. That being the last week of term, there was a bit of a wild atmosphere. The kids weren't much interested in doing any work – even less than usual!- and the teachers weren't trying too hard to keep them at it."

I nodded. End of term had been like that in every school I'd been at, a mingling of excitement and impatience that effected everybody.

"So when the teacher stepped out of the room for a minute, some of the lads started a water fight with Bunsen burners. Did you ever do that? Put the Bunsen burner on a water tap instead of the gas and you got a terrific jet of water. They'd soaked half the classroom before the teacher came back in.

"While he was sorting that out, Vera grabbed me, pulled me into the storeroom at the back of the classroom. Which no one was supposed to go into without the teacher's permission.

"I was nervous, of course. I was always nervous around Vera, especially when we were alone together. But mostly I was worried that she'd have some new nasty scheme that she was going to drag me into. I was trying to think who might have upset her recently.

"She gave me one of those little smiles of hers. Which moved me up from nervous to scared, because Vera only smiled when she was planning something. When she smiled it meant that someone was going to suffer.

'There's going to be some changes soon, Kay,' she said. 'I expect to be going away.'

"I remember a little burst of hope when she said that. Vera going away was my dream. It was what I lived for, that someday she would go and I'd be free of her.

"But what I said was 'Oh. You mean on holiday? With your family?'

'No. Not with my family. I've decided to finish with the family. Father is becoming too demanding, and I have to put a stop to it. But that's not your concern. I want to talk to you about us.'

"And now I was more than scared, I was really frightened.

"Vera reached behind a pile of new exercise books and pulled out a bottle that was hidden there. It was one of those little glass bottles that they put acid in for experiments. All the dangerous chemicals were supposed to be in a metal cabinet that only the teacher had access to, but Vera had a way of getting things that she wanted.

"She took the top off, and waved the bottle, sloshing it around. 'Sulphuric acid. Not the diluted stuff they let us use in experiments. This is pure. The real deal.'

"I wanted to get out, but Vera was between me and the door, and she had that bottle in her hands. 'Vera – please...'

'You see, Kay, I've been thinking – if I'm not around to keep an eye on you, you might forget yourself. Say something silly, cause some trouble. I don't want that happening.'

'I won't say anything, Vera, I'll never say anything... please, we're friends...'

"She just shook her head. 'I'm not sure about being friends, Kay. After all, you were going to tell on me, and friends don't do that. So I think you need a little reminder. Not to tell. Because even if I'm not around, if you tell anyone, I'll hear about it, and I'll come for you.'

'I know, I know, I'll remember, I'll never tell, never tell – please Vera...'

I had my hands up, to protect myself, and I was moving back, trying to get away, but I couldn't go far. She had me trapped up against a shelf. Then she grabbed one of my hands, pulled it out of the way, and threw the acid in my face.

"It hurt so much. I could feel it burning on my skin. I was screaming. And I heard Vera screaming as well. She smashed the bottle on the floor, and rushed out into the classroom, screaming.

"I don't remember much about what happened then. I just remember the pain. And the fear... someone was pouring water on me, then there was an ambulance. And I suppose they must have given me morphine or something, because the pain finally went away. For a while."

Some things made more sense now. I finally understood why Kay hid in the darkness. And why she was so terrified at the thought of Vera coming back.

'Some time afterwards people came to see me, and asked what had happened. I told them it had been an accident, that I was trying to get a new exercise book and the bottle had been on the shelf above, that it had fallen on me. Apparently, Vera had told a similar story. So they accepted that. The teacher was blamed for negligence, for leaving the bottle out – he denied it of course, but he was forced to leave the school anyway.'

"And Vera?" I asked. "Did she go away?"

"While I was in hospital, there was a fire. The Staysworths house burned down. Gas leak, they said afterwards. But only Vera escaped. I think she had some distant relatives down in London, she went to live with them. I felt sorry for them, but I was glad she'd gone."

"You think she caused the fire? Killed her parents?"

"Don't you?"

The most shocking thing was that I had no doubt at all.

"You didn't tell anyone that? Or about any of it?"

"Just Liam. When he was a bit older... I got to be a bit of a recluse; you see. I was scared of going out. I didn't want people to see me. And when I was out, I always felt like Vera was there, watching me. I kept catching glimpses of her. My sight isn't good. I lost one eye to the acid, the other one was weak anyway. So I kept thinking that I could see her. Anyone who even looked like her could trigger a panic attack. So I stayed indoors. Liam was my only friend. Since our parents died, he's been my connection to the world."

She gripped his hand, and he hugged her again.

"Is that when you moved up here?"

"After Dad died. Mum went first. I hated living there, even after they built some new houses where The Grange used to be. I wanted to go somewhere that Vera wouldn't know about. So we came out here. Liam keeps in touch with people, though. Jackie, at the shop, she's our cousin – she doesn't know what really happened, but she knows to call us if if she hears that name."

"Vera Staysworth."

Kay shuddered. "Yes. So now you know all about her."

"Well, I know a lot more than I did. I don't suppose you have any idea where she might be now? Anywhere nearby that she might stay?"

A little sob went through Kay. "Nearby? Oh please no! Just the thought that she might come back... I've no idea where she might be.

But if you do find her – you won't tell her about me, will you? You won't tell her where I am?"

"Of course not. But if we can find her, if we can connect her with this bomb, with murdering the Judge – then she'll go away for good."

There was a long pause. "That would be wonderful," Kay whispered. "To know that she was locked up. You'll let us know, won't you? If you find her and get her put away?"

"Yes. Of course."

"Thank you."

"And if you think of anything, any idea about her, give me a call. Let me give you my number..."

Liam rummaged round in the semi-darkness and found paper and pen. We exchanged contact information. "If you need to get in touch, call me first," he said. "Please don't come back here. It makes Kay very nervous if she sees anyone she doesn't know, even out in the street. I'll take you back to Frayhampton. Kay – you'll be all right for a bit on your own?"

"Yes. Thanks Liam."

I stood to go. "I do appreciate your help, Kay. What you've been through has been terrible, and talking about it must be very hard. But if it gets Vera Staysworth put away, it'll be worth it."

"Alison?" said Kay. "If you do find her – be careful. She's more dangerous than you can imagine. She's evil. Don't trust her for a moment."

"Believe me, I won't."

"Liam, pull back the curtains."

Liam hesitated. "Are you sure about that, sis?"

"Yes. Alison needs to understand what she's up against. She needs to see what Vera can do."

The sunlight was weak and grey outside, but dazzling when it was let into that little room. When my eyes adjusted again, I could see the battered old furniture, the peeling wallpaper, and the worn dark leather of Kay's armchair.

Kay herself, a big lady about my age, with long dark hair across most of her face. She slowly pulled it back and looked at me.

On the right side of her face, she was round-faced, quite pretty.

"They did their best, with skin grafts and a glass eye. But there was a lot of damage."

The scars were obvious, but not as bad as I might have expected. She wasn't hideous. But of course, the real scars were inside.

Chapter 12

Things not to discuss with your boyfriend's mother:
murders, crime scenes, insensitivity, her choice of evening wear. Safe
topics: tea, coffee, walking.

I wanted to be with Sam. To tell him everything that had happened, but even more than that, just to be with him. After Liam dropped me off – we dispensed with the sack for the return trip – I checked my phone for messages, hoping he'd planned dinner again.

Instead, I got an apology.

'Sorry, photo job just came up, could be a while, I'll let you know when I'm back. X'

I appreciated the kiss at the end, but it wasn't much of a substitute for the real thing. Still, better than a poke in the eye with a sharp stick, I told myself as I headed back into town.

Kay's story had left me with a turmoil of emotions to cope with. Shock and horror. Pity for Kay.

Not a little fear about what Vera might be doing now, what she was capable of. But also vindication.

I had been right about her. She was a very credible suspect for the murder of Ruth Darnley. Character, motivation, opportunity, presence at the scene – the list was growing.

I just needed to convince Special Branch of that. Last time I saw him, D.I. Halse hadn't seemed very open to anything I might have to say, but I was pretty sure that he was far too professional to let a small misunderstanding over a mug affect his judgement. The problem was getting his attention in the first place. I could try going through DC Dotheridge again, but she was a long way down the pecking order, and that route might take a while. I didn't like the idea of taking a while, not whilst Vera was still out there and perhaps still bent on revenge for Mickey Fayden.

I wondered why she'd waited for so long after he'd been sent down. Of course, his death might have been the trigger, but that was over a year ago. Why now? Or was it that she'd been planning all this time? That sounded like Vera.

The route back into town took me close to Monument Hill School. On impulse, I turned off the main road and went up to look at it.

Nothing very impressive. Typical jumble of different architectural styles, added to in dribs and drabs over the years. The central building was probably the one that Kay and Vera had attended, a three story block of 70's concrete, flanked by a more recent construction whose plastic panels had probably once looked bright in blue and red, but which were now dull and faded. The sports fields were on the right, partially built over with another, even newer block. I wondered where the old pavilion had been?

Above and behind the school was The Bowl, or Monument Hill to give it its official name. I stood up there just a few days ago, looking down, without the slightest idea of the terrible things that had happened there fifteen years ago. I doubted if anyone at the school now knew its dark history. I hoped not. It wouldn't make for happy school days – though kids being kids, they'd probably think it was really cool.

I needed Sam more than ever, and going back to my flat with at best only Ollie for company didn't appeal at all. Another impulse had me turning the other way along the town by-pass. Ten minutes or so later I pulled up outside Sam's house.

Properly speaking, his parents' house. I'd been there once before, sometime back, on official business: an arson attack. Standard stuff, liquid accelerant through the letterbox, followed by a rag ignited from outside. No major damage, though as usual with fires it had left a huge mess. But Sam's dad, Graham, had been injured in the fire, making it into a major incident so I'd been there all day.

Ironically, and sadly, just a few days later Sandra, Sam's mum, was nearly killed in a major fire that had engulfed a huge swathe of old buildings around Delford Mills. The family, I reflected, had had their share of troubles.

It was starting to get dark now, and I hesitated before getting off the bike. Sam probably wasn't there, or he'd have texted me. I'd just be disturbing his parents, and I'd be better off going home myself.

On the other hand, since I was here anyway, why not?

From past experience I knew that they didn't use the front door much, so I went round the back, and knocked. After a delay, it was opened by Sandra. A middle aged woman with a warm smile, wearing a dark blue cardigan over a pink rabbit onesie, with a purple headscarf.

I assumed she hadn't been expecting visitors.

"Oh, hello – Alison, isn't it?" A whole jumble of emotions crossed her face, too fast for me to read, but settled into a polite welcome.

"Yes, that's right. Hello Mrs Deeson. Sorry to bother you, I was just passing and I wondered if Sam was home yet?" Passing by going in the opposite direction from my place and up a cul-de-sac, but there was no need to go into that sort of detail.

"No, not yet. I'm not expecting him back for a while. He's gone to Leicester with his Dad. But please come in."

I shook my head. "No, it's OK, I just dropped by on the off chance – I won't disturb your evening."

Sandra laughed. It seemed a little forced, somehow, and I wasn't sure why. Embarrassment at being caught in her onesie, perhaps. "You know what? I was just sitting here thinking how boring it was being on my own and wishing someone would come by – so do come in, at least long enough for a cup of tea. Or coffee. I usually make coffee, Graham's the tea expert, but we've got both. Real or decaf as you prefer. Oh, and do call me Sandra. I hate being 'Mrs Deeson'. Well, not being Mrs Deeson, of course, just being called it. Sounds so formal. I'm not a formal person."

"Oh. All right then." It seemed rude not to, and I really didn't want to be rude to Sam's mum. Besides, as social situations went it wasn't too bad, just two people having a natter, I told myself. "Decaf coffee, please."

Sandra led the way into the kitchen, and busied herself with kettle and mugs. "Hope you don't mind mugs. I always prefer them for coffee. Cups for tea. I don't know why, just a habit I suppose. Except espresso, but I don't drink that very often anyway."

A small black dog hauled itself out of a basket, and wandered over to sniff at me.

"Hope you don't mind dogs. That's Brodie. Not the world's greatest watchdog, but he does like to say hello to visitors."

Brodie accepted a stroke from me, but snorted contemptuously and went back to his basket. Probably put off by the scent of cat.

"Did you say Sam's gone to Leicester?" I asked.

"That's right. You know Graham used to be a sports reporter? Mostly retired now, but he does a bit of free-lancing, and he got an opportunity to interview that controversial rugby player – what's his name? Hoolihan?"

"Hoolihan the Hooligan?"

"Yes, I think so. Smashed up a bar in London after a match, and his career has been on hold ever since. Well, apparently he's trying to make a comeback. Graham was offered the chance to talk to him about it, but it had to be in Leicester and it had to be today. So he rushed off at once, took Sam with him to take photos and help with the driving."

She put two mugs down on the table. "Are you all right at the kitchen table? Only the lounge is a bit of a tip at the moment, I'd just started sorting a few things out, old clothes for the charity shop, we get a lot of donations at church but they need looking at, some of them are a bit – well, they need washing, shall we say, so I'd taken that on but I wasn't getting on very well with it."

"Oh, the kitchen's fine." I pulled up a chair and sat down. Sandra produced a plate of biscuits and sat opposite me, talking the whole time. I hadn't realised from our previous meetings that she was so chatty.

"Actually, I often think the kitchen's a nicer place to sit and talk. A bit cosier, somehow... anyway, Graham and Sam went to see this Hoolihan, sounds like a bit of a character, doesn't he? Funny name, I thought it sounded Irish but apparently he's from Leeds. Though over in the States a 'Hoolihan' is something to do with Rodeos, I think. I read it somewhere. Some way of wrestling a bull or maybe using a lasso, I can't quite remember. Interesting word, though."

She suddenly stopped talking, took a deep breath, and shook her head. "I'm sorry. I don't usually gush like that. I'm not even letting you get a word in."

It was only then that I realised that Sandra was actually quite nervous. And that it was me who was making her that way. And I couldn't understand why I would make anyone nervous – least of all this strong, resolute woman who I knew for a fact had discovered two murders, solved them both and had survived two serious fires in the process. If anyone should have been nervous it was me.

And because I was nervous, and because I'm the person I am, I blurted it out. "Why do I make you nervous?"

She sighed, put her cup down, then very deliberately looked me in the eye. "It's that obvious?"

I felt myself blushing. "Sorry. That was blunt. I didn't mean to be rude."

She shook her head. "No, not rude. Honest. Sam says that about you. That you're honest and open and say what you think."

"I... Sam talks about me?"

Sandra was smiling. "Oh yes. All the time. Especially recently, but you've been dropping into the conversation ever since Rob and June's wedding."

"Oh." I knew I was smiling. Grinning like the Cheshire Cat, actually, but I couldn't stop myself.

"That's why I'm gabbling on so much. Nerves. Because I know you mean a lot to Sam, and as soon as saw you at the door I was terrified that I might make a bad impression. Especially because..."

I waited for her to finish.

"OK," she continued. "You like to be honest, so I'll be honest as well. Do you remember the first time we met?"

"Yes. Of course. That murder at the library. I was working the scene and you had to come in for something." I was aware of a growing discomfort in my gut, the sort of thing you get when you realise you did something wrong but don't know what it is. I get that a lot.

"That's right. And while I was there, you asked me to look in the Memorial Wing."

"Oh, yes. That was where the body..." I stopped, suddenly seeing where this was going.

"Yes. The last time I'd been in there, I'd found a body. And then you asked me about the fire extinguisher."

"The murder weapon." I swallowed. "I suppose that must have been difficult for you."

"It was. But I know you didn't realise that."

"I was probably focused on the job. On the examination. I don't get emotionally involved. But of course it was different for you. I'm sorry. I'm really insensitive sometimes."

I was gripping my coffee cup hard, but I couldn't drink any of it. My guts were in turmoil. Once again, my stupid ignorance of people, my sheer dumb blindness to their feelings, had come back to bite me. And of all people, Sam's mother! Before I'd even met the most important person to ever come into my life I'd already sabotaged my relationship with his family, trampled over her feelings at a time when she was really vulnerable.

"It's all right. It's OK, Alison."

Sandra reached across the table and touched my hand: I, of course, on edge and not thinking, reacted as I normally do and snatched my hand away. Regretted it immediately, put my hand back on the table, but of course it was too late and we stared at each other in mutual embarrassment.

"I'm sorry!" I said again, but talking right over Sandra as she also tried to apologise. "Sorry, Alison, I know you don't like to be touched - Sam said..."

It was too much. I stood up (too quickly, the chair nearly fell over). "I'd better go, I shouldn't have come, I.. I.."

"Please don't! Please don't go!"

I was desperate to get out, to escape the awful situation I'd created, but Sandra's plea was just as desperate.

She was standing as well. We looked at each other across the table.

"Please," she said again. "I haven't gone about this the right way at all, but I need to tell you... That thing with the body, it was a long time ago, and I'm over it. It was just, well, that past history between us was on my mind. That's why I was nervous. Because I was afraid it might come out somehow and you'd think I was being ridiculous, being stupid, carrying on about something in the past that wasn't an issue at all to you, just part of your job." She took a deep breath. "And – while we're being honest – I was afraid that if you were annoyed at me it might affect how you saw Sam. And if I was responsible for spoiling your relationship, I couldn't forgive myself. Especially because..."

She broke off, mid-sentence. I met her eyes, and saw tears in them.

"You're going to think I'm a silly selfish old woman," she continued. Her voice had dropped till I could hardly hear her. "The thing is – Sam was away for a long time, you know. When he dropped out of Uni and went globe-trotting. We didn't have much contact with him at times. I used to worry so much. And I blamed myself as well. For a long while. He says it wasn't me, but it's hard to get out of the habit. So the thing I'm most afraid of is that he'll go away again. That I'll do or say something to make him go. I was so glad when he started talking about you, because I thought that you'd be a reason for him to stay around. But if I got between you somehow, broke it up, he'd leave for sure, and it really would be my fault this time."

I sat down slowly, and so did she. I took a deep breath, reached out and touched her hand lightly while I struggled to find words.

"That's why I'm nervous." She sighed, shook her head. "Put into words it sounds ridiculous, doesn't it?"

I found it hard to speak round the lump in my throat. "It – I don't think it's ridiculous. Not any more ridiculous than not realising that a murder scene might be hard to re-visit for the person who discovered the body. And not more ridiculous than being afraid that she'll hold a grudge and turn Sam against me because of it."

"No. No, of course not. Never. And I hope you won't give up on Sam because of me, either."

"No! I'll never give up on Sam." As I said it, I felt a total certainty in my words. More than I'd realised was there. "I couldn't. I.."

She raised an eyebrow, but I just shook my head. Not appropriate, to be blurting out 'I love him' to Sam's mother, especially when I haven't told Sam himself.

In any case, I didn't need to. Sandra knew. "Good. Because, you know a lot of people like him, he's good with people – but we all need more than that. And he deserves to be loved. Of course, I'm his Mum, I would say that – but what I mean is, he deserves *your* love, Alison."

"Thank you. I just hope I deserve his."

"Oh, I think so." She gave my hand another squeeze and let go. "In any case, you've already got it. I'm sure of that."

She picked up her coffee, put it down again. "Getting a bit cold, I'll make some more. Well, honesty's not a bad thing, is it? Hard work, but worth it!"

I stopped for another coffee and we talked more normally. Avoiding all topics relating to CSI work and shared past history and even Sam.

My phone chimed to indicate a text, and a moment later so did Sandra's

"Sam," I said. "They're stuck in traffic."

"Yes. Just got the same thing from Graham. Some sort of incident on the motorway."

"Could be hours." We exchanged glances. "No point in waiting for them, then. I might as well get off."

"Yes. It's getting late enough – have you got to go far?"

"No, shouldn't take more than twenty minutes at this time." I stood up. "Thanks for the coffee, Sandra. And for the chat."

She stood as well. "I'm glad you came round, Alison. I know we've met before, but I think we actually got to know each other properly this time. And got a few things sorted out." She laughed a much more natural laugh than the first one I'd heard from her.

By the time I got back to my flat the events of the day were catching up with me, leaving me feeling exhausted. Not just physically tired: there was a deep weariness in me, an emotional draining that came not just from today but was an accumulation of all the recent events. And, at its heart was the appalling thought that all this pain, all this grief and loss and sadness could be traced back to just one person. One sick, twisted individual.

As a CSI, you can't be long in the job before discovering just how nasty some human beings could be. You can't last long in it if you let it get to you. But Vera's one-woman career of constant warfare against the rest of the human race – that was a whole new level of sickness. And it had got through my armour, inflicted an energy-draining wound in my soul.

I went through my return-home check list, using routine as a protection. Door locked, bolted, checked. Coat hung up behind the door, keys on the hook next to the door, helmet in the hallway cupboard, boots on the shoe rack by the cupboard. Mentally ticking things off as I did. There was comfort in security, there was security in everything in its place, everything where it belonged.

There had been a few letters for me in my box on the ground floor. Mrs Edmondson, who has the ground floor flat, always sorts everyone's mail into their respective boxes: she has her routines as well. I dumped them on top of the cupboard, where I put items awaiting attention. All probably junk mail anyway, but I'd check it in the morning.

Something out of place caught my eye. The leaflet – tract? - that my curate neighbour had given me, dropped there and still not given attention.

I'd misread the title. In the quick glance I'd originally given it, I'd thought it said 'Do you deserve God's love?' But looking at it now, it was 'Does God deserve your love?'

Not what I'd expected to read. But on the basis of today, of all the last few days...

"No, he doesn't," I said aloud. "Not if he allows people like Vera to go round destroying lives!"

I opened up my laptop, and did a search for tragic deaths at local schools. It didn't take long to find it. Headlines in local newspapers, shorter stories in some nationals. All pretty much confirming what Kay had told me, but without the details, of course.

Enough grief for one day. I hurried through the rest of my routines and went to bed.

Chapter 13

Preparing a Statement for Court: 1) Be clear and concise. 2) Stick to the facts – use what's in your Scene Examination Report. What you did, what you saw, what you recovered. 3) If for any reason you include information from outside the Scene Examination Report, be clear about its source and relevancy. 4) Don't speculate.

N ext morning, Sam woke me with a phone call. Again.

"Umm?" I'm not chatty at the best of times. Especially not when still half asleep.

"Sorry, did I wake you? Terrible when that happens, isn't it?"

If it had been anyone else I would have cut them off. But it being Sam...

"Tha's twice. I only woke you once," I mumbled.

"Not a problem, I won't charge extra for it."

I said something rude.

"That's not the sort of language I'd expect from a lady!" He sounded amused rather than upset.

"I'd give you a ladylike kick in the..."

"Alison!"

"...buttocks if you were here. What time is it anyway?"

"Half past eight. Bad night?"

"Half eight? Already?" I sat up in bed. "Not great. Too much on my mind." No actual nightmares, but the thoughts that had filled my head when I was half-awake were as bad, if not worse. Kay's story was not something that could be easily dismissed. "What about you? What time did you get back?"

"About midnight. Mum told me you'd been round – sorry I missed you. But I understand that you two had a good chat."

"Yes. We did. How was your photo thing with, what's his name, Hooligan?"

"Hoolihan. Yes, that was an interesting experience. Great rugby player, but very full of himself. Wanted to keep posing for pictures whilst Dad was trying to ask questions. Well, made a nice change from weddings. I managed to get some good shots, I think. Especially the ones where he wasn't posing."

"And how come you're so chirpy if you were back so late?"

"Oh, I'm a morning person. Been up since six-ish, doing that bit of research I promised you."

"What – Cadenti?"

"That's right." There was a pause. "I managed to find something on him, but it's not good news."

I felt suddenly, coldly certain of what Sam was going to say. "He's dead."

There was a long pause before Sam replied. "Did you know, or was that a guess?"

"Call it an informed guess. How did it happen?"

"Well – according to some newspaper reports I found, it was a burglary that went wrong. Apparently someone forced the back door, perhaps believing the house was empty, and they were surprised when Cadenti came down to investigate. There were signs of a struggle, but Cadenti was hit several times on the head by a heavy object. They don't say what, but the implication is that it was something from the house – ornament, perhaps."

"Rather than something the offender brought with them."

"Yes, I suppose that's the point. No indications of a premeditated murder."

"And I take it they didn't get anyone for it?"

"No. Cadenti lived alone, worked as a Security Guard – his absence wasn't noticed for a few days, until he didn't turn up for his shift, then it was another day before they made a serious effort to check up on him. A colleague went round and found the body."

I thought about it. "You're sure it's the same person. The same Cadenti?"

"Pretty sure. I'll send you the links to the articles I've found but his full name is Carlo Cadenti, and they mention that he was a police officer in 'a southern police force'. Which, since this was up in Newcastle, would include us down here."

"When did it happen?"

"Not long... just over a month ago."

"Right. So he was probably the second person she targeted. The lawyer was first, then Cadenti Getting the long-distance ones out of the way first, before she came down here."

"So you're assuming this was Vera. It's still a big jump, Ali. From someone who's sneaky about getting her own back – to murder."

"It's not. Not when you take her past history into account."

I summarised the story I'd heard from Kay. Sam was shocked into silence.

"Of course, none of this can be proved," I admitted. "Even with Kay's evidence – we only have her word for it. But put it all together – that's not just my imagination. Is it?"

"No," Sam agreed. "No, that's far too much to be coincidence or imagination."

"Thank you."

"Ali – you remember what we talked about before? About how you could have been a target for that bomb? Well, you could still be a target. That level of vindictiveness, that doesn't go away. It doesn't just stop. If Vera's behind these murders, if she's really driven by revenge for Mickey, then from her past history she might not be satisfied until everyone who was involved in the case is dead!"

"Everyone? That's a lot of people. Do you think she'd extend it to anyone with any connection at all? What about the Jury – could she track them down?"

"I wouldn't put it past her to try."

A thought struck me. "Rob and June! They were both involved in the whole thing. In fact it was mostly due to them that Mickey was exposed. They'll be on her list for sure."

"Yes! Of course they would."

"I need to warn them."

"Better yet, you need to hand this over. Give it to someone who can act on it with the proper resources. To protect yourself and anyone else who this madwoman might have a grudge against. Please, Alison. No more lone wolf on this."

His concern warmed me even as the potential threat chilled me. Weird sensation.

"No, you're right Sam. I've done enough digging around. I'm going to offload this as soon as I can find someone to listen. The only problem now is getting some attention. Special Branch are handling everything connected to the bombing, and they haven't really been very open to what I've had to say."

"Yes, I see the problem. I suspect the political agenda is what's driving their investigation at the moment. A lot of elements, in and out of government, are using this to push the 'War on Terrorism'. Is there anyone else you can approach? Your own superiors, perhaps?"

I considered that for a moment. "I could go to my line manager. Or direct to Head of CSI. But the best they could do would be forward it on to Special Branch, and I don't know how much priority it would get. I really need to give this to someone with a bit more clout, to get action taken immediately. Perhaps even outside the Special Branch investigation."

"OK. Let me think for a moment."

I got out of bed, headed for the kitchen and coffee. "Call me back, then, I've got to finish waking up."

"Hang on, I've had an idea. Why don't you go outside the bomb-investigation thing? Make this about Vera. And Mickey."

"How do I do that?"

"Well, I was thinking – the Senior Officer in the original investigation. The one who took Mickey to trial. They would probably still be interested. All the more because Vera might have them on her death list! Go to them with all this stuff."

"Detective Superintendent Grombert. He was a DCI then, SIO – that's Senior Investigating Officer – for the whole Fayden thing. But he retired a few months ago."

"All the better. If he's retired he might have more time on his hands. And I'll bet he'll still have contacts. Enough to get some attention."

"Sam, that's a great idea. Listen, send me those links and I'll use this morning to write everything up. Everything we've learned about Vera, all Kay told me, the possible links to Fayden, Plus Cadenti's murder and then the bomb. Finish with that, not start with it. And afterwards – how about lunch?"

"Lunch it is. The usual?"

"See you at the Nook!"

A good night's sleep and a conversation with Sam made a huge difference to life. Of course, Vera was still an unpleasant reality, who had done some terrible things and would probably do more if she wasn't stopped – but we had put it together, Sam and I, we'd worked it out and we'd expose her. We'd put a stop to her twisted little career. We had the story, we had the strategy, we'd bring her down.

And in spite of Vera, in spite of all the Veras of the world, outside it was a bright morning and inside even Oliver seemed to be in a good mood and consented to being made a fuss of after feeding.

I worked my way methodically through my morning checklist, deliberately not rushing into the morning's main task of writing up a report on Vera. I knew from experience that I'd concentrate better if everything else was done.

That included going through the accumulated mail. Mostly junk, as expected. I'd picked up the tract as well, and sat at the kitchen table to glance through it. The title had caught my eye, I had to admit, mostly because it was just the opposite of what I'd expected.

"Does God Deserve Your Love?' Not the question I'd expect to come from a Church leaflet. That was usually taken for granted.

Inside, it was short and to the point. A few bullet-point headings – all the reasons people give why God didn't deserve to be loved. i.e. war, famine, disease, injustice.

Add 'Vera' to that list, I thought to myself.

I anticipated a matching list of all the good things God has done for us but instead, on the back of the paper was the question repeated. 'Why does God deserve our love?' and a picture of the Cross.

Underneath it said, 'Because he has sacrificed everything to share everything with us.'

A slightly ambiguous statement, I thought. Share what, exactly? Presumably the writer knew what they meant, but as with a lot of religious tracts, they assumed a similar point of view that for me didn't exist. Still, I supposed it might work as a starting point for a discussion, should I ever take up Curate Pat's offer for coffee and chat.

More important things to do first, and with everything else out of the way, I could get on with it. I dumped the tract and the junk mail into the recycling bin and fired up my laptop.

I laid it out as I would a formal statement for court, starting off with my name, rank and current station. But after that, the question was, where to start? I didn't want to go straight into the bombing and my glimpse of Vera at the gate. This wasn't just about the bomb. It had been my starting point, but not Vera's.

On the other hand, beginning with Vera's school crimes didn't seem right either. Too long ago and too reliant on Kay's story. No chance of any supporting evidence after all this time.

This was for the attention of D. Supt. Grombert (Retired). Initially, at least. It had to get his attention. So the best place to start would be the point at which he got involved. Which was Mickey Fayden.

'In (add date and time later) I was involved in the police investigation of Michael (Mickey) Fayden, at that time a Detective Sergeant based at the same station. Specifically, I carried out a forensic examination of his home address, during which I recovered various items including some tablets later identified as being a Class A illegal drug with the street name of La Paz, or Lappies. I later gave evidence in court at Fayden's trial.

I have recently been made aware of certain information that I believe may have a bearing on this case...'

I went on to carefully detail all the information I'd gleaned about Vera Miranda Staysworth.

Finishing with my sighting of her outside the court, and finally drawing everything together.

'In light of this information, I believe that it is a credible possibility that Staysworth may be involved in the murders of Cadenti and Darnley, and that she may be planning further actions against persons involved in the arrest and subsequent trial of Fayden. I further believe that resources should be allocated to a full investigation of her current and past activities, with a view to identifying crimes she may have committed, obtaining evidence regarding these crimes, and preventing any further crimes.'

Should I include the lawyer, Aberson, in the list of victims? I was pretty certain that Vera had pushed him off the platform at Victoria

Underground station, but there was no proof at all. I decided to leave it out. At this stage, it would weaken my case, and if a proper investigation was carried out, it would come up anyway.

I read it over. It wasn't a textbook example of statement. No supporting documentation, like a Scene Examination Report – though I could make reference to the one from Mickey's house? I considered it, but decided not. Without a copy of the actual report to hand, I couldn't risk making references that might later prove to be inaccurate. As it was, I felt uneasy about straying into speculation and suggestion. Still, this wasn't actually for court, it was to get Vic Grombert interested, and I needed to make sure he got the point.

I corrected a few typos, printed it out, signed and dated each page.

Done.

I just needed to get a copy to Grombert. Post? No, I thought, I'd hand-deliver it. It would have more impact that way. As long as I didn't manage to upset him. Fortunately, I'd hardly ever met the man, so hadn't ever been on his wrong side. As far as I knew.

The downside of that was that I had no idea where he lived or how to contact him. No problem, I knew people who knew people.

I picked up my mobile, flicked through the address list and made a call.

"Hi – Helen? Is this a good time to pick your brains?"

"Alison! Finally, I get to hear from you!"

I laughed. Helen had a way of raising my spirits just by being there. I could imagine her smile lighting up the office. "Sorry if I've been out of touch. But you could have called me, you know."

"No I couldn't! Derek's told everyone that you're to be left alone while you recover. No calls, no visitors."

"Derek should keep his nose out," I said. "But for goodness sake don't tell him I said that! I'm fine, really."

"Glad to hear it. I just hope you're getting plenty of rest."

"I'm... just keeping myself occupied." By tracking down a serial killer, but I didn't say that. Too much explanation required. "How about you? I knew you were due back off maternity leave – are you in the office now?"

"Yes, just easing myself back into the routine this week, catching up on some paperwork, making Charlie multiple cups of tea, all the usual stuff... he says 'Hi' by the way."

"Tell him 'Hi, and isn't it about time he actually went out and examined a scene?"

There was a brief pause while the message was passed, and Helen's voice, slightly muffled - "I can't say that!" before she came back to me.

"Charlie said something very rude, even by his standards!"

I sighed. "Not missing the office banter! But I didn't call to catch up on how Charlie's doing with his eternal statement. I was actually wondering if anyone there had an address for Vic Grombert. The Detective Superintendent who retired recently?"

"Oh, I've got that somewhere. He and his wife hosted a charity thing just before I went on leave. I didn't go, but I think I kept the invite. Hold on."

There were drawer opening noises, paper shuffling noises and drawer closing noises.

"Here it is," Helen announced. "It's not far from you, actually. Warkestone Abbey – that's just past your place, isn't it?"

"A couple of miles up the road."

"5 Abbots Walk. Do you need the postcode?"

"No thanks, I can find it. Thanks Helen."

We chatted for a few more minutes whilst she brought me up to date on the new baby. Her first, and to go by her description, not a good advert for motherhood. "All appetite at one end and no self-discipline at the other!" she complained.

"I'm told it gets worse when they hit the teens!" I said encouragingly, and promised to be in touch again soon before disconnecting.

It was just past 11. I would have time to get to Warkestone Abbey and see Grombert before going back into town to meet Sam for lunch. I could leave my report with him, ask him to read it and get back to me, which might actually be better than hanging round while he looked at it. I didn't want to give the impression that I was pressurising him.

I folded the printout and slipped it into an inside pocket of my jacket. Ran quickly through my check list. Finished with my usual question.

"Are you OK, Alison?"

I was making serious progress in tracking down a murderer. And I was making serious progress in a relationship.

"I'm better than OK! A lot better."

I smiled at myself. It was nice to feel so positive about life.

I was sitting on the moped and adjusting my helmet strap when my phone rang. I sighed, pulled the helmet off again and answered it without checking.

"Hello? Alison – is that you?"

Liam's voice. I'd half expected Sam. "Yes. Liam? What's up?"

"Where are you just now?"

Why did he want to know that, I wondered. "I'm just on my way out. Has something happened?"

"Vera," he said, and I felt a coldness in my stomach. "She's been in Frayhampton, asking about us. Cousin Jackie at the shop just called."

"OK. Has she been anywhere near your house?"

"No. I don't think so. Jackie wouldn't tell her where we are, of course. But someone in the village might. She could turn up at any time."

I thought for a moment. "Liam, I think you should get out of there for a while. Pack a bag, and you and Kay go and find somewhere else for a day or two. It won't be longer than that, I don't think. I'm just on my way to see someone who can make this thing official. Someone who can start a search for Vera, launch a proper investigation. You just need to be safe for now and we'll get this sorted."

"But where would we go?"

"Anywhere. Friends – relatives..."

"There's no-one who'd put us up. Not at short notice. Perhaps not at all. We don't really know many people, and the family – well, that's Jackie's family and to be honest, we don't get along. They think Kay's a bit weird. It would be difficult."

"I see. Well, a hotel, bed & breakfast – take a holiday, go to the seaside!"

"Can't afford it. Honestly. A night in a hotel would clean us out."

"Right. Well, let me think."

There was an obvious solution, but it wasn't one that I liked. I couldn't see any other possibilities, though. And it would be short term. "Liam? You can stop at my place if you like. It'll be a bit cramped, but for a day or two, we can manage."

"Really? You'd do that? Alison – I..."

"Yes, well it's an emergency isn't it? Listen – here's the address..."

"Hang on, getting some paper – go ahead..." I reeled it off and he read it back.

"Get down here as soon as you can," I instructed. "Ring me when you arrive, if I'm not back I'll come and let you in."

"OK – hang on..." There was a muffled conversation in the background, then Liam came back on. "Kay says she won't go. She's as frightened about leaving the house as she is about Vera finding her." He lowered his voice to a whisper. "Do you think you could come and talk to her? She might listen to you."

I took a breath, thinking about it. The time it would take to get to Frayhampton and talk Kay round – even if I could – would seriously delay me getting to see Grombert, and I had a sense of urgency about that. Once Vera was officially a 'Person of Interest' in the case, then we'd all be a lot safer.

Plus which, I'd miss lunch with Sam. Not the main consideration, of course, but I needed to bring him up to date on all this.

"I can't come just now. I'll get over to you as soon as possible. In the meantime, keep the doors and windows locked. Don't let anyone in. If Vera shows up, just stay quiet and ring me. Better yet, ring the police. With any luck they'll be looking for her by then anyway."

"Yes. Yes we'll do that. Look, don't worry about us, Alison. I know Kay's scared, but I'm sure we can deal with Vera if she turns up."

Typical young male bravado, I thought. "Liam, don't underestimate Vera. She's seriously dangerous, and Kay has reason to be scared. Really, it would be best if you got out of there for a while."

"I know. But it's OK. Listen – I've got a gun."

I went cold all over again. "Liam – do NOT start shooting at her or anyone else!"

"Relax. It's just an old shotgun that Grandad used to keep for rabbits. Not been fired in years, I don't think we've even got any ammunition for it. But if Vera turns up and gets nasty, I'll just wave it at her. Scare her off."

"Well, it would be better not to get guns involved anyway. I bet you don't even have a licence for it, do you? Don't answer that, best if I don't know. Just try and persuade Kay to get out and I'll be there as soon as possible."

"Ok. Thanks. Where are you going now, then?"

"Never mind. I'll tell you about it later. It'd take too much explaining just now, and I need to be on my way. Bye for now."

He started to say something else but I'd already cut him off. The quicker I got to see Grombert the better. I put my helmet on, started the moped and headed for Warkestone Abbey.

Chapter 14

Road Safety Checklist – Junctions:
Always approach junctions at a safe speed, be prepared to stop if your
exit is not clear.

Actually, it's a bit of a misnomer. There was an Abbey at Warkestone once, but not since the 1500s.

Henry VIII shut it down along with most of the other monasteries, friaries, convents, and priories in England in what some regard as the biggest land-grab in British history. Otherwise known as the Dissolution of the Monasteries. The building was stripped of all its valuables and then set on fire, this being the easiest way to get at the lead on the roof. What remained was re-purposed as raw material for new houses, barns and other structures. All that now remains of the Abbey are buried foundations and the name.

The principal street – Abbot's Walk – runs up to a field where the foundations are marked by a badly weathered wooden sign. There are some nice properties along the walk, a pub at the end, and a handful of cottages scattered around nearby. A very quiet little place, with nice views and jaw dropping property prices. Even a Detective Superintendent was doing well to have a place in Warkestone Abbey. Though I'd heard that his wife was a Consultant Gynaecologist, so I supposed that they'd managed it between them.

Perhaps they'd done so by cutting down on other expenses. As I turned up the drive, the only vehicle I could see was an old van, painted matt black with decorative rust streaks. It didn't match the property, which, whilst not the grandest along the Walk, wasn't the smallest either. A relatively new building, it probably didn't incorporate any of the Abbey's stone, but it was still very nice – red brick framed in wood, mullioned windows and a large conservatory stuck out at one end, ideally situated to catch the sun and make the best of the view out across the valley.

I went past the van and parked near the front door. From here I could see a detached garage at the far end of the house, the door open to reveal a big 4x4 and a vintage Jaguar – much more in keeping. The van was probably a workman's.

I took off my helmet, put it on the seat and headed towards the front door. There was a polished brass bell push next to it and a CCTV camera above it. I put on my professional face, smiled for the camera and rang the bell.

I could hear a musical chime sounding inside, but there was no sound of any response. I waited for another minute, then pressed it again. And, after a further delay, tried knocking.

Still no answer.

Something felt wrong. If they were out, why was the garage full? They could be walking, they could have taken a taxi – but the garage door was wide open, with two expensive cars inside and clearly visible. Some people might do that, but police officers, even retired ones, are usually quite security conscious.

But there was the workman's van - so where was the workman? Perhaps they were in the house – or behind it? It was quite likely that the Gromberts had a gardener. I didn't know how far back the grounds went, but it was certainly possible that someone could be busy there, out of earshot.

Which was the best way round, I wondered? The garage was connected to the house with a high wall, no obvious gate. There might be access round the back of the garage, but a paved pathway ran in the other direction, past the conservatory.

I started to walk in that direction, pausing on the way to try and look into the house. However, peering into a dark room from outside is always difficult, and all I could make out was some heavy looking furniture and a large TV, switched off.

The conservatory would have been easier to see into, except that the blinds had been pulled down. The path took me all the way round and it wasn't until I was at the back of the house that I saw a gap big enough to peer through.

The Gromberts were in.

Vic Grombert was sitting in a wicker armchair just opposite me, apparently asleep. At least he seemed very relaxed, and his head had dropped forwards, so I couldn't see his face.

I could just make out another person. A grey haired woman, sprawled over a sofa that matched the armchair. It didn't look like a comfortable position; her head was hanging over the edge.

There was a bottle on the low table between them, and a couple of whiskey glasses, half full.

A coldness had crept over me as I looked through the window. I tapped on the glass, knowing full well that there was nobody there to hear me.

It could be that, in the middle of the day, Mr and Mrs Grombert had drunk themselves into a stupor. It could be that the worst they'd suffer would be a severe hangover. But I didn't think so. Their positions, their unnatural stillness, told me that I'd arrived too late and that I was looking at a crime scene.

First thing to do, call for help.

I dialled 999, got through to the Ambulance, gave them my name, the address, the bare details.

"Yes, I'm looking at them now, through the window. No, I don't have access, though I haven't checked all the doors yet. No, they don't appear to be conscious..."

Round at the front of the house, an engine started.

The black van.

I cut off the stream of questions. "I've got to go! I think there's someone else here. They might have access."

I hung up and broke into a sprint, going back the way I came, round the conservatory to the front of the house, just in time to see the black van disappearing down the drive.

Workman or gardener, finished and going home? Perhaps. Or perhaps not.

Acting on instinct, I flung myself on the moped. For once it started first time. I dragged it round and headed down the drive, trying to jam the helmet over my head at the same time.

Not very successfully, it was still over my eyes when I reached the road, and I was forced to take a moment to adjust it. Which way had the van gone? Surely not left, that was a dead end. So I turned right.

Bottom of the road, and a glimpse of the van heading out of the village. Not going back towards town but heading in the other direction, which would eventually take it down to the dual carriageway that led out towards Anniston. I swung out to follow it and pushed the moped up to its maximum.

Which wasn't much. Somewhere between 30 and 40 mph, downhill. The van was already out of sight as I passed the last house. There was a long straight stretch from here, then a series of bends as the road wound its way downhill. Perhaps that might slow it down? There were also some side roads it could turn into, but my best bet was that it was heading for the main road. There was a roundabout at the bottom, if I remembered rightly. If it was busy, the van would get held up there. I still had a chance of catching it.

And what if I did? I hadn't stopped to think about that. I wasn't going to pull it over, was I? And once out on the dual carriageway I would never be able to keep up with it. So no chance of following it.

But if I could get the registration, that might help trace it. Or just a good look at the driver.

It was Vera, I was sure of that. She'd gone after Vic Grombert because he'd headed the investigation that brought Mickey down. His wife was probably just collateral damage in Vera's warped vision of justice. But I still needed some evidence, some proof. Too much to hope that she'd left any useful forensics at the scene, but if the van could be traced, if she could be linked to it...

All ifs, and none of them counted at all unless I managed to catch up. I entered the first bend without slowing down. It was a right-hander, not too sharp and I got round it all right but it was immediately followed by a vicious left-hander that sent me skidding and drifting across the road, almost into a car coming the other way. It slammed to a stop with a wild blaring of its horn and I managed to get back to the proper side of the road, just a few feet from collision and a glimpse of a man's face white with shock.

It wouldn't help anyone if I killed myself. I really should slow down, never mind catching the van. Stop, in fact, then call the police and tell them about the van and about Vera.

I thought all that as I swung into the next set of bends without slowing. I'd do it if I couldn't catch up at the roundabout. It was only a matter of a few minutes.

A minor road branched off to the left, I shot past the entrance too fast to look for the van. Another one came up on the right and this time I managed a quick glance but there was no sign of anything there.

Only a few more bends to go. I could see the next one was clear, so allowed myself to swing wide.

Fortunately this was a very quiet road. I hadn't had to brake once since I'd turned onto it.

And now I was coming down the last stretch, quite steep in parts but perfectly clear and I could see all the way to the roundabout.

No van.

It had beaten me to it, was already gone. I swore to myself and started to slow down.

And then – there it was. Just a glimpse, out of the corner of my eye. In my mirror. Matt black, even the radiator grille, and bearing down on me fast from behind.

In that moment I suddenly realised that chasing after a killer is not a course of action to be entered on impulsively. Especially not when you're on a moped, and they have a van.

Clearly it had pulled into one of the side roads, turned round and then come out behind me as I passed.

I sped up again, pushing the 50 cc engine to its absolute limit. The van kept up easily. Catching up, now only a dozen yards behind.

Ahead, the road began to flatten out as it approached the roundabout – which was typically busy, traffic on the main dual-carriageway was always heavy, a near constant stream of cars, vans and everything up to big artics thundering past in both directions.

I wouldn't be able to stop. The van would push me out into the traffic, and no one would even know it was murder, just a nasty accident. Or I could slow down and it would run right over me. It had all the advantages – position, speed, momentum. And I was running out of road.

The lane had no footpath. Just a narrow grassy verge and a stone wall on each side. Not a good place for walking. Not a good place to get caught by a homicidal maniac.

I had to get out from in front of the van. There was nothing coming up the lane, I swerved across and tried to brake, but the van had been hanging back enough to see and counter my move. It followed me, bumper nearly touching my back wheel as I accelerated again and went back across the lane to try and get some space but the van matched me. And even if I managed to drop back beside it, the driver – Vera? - had only to turn the wheel slightly and I'd be crushed up against the wall.

The roundabout was just a hundred yards away, I was doing forty miles an hour, cars were hammering past, barely slowing down for the roundabout, and I only had a second to think of a way out, only half a second...

A massive artic was on my right, just entering the roundabout, the driver staring ahead, not even seeing me. And behind the van had slowed, pulled back slightly. Not wanting to shoot out into the traffic itself, but staying just close enough to nudge me out if I tried to stop.

So don't stop.

I kept the revs up. Swung right again and the van followed, but I wasn't trying to get round it this time, just giving myself room...

Just before I reached the roundabout I went left. I couldn't slow down and I couldn't avoid going out of the lane, but I could change the angle that I came out at, making it as sharp as possible, turning as hard as I could with the tyres screeching and skidding and the side of the artic looming over me, the huge thundering rear wheels rushing to meet me.

There was room. Just enough room to fit a moped and rider between the artic and the edge of the roundabout. There was room, and the angle was sharp enough and my turn was tight enough. And there was a narrow strip of pavement round the edge, just enough so that my knees and elbows were hanging over it as my sadly abused tyres scraped along the curb and the artic's wheels were close enough to touch, without even extending my arm.

Then they were gone. Passed. The back end of the artic's trailer was above me, in front of me, drawing away from me. I could read the sign on the back that said 'In case of dangerous driving, call...'

I didn't get the number. I hardly noticed the frantic blaring of a horn behind me, as I suddenly appeared from nowhere in front of the car which had been following too close behind.

Chapter 15

First three things to do after a burglary: 1) Phone the police. Dial 101 if the offender has left, or 999 if they are still present. DO NOT confront them. 2) Avoid moving items or disturbing the scene – you may damage forensic evidence if you do. 3) Try and note items moved or taken.

I t was hard to keep on riding, I was shaking so badly that I couldn't steer straight. I did manage to slow down. The car passed me, with someone in the passenger seat making rude gestures in my direction. I hardly noticed, and certainly didn't care.

I kept an eye on my mirror, but there was no sign of the van, just a steady stream of traffic coming from town. It would have had trouble getting out from the lane, and might have headed back into to town rather than pursue me.

I was sure it must have been Vera. Who else would be trying to kill me? I hadn't actually seen the driver properly, but it must have been her.

It was several miles before the next roundabout, where I could turn round and head back into town. But there was a lay-by coming up before then, I remembered. It usually had one of those roadside café places parked up there. A converted ambulance: I'd done forensics on it once, when the owner had left it parked up and it had been broken into. He made strong tea, and I needed something like that.

The lay-by came up and I pulled in. The café was there with a lorry parked up in front of it, the driver leaning on the counter and chatting to the owner. I pulled in behind it, put the moped on its stand, took off my helmet and sat for a while, struggling to cope with the aftermath.

At least I hadn't burst into tears, I thought. Well, my cheeks were wet, but I wasn't sobbing. I wanted to, but I wasn't. And I was still shaking, but I was also still breathing and that was the important point.

Checklist: arms, legs, fingers, toes, head – all intact. Moped – surprisingly undamaged. Tyres would need checking. And the engine. It wasn't used to that sort of punishment.

When I'd convinced myself that everything was all right, I took out my phone and called Sam.

"Hi – are you there already?" he asked.

"N..no. Um, something, something – er – happened." There was an annoying tremor in my voice, and Sam caught it at once.

"Ali? What's happened? What's wrong?"

"Sam, it's OK. I'm OK. But – I went to see Grombert. The retired Detective Superintendent I told you about. And – he's dead, Sam. Him and his wife. Probably dead. I saw them through the window, I think they were dead."

The mental image of Vic Grombert and his wife in their conservatory had been suppressed by subsequent events, but it came back now, and with it the shock. I've seen plenty of dead bodies, it goes with the job. Most of them in much worse condition. But the thing about going to a body as a CSI is that you already know that they're dead before you go. Going to talk to someone and finding them unexpectedly dead was an entirely different experience.

I found myself choked up and unable to go on for a moment. Sam said nothing, which was the right thing to say. I got my voice back and carried on. Trying to be professionally dispassionate, possibly succeeding.

"There was a van," I explained. "On their drive. I heard it start while I was phoning the ambulance. So I chased after it. Stupid thing to do. I suppose I was hoping to get the licence plate. Or see the driver. I was thinking it might be Vera."

"And did you catch it?"

"No. It caught me. Came up from behind, tried to run me over or push me into an accident."

"What? Ali..."

"I told you, Sam. I'm OK. Mostly. Just a bit - shaken up, that's all. Look, I'm not sure I'll make it to the Nook for a while."

"Where are you?"

"Lay-by on the way to Anniston. The one with a converted ambulance made into a burger bar."

"I know it. Stay there. I'll come and collect you."

"No, it's OK. I'll be fine, I'm going to get a cup of tea, calm down a bit, then I'll come to you. And besides, I'm on my moped."

"Right. And do you want to be on your moped if Vera finds you again?"

He had a point. I felt vulnerable just sitting on it in the lay-by.

Sam continued. "There's a neighbour of ours who has a pick-up. I'll see if I can borrow it, to move your moped. Then I take you home, help you pack and you move out until this is over."

"What? Where? Why?"

"What is move you out. Where is something we can sort out later. There's a spare room here at my Mum and Dad's, or we'll put you in a hotel. Whatever you prefer. As for why, well, think about it. If Vera could find the Gromberts, she can find you. And if you weren't on her bucket list before, it looks like you are now!"

My flat was my safe place, my refuge. To think of it having become a danger zone was another blow to my fragile composure. My first thought was denial. My second was that Sam had a point.

"Right. Yes. OK, But I've offered Kay and Liam a place to stay! They could be turning up there any time."

"Oh. Well, that's not going to work now. We'll think about it. I'm sure we can come up with some options. The main thing is to get you safe."

"Thanks. I do appreciate that, Sam."

I'd never heard a smile before, but it was definitely there in his voice. Warm and gentle. "I'm glad you do! But seriously – just stay put until I get there. And stay safe."

"Yes. I'm fine now. Mostly. Just a bit shaky. I'll get that tea now. See you soon."

Tea from the ambulance café came dark and strong and in large, comfortable mugs. I loaded mine with sugar and started sipping at it, feeling warmth and comfort from both the mug and its contents.

"You all right, luv?" asked the owner. "Only you're looking a bit pale."

"Near miss on the roundabout. I'm OK."

I drank the tea slowly, letting it calm me. How long would it take for the ambulance to get there, I wondered. The target response time for situations where there was danger to life was – what? Eight minutes, I thought. They didn't always manage to get that, but they were pretty good round here. That was if I'd managed to convince them of the urgency. I'd only seen the Gromberts through the window, after all. I'd said that they didn't appear to be breathing. Surely that would be urgent enough.

Assume they made it in eight minutes. They'd be there by now. Then they'd look through the windows – I'd told them where to go. They'd probably bang on the glass, try and wake someone up. Natural response, but they'd be looking for access as well. Would they force entry or did they need to get the police for that? I didn't know. But I'd told them that the place appeared locked up, though I hadn't actually checked the back door. They might have requested police assistance while they were on the way, that happened quite often.

So, they could be inside within a few minutes. How long to check for signs of life? No idea, but not long. I would guess that within fifteen minutes, perhaps half an hour at the most, the police would be recording a suspicious death incident, and CID would be notified. And having a senior officer involved – even a retired one – would make it a priority.

I could probably expect a call back within an hour, and I'd be in the station giving a statement not long after that. Then I could tell them the whole thing. And give them the statement about Vera I'd already prepared. I wasn't sure what the reaction would be, but for sure they'd be on the lookout for the van and for Vera. They'd also be finding out who'd dealt with Cadenti's murder, and talking to them. And once they'd joined the dots for themselves, it wouldn't be long before they called in Special Branch about the bomb connection.

It was almost over, I realised, and felt a strange sense of peace flood over me. A tension I hadn't been aware of suddenly eased and only then did I realise how much I'd been carrying. Ever since the bomb, ever since I'd half-seen someone by the courthouse gate.

Vera's murderous revenge spree had claimed too many lives, but it would all come out now, and she'd be stopped. Liam and Kay would be safe. Rob and June would be safe.

I'd be safe.

The relief must have been obvious in my face. "You're looking better already," said the café owner when I went back for a second cup. "Can't beat a good cuppa tea, can you?"

"Best medicine I've ever had from an ambulance," I agreed. And, bearing in mind that lunch at the Nook was probably not going to happen, I had a burger as well.

Not as good as the tea. Cold bun, greasy onions and overdone beefburger. I was still picking bits out of my teeth when Sam arrived in a battered blue pick-up. He jumped out with the engine still running and enfolded me in a rib-crushing hug that was followed by a kiss that might have got more passionate except that I was suddenly self-conscious about the burger bits.

"You can't know how glad I am to see you," I told him.

"Can't be more glad than I am to see you – and still in one piece!" he said.

This might have gone on for a while, but I glanced over at the Café and saw the owner staring at us with misty eyes and a soppy smile on his face. I bet he loved soap operas.

"Come on. I'm expecting CID to get in touch before long."

"We're still moving you out. You're not getting out of my sight until I'm sure you're safe."

I smiled. "I've got no problem with that!"

Typically, Sam had had the forethought to bring a few planks along, which made getting my moped into the back of the pick-up a relatively easy job. Out on the road, I felt a lot more secure than I had on the moped. Perhaps it was time to get a car, I thought.

We arrived back at my flat without incident and no calls from CID or anyone else. There was no sign of Kay or Liam either.

"Right. How long will it take you to pack?"

"Ten minutes. Just toss a few things into a rucksack, grab my laptop and feed Oliver – that's the cat. I'll need to come back tomorrow to check on him."

"We'll come back."

"Fine with me." I paused. "You don't have to come up now. Not that you're not welcome, but I wasn't expecting visitors... and I sometimes leave washing drying on the radiators. I take it that a few items of underwear won't shock you too much?"

"I shall avert my gaze from anything unseemly," he promised. "But, like I said, I'm keeping my eyes on you!"

"Right then." I led the way into the house and upstairs. "Don't be too impressed by the Georgian grandeur, I do only have a few rooms at the top. Servants quarters, basically."

I reached my door, turned the key and glanced back at Sam as I opened it. "Though it is quite an interesting building, over two hundred years old... what?" Sam was looking past me into the flat.

His expression had changed.

"Stay here," he said, pushed me aside and went in.

I turned and stared after him. "Sam?"

Then I saw my flat. But it wasn't my flat. It couldn't be. I must have gone into the wrong building, opened the wrong door.

In all honesty, I couldn't remember if I had left any undies drying on the radiators. Quite possibly. But I certainly hadn't emptied my hallway drawers all over the floor.

"What?" I said again. "What?"

I've seen plenty of burglaries. I've seen many victims of burglaries. I know what a shock it can be to see your home after a messy search. But I'd never experienced it myself. I'd never had my brain freeze up in disbelief, unable to understand what I was clearly seeing.

Sam had disappeared into the bathroom. He came out, went into the bedroom, then down the hall to check the kitchen / living room at the end.

"All clear," he said, coming back down the hall. "Whoever it was has gone."

"Wh.." I started to say yet again. I was shaking. There was a little sobbing sound: I knew I was making it myself, but it seemed very distant. I was disconnected from it. From everything. Because it couldn't be happening. Not to me. Not in my safe place.

Sam touched me, gently. "It looks like you've been burgled, Ali."

Light as it was, his touch gave me an anchor. Something known and safe in a world that had suddenly becoming strange and threatening. I grabbed his hand and clung on.

"Burgled?"

The only thought that came to me then was that it was really bad luck to suffer a burglary on top of everything else. I took some deep breaths, forced myself to step aside from the panic, to put on my CSI persona.

"Did they take anything?" I asked. It's what you ask at a burglary. But you ask the victim. You ask the 'Injured Party'. And that was me. "Sorry. Daft question. How would you know? I need to see for myself. I need to make a list."

"OK, but don't touch anything."

Which was supposed to be my line. "Yes, I know. I'm a CSI, remember?" Or would be, once I had the right head on.

He had the good sense to look embarrassed. "Oh. Yes, of course. Sorry, I didn't mean to sound like..."

"Yes," I interrupted. "We both know what you sounded like!"

I stepped through the doorway and went down the hall, being careful to avoid disturbing the scattered items. Sam's little faux pas had helped me get fully into professional mode. I pushed aside the horrible sick feeling that came from seeing what someone had done to my home. I noted but then ignored the feeling of invasion, even violation, that so many burglary victims had told me about but which I now understood on a visceral level. I shunted aside the tears and the anger and focused on looking. Even more important, seeing.

My initial training, by an old-school SOCO (Scenes of Crime Officer) had started with a few simple rules on how to approach a crime scene. 'Look before you touch.' 'Think before you step.' 'Never enter a scene without wearing gloves.'

I didn't have any gloves, but that mattered less in my own flat, which of course would be covered in my fingerprints anyway. Nonetheless, I avoided touching.

The bathroom was off to the left. Bottles of shampoo and conditioner had been emptied over the floor, the loo was filled with toilet rolls, and my clean towels had been thrown into the bath. The taps were on. I turned them off, the surfaces were poor for fingerprints in any case.

Opposite the bathroom was my bedroom. The wardrobe and every drawer was open, contents everywhere.

I didn't linger, but went on to the end of the hallway, and the living room / kitchen beyond. Quite a large room, light and airy.

Furniture up-ended. TV knocked over, broken glass everywhere. Not just from the TV. Ornaments had been destroyed. Most of my crockery. The fridge was open, food emptied out...

In spite of my determination to remain objective, there was a lump in my throat. And once again, my cheeks were wet. Second time today, I didn't know I had that many tears in me.

Sam had been following me carefully. He rested his hand lightly on my shoulder and I leaned into him.

"Very untidy search," he commented. "They must have wanted something really badly."

"Not just a search," I said. I thought I managed to sound very calm, considering. "This was – angry. Deliberately destructive. Personal."

"Personal? Who would hate you this much?" He only had to pose the question to realise the answer. "Oh. Vera?"

"I think so. If she was in the van... after I got away, she must have come straight here. Perhaps hoping to find me again. When I didn't show, she took it out on the flat."

Sam glanced round him. "That is actually more frightening than a real burglary. Are you sure there's nothing missing?"

"Hard to tell with all this... mess." I looked round again. "My laptop! That was on the table. No sign of it now."

We looked at each other. "Was it unlocked?" Sam asked.

"I don't think so. I don't usually leave it like that. I'd just finished printing out my statement when I left, so it's possible, but I would normally shut it down. Why take just that though?"

"I think that after trying to kill you, Vera started wondering why you'd turned up there. What you were coming to see Grombert about."

"So she came here to find out what I knew?" I had a sudden shift in my thinking as another pattern suddenly emerged. "She saw me! At the courthouse. When I saw her at the gate – of course she saw me at the same time. But she recognised me straight away. So she'd have been wondering if I'd recognised her and told anyone!"

"Then you arrived at the Gromberts while she was still there. Which must have confirmed for her that you knew something. Or had guessed. Maybe she thought you were there to warn them? But in any case, she came here to find out what you knew and who you'd told. And to wait for you. Had a good search round while she was waiting, took your laptop to try and hack into it."

"Or to stop anyone else from reading what I've got on it."

"Did you send anyone that statement?"

I shook my head. "I only made one copy. This one in my pocket."

"I wonder how she got in? I didn't see any damage to the door."

"Oliver!"

Sam looked puzzled. "Your cat let her in?"

"No. Well, not deliberately. I keep the bathroom window open for him. It lets him out onto the roof, and there's a fire-escape at the back of the house. Vera might even have seen him going in and out."

"Which means she was watching the house. Maybe for a while." He saw my expression and broke off. "Sorry, didn't mean to make things worse."

"They're bad enough. What's worse is wondering where she might be now. How come she left if she was waiting for me?"

"Perhaps she saw us both turn up and decided that that was more than she wanted to deal with."

I wasn't sure. Vera didn't seem like the person who backed off easily. On the other hand, she did like to plan things. So maybe Sam's presence had caused a change of plan. I suggested as much, and he nodded in agreement.

"In any case, I don't think we should hang around waiting for her to come up with any new ideas. Let's just get out of here. I think we should go straight down to the police station, never mind waiting for CID to call you. Go and report this, we can talk to CID about the Gromberts while we're there, let them make the connections."

"That's a good idea." I looked round again, wondering what had happened to Oliver. But he was a survival expert. If there was trouble, he'd make himself scarce, and come back when he thought it safe. "Let's do that."

Sam led the way to the door. He turned as he reached it and smiled back at me. Warm and reassuring. "We'll sort this," he promised as he turned the handle and opened it.

And screamed, and fell back onto the floor.

A slender figure was standing there. Someone with short dark hair. She had something in her hand that she raised and pointed at me.

"Hello," said Vera. "Alison, isn't it? Goodness, it's been a long time!"

Chapter 16

ASP: 'Armament Systems and Procedures:
US company, major manufacturer of police equipment. The acronym is
often used to refer to their range of extending batons.
(Not to be confused with an asp, a venomous snake allegedly used by
Cleopatra to commit suicide).

A stun gun uses a hi-voltage, low-amperage burst of current to disrupt the body's nerve signals. It produces a temporary weakness in the muscles and disorientation in the brain. Also, it hurts a lot.

Sam was on the floor, twitching. Vera stepped forward, and the gadget in her hand snarled and flared with electricity.

"Don't move, or I'll use it again."

I looked at her, and at the stun gun, and at Sam. The effects of a stun gun aren't permanent, and she hadn't used it for long. He'd recover quickly – as long as she didn't give him another shock.

"Vera." I inclined my head. A cordial greeting between two colleagues who hadn't met in a while.

"Oh, you remember me? How nice. Aren't you going to invite me in?"

"You've already been in."

"That's true," she agreed. "No need to sound so surly about it!" Stepping forward again, she stood over Sam, whilst reaching behind her and pulling the door closed.

Sam groaned and stirred, trying to get his muscles to work
properly. Vera frowned, and triggered the stun gun again. Just as a
warning.

"I think you should just stay where you are and keep still," she
said firmly. She took another step forward. "Now then Alison, I'm
sure we'd both enjoy a nice chat, but what I really want to know is,
what you were going to talk to Vic Grombert about?"

"That would be the Vic Grombert you just murdered? And his
wife?"

"Yes, of course. Who else would we be talking about?"

Vera spoke with a strange sort of intensity. Like someone very
angry but in control. She was smiling, but it was a forced smile, on
the verge of becoming a snarl at any moment.

Sam had fallen backwards from the door. She was standing level
with his head now. I could see his hands moving, very slowly, as he
worked his fingers, testing how much control he had. I needed to
keep Vera's attention away from him, give him chance to recover.

"I can't believe that you can talk about it so casually. You took a
life, two lives..."

Vera triggered the stun gun again to interrupt me. "Just tell me!"

"OK. OK. I was going to ask him if he knew anything about you.
If he knew where you might be living now."

"And why would he know that? Never mind, I know there's
more. What did you print out to show him?"

"I didn't print anything."

Vera shook her head. "Don't lie to me. Your laptop was switched
off, but still connected to the printer. Which was still switched on.
You printed something recently. Something you were going to show
Grombert. I want to see it. Now!"

I was very aware of the printed sheets in the inside pocket of
my coat. If she read them, she'd not only know how much I knew,

she'd also know where I'd got the information from. It would lead her straight to Kay and Liam.

(Who might turn up here at any time, I remembered. I put that aside. Not something I could deal with just now).

Stun guns work best on bare skin, or through thin clothing. Sam had only been wearing a t-shirt beneath a fleecy jacket, which was unzipped and hanging open. Vera had had an easy target, especially as he'd been caught by surprise.

But surprise was no longer on her side. And I was wearing my moped riders kit. Thick waterproof coat and trousers. Good luck trying to stun me through that, Vera. And if she did managed to catch me on a hand or my face – well, I only needed to distract her for a second or two. I was pretty sure that Sam would be back in control, he only needed a moment. She wouldn't catch him by surprise again.

"I always leave the printer like that," I said calmly. Trying to keep her attention, while I tensed to leap forward. "Not good practice, I know, but I usually forget to switch it off, so it's probably been on for days."

Vera had the stun gun in her left hand. She flicked her right hand, and something slid out of her sleeve. She caught it, flicked again, and was holding a steel baton, nearly two feet long with a metal ball at the end.

"Do you like my ASP?" she asked brightly. "I borrowed it off someone. Forgot to return it. I think they got into a lot of trouble over that, but then they shouldn't have upset me. You're not going to upset me, are you Alison? Give me what you printed out."

The ASP gave me pause for thought. With that and the stun gun she had a big advantage. I needed some weaponry of my own.

There were knives in the kitchen. A tool box as well, with a hammer.

"Yes, alright. I printed it out but I didn't take it with me. It's in the kitchen. I'll go and get it..."

"I searched the kitchen," said Vera calmly. She took a step to one side, and swung the ASP down hard. There was a horrible thunk sound as it impacted the side of Sam's head.

I screamed, moved forward, but she was holding the stun gun towards me, probes flashing raw voltage, and had the ASP ready to strike again.

"Stay where you are!" she commanded.

"You've killed him!" I shouted. "You've killed Sam!"

"No, I don't think so. I know what it sounds like when a skull breaks open. I didn't use full force on him, so he's probably just a bit concussed. Depends how thick his skull is! But if I have to do it again it might well be fatal. So are you going to give me that printout, Alison, or will you risk another lie?"

Numbly I reached inside my jacket, pulled out the folded sheets of paper, and tossed them over to her. I'd been wrong about the surprise factor.

Sam had gone very still. His eyes were closed. There was blood in his hair.

Vera put the stun gun in a pocket, but kept the ASP ready for use as she bent down to pick up the printout.

Now was my chance, I thought. Hurl myself forward as soon as she takes her eyes off me.

But the moment came, and I didn't move. Couldn't move. Couldn't take the risk, the risk of her hitting Sam again. Killing him.

I stayed perfectly still as she quickly scanned through the pages. "Well, you have been busy, haven't you?" she said, standing up again. The paper went into a pocket, the stun gun came out again. "And just think, if I'd got you earlier today, all this would have come to light when they searched your body. "

She could have been talking about an amusing coincidence.

"So it was you in the van," I answered. Not sounding anywhere near as cheerful as she did.

"Of course. When I realised that it was you trying to chase me on that silly little moped, I couldn't believe my luck! I thought this would be the ideal time to tick you off my list – but I suppose luck works both ways, doesn't it? You've certainly used up your share today! But then, I was lucky as well. Because I thought afterwards, how much does she know? Who has she told? Better find out, I decided. And now everything has worked out even better than I'd hoped."

"I've emailed it already. To CID, to Special Branch, to everyone who'd interested."

She shook her head, smiling. "Nice try, but you're way too late with that. I heard you talking. You were in a hurry to go and tell CID – so, no emails. I'll check your laptop – you'll give me access, of course, you know you will – but I think that this" - she tapped her pocket - "will stay between us!"

Then, quite abruptly, her voice changed. Her whole face changed. The bright smile vanished and the anger underneath was naked on her face. "There won't be any more lucky breaks for you or your boyfriend! I'm not taking any more chances with you, you little sneak!"

The change was so sudden that I actually stepped back in shock. But before I could complete the step, Vera had put her mask back on. Smiling again.

"Now, there are few things I need you to do before we can leave. First of all, your rucksack in the bedroom. I noticed you kept a few things in it – all ready to go for a walk whenever you want, eh? Very useful. You need to get that. And those are your hiking boots over there, I suppose? Well, put those in as well."

"Why?"

"Oh, you'll see. Hurry it up, now!" She poked the end of her baton into Sam's face, playfully tapped his nose with it. "Chop chop!"

She watched me the whole time, coming to the bedroom door as I found my boots and put them in.

"All done? Good! Give it me, then, and let's go. Sam has the keys to your vehicle, I assume? Find them and toss them to me. And after that you'll have to help him down the stairs. I'm afraid he's still a bit out of it."

And all the time her eyes were on me. Not once did she let me get close enough to reach her before I could reach Sam. There was never a point where I could take the risk of him getting another, and perhaps fatal, blow.

Getting him out of the house was hard work. I'd been trained in using a fireman's lift, but I'd never had to do it with anyone unconscious. Once I'd managed to get him on my shoulders it was easier, but still difficult going down the stairs with his weight threatening to topple us both at any moment.

I concentrated on each step. Thinking only about the step. Thinking about the fact that Sam was still breathing. Not thinking beyond that.

Out of the front door, back to the pick-up. Vera opened the cab door, and had me put him down on the long bench seat.

"Get him sitting," she ordered. "In the middle. Sitting up and with the seat belt on.

"He needs to go to a hospital," I said.

"Don't be ridiculous. Get in the other side, you're driving."

I went round to the right, climbed in. Vera was already in on the passenger side. She'd put the ASP away, but was sitting with an arm round Sam's shoulders and the stun gun held just under his chin.

"I've no idea what would happen if I used this on him while he's unconscious. Do you want to find out?"

"No."

"So drive carefully. Don't do anything silly." Vera slid the keys along the dashboard. I started the engine.

The pickup wasn't easy to drive. The clutch was very stiff, and I kept crunching the gears through not pushing my foot down hard enough. Fortunately the traffic was light, and even less when Vera had me turn off down a side road.

I knew where we were. I know all the roads, paths, tracks and bridleways round here. So did Vera, it seemed, because the side road dwindled to a lane, then a cart track – just two long ruts with grass in between. If you weren't familiar with it, you'd think it was going to come to a dead end. But if we kept on along here we'd come out on a B-road that led up over the ridge where I'd walked a few days ago and down into Frayhampton.

From there it was only a short drive to the little hamlet where Kay and Liam lived. Was she planning her revenge on them? Now she knew how much they'd told me about her?

I felt my guts clench at the thought. But surely she wouldn't go after them whilst she still had Sam and myself to deal with?

Thinking of Sam, I glanced over at him again. He was still breathing, still unconscious. Very pale.

"This is all about Mickey, isn't it?" I said.

"Shut up and drive."

I said nothing for a few moments, then "Sam had nothing to do with Mickey. He never even met him. If you've got an issue with me, take it out on me. But let me get Sam to a hospital. Or at least somewhere that he can get help."

Vera sighed. "Do you really think I care? You saw what I did to the Gromberts – Mr and Mrs! And your Sam knows too much anyway."

"So why did you kill Mrs Grombert? She didn't know anything."

Vera shrugged. "Collateral damage. To be honest, I couldn't really avoid it. Vic Grombert – pardon me Detective Superintendent Grombert, retired, now deceased – poured drinks for us all. I'd already poisoned the bottle while he was out of the room. He went to fetch his wife, that was nothing to do with me. She hadn't even seen me up till then, I wouldn't have had to involve her at all."

Keep her talking, I thought. Isn't that what they tell kidnap victims? Establish a relationship with your captors?

Or was it the other way round – avoid building a relationship? Something to do with Stockholm Syndrome? I'd read a lot about it, but I couldn't remember anything useful.

So go with your gut, I decided.

"I'm surprised he let you in, offered you drinks. I didn't think he knew you."

"He didn't, really. I was just one of the PCSO's in the station, he was a Senior Officer. You know how it is, Alison. But when I turned up on his doorstep, telling him I was researching a book about my time on the Force, he couldn't do enough for me. Typical ex-copper. Bored with retirement, always ready to talk about the old days, all his great cases!"

She snorted contemptuously. "And the nonsense he came out with! I didn't mention Mickey until he'd already had a drink or two. And his wife. It was too late for him then. But as soon as I mentioned Mickey's name he started on about how much he hated 'bent coppers'. Then he started feeling the poison. They both did. It was a pleasure watching them die."

The cold viciousness in her voice sent a shudder through me.

"Right here," she told me. We'd come to the end of the track, and turned towards Frayhampton.

"I suppose you killed the Gromberts because he headed the investigation into Mickey?"

"I killed them because they betrayed him!" Now she'd started talking, Vera didn't want to stop, and her inner rage was starting to slop over the edges of her self-control. "You all did!"

That was directed at me.

"I just did my job," I said, as calmly as possible. "They sent me to examine a scene – Mickey's house. I examined it. I recovered several tablets that were later identified as being 'La Paz', a Class A drug. The lab also confirmed that they were part of a batch manufactured in the hidden factory that was run by Mateo Canoso, who was known to have been in contact with Mickey. I wrote a statement and gave evidence in court – all just part of my job, Vera."

"Except that it was a bit more than 'just doing your job', wasn't it?" she hissed at me. "You went above and beyond. Embellished things a bit, didn't you!"

"What? What do you mean?" I was genuinely puzzled.

"Those tablets you claim to have found – you brought them with you. Or you were given them at the scene. Who was it? Vic Grombert? Was it him who told you to set Mickey up?"

"No! That's absolutely not what happened! I found those tablets just as I said, in the bathroom cabinet. Three tablets and some powder and broken pieces. Nobody set Mickey up, Vera. He was taking that stuff from Canoso, as part of his payment."

"LIAR!" she screamed. She leaned over Sam, waved the stun gun in my face and triggered it. Brilliant electric blue flashes, just inches from my eyes. I recoiled, the pick-up swerved and nearly ran into the ditch that ran alongside the road. The near miss brought Vera back to her senses, and she slumped back into her seat.

We were approaching the climb up to the ridge. A distant part of me noticed that it was a beautiful afternoon: clear skies and sunshine, quite warm even though the trees were showing their autumn colours quite clearly now. Much more than when I'd walked the Ridgeway, just a day or so ago. I wished I was up there now. Or in the hills ahead of us. Out walking, with nothing more to think about than the path ahead. Out walking with Sam.

"Slow down," Vera said. "There's a turning coming up. On your right."

"I know the one you mean. It doesn't go anywhere, though."

"Just take it. Here."

I obediently turned into the narrow track. It took us down through some trees and out into open fields. There was a farmhouse a few hundred yards further on, with a gate across the end of the track.

"See? It's a dead end."

"Turn right just before the gate."

There was a gravelled parking area. We turned into it, drove past a parked tractor and a Landrover, then came across a continuation of the track that I hadn't known about. It took us round the farmhouse then on across the fields.

"See?" Vera mimicked "You don't know as much as you think."

I said nothing, concentrating on driving. The track was narrow, and muddy, so I took it slowly. Plus which I was in no hurry to get to our destination, whatever that was. At least Kay and Liam wouldn't be involved, or not yet. I hoped they'd taken my advice.

"And I know that you must have planted those drugs," she continued.

I shook my head. "Come on, Vera. Mickey was addicted to those things."

"Yes, I knew about that. But there weren't any lappies at his house when you searched, so you must have planted them."

"I told you, I found them in the medicine cabinet. Photographed them in situ, diagrammed and measured the location, properly recovered into evidence."

"They were never in the medicine cabinet!" Vera announced triumphantly. "There was a hidden compartment behind it. You had to take out a shelf to open it, and then pull away the back. But even if you'd found it, it would have been empty. I got there before you did. While the first-on scene officers were setting up a cordon, I was inside clearing out the drugs!"

I had a sudden, vivid memory.

Night time. Police vehicles lined up along a suburban road, their flashing lights painting the surrounding houses with flickering blue. Detached houses, not the most prestigious area, but comfortable.

Officers milling around. One of them pulled aside the scene tape, allowing me to drive the CSI van inside the cordon. They waved me over to a parking spot.

DCI Grombert, Senior Investigating Officer, came over to meet me. "Ah. CSI – Kepple, is it? Just you, then?"

"Yes sir. For the moment. I'm the on-call CSI. The duty Senior was called out to a job earlier, he'll be back as soon as possible. In the meantime he's instructed me to take photographs and start the scene examination."

"I see. Have you been briefed?"

"Yes sir."

"Right, I'll leave you to get on with it. Let me know immediately if you find any drugs. We're particularly interested in 'La Paz'- have you come across it?"

"No sir, but I've seen the briefing material. Pinkish white tablet with the letters LP on it. Or a granular powder of the same colour, usually in a plain white capsule."

"Right," he said again, and turned away. "Hey you. PCSO!"

A slender figure, short dark hair, stepping out from the alleyway that ran alongside the house.

"Sir?"

"Were you on the cordon at the rear?"

"Yes, sir. Just came to see if there were any refreshments going."

"What, already? We've barely got set up. Get back to your position. I won't see this crime scene compromised because someone wasn't doing their job!"

"Sir!" said Veranda. She caught my eye as she turned away, face expressionless.

Then she was gone, and I was opening the van and getting out the kit.

"You were there!" I said. "When I arrived at the scene!"

She stared at me for a moment, searching her own memory. "Yes. I remember seeing you." She turned her attention to the track ahead. "I was in the station, just finishing my shift, when it all kicked off. First there was a firearms incident over at Delford Mills. Then people were asking about Mickey. Not in a good way. The rumour went round that he was going to be arrested. So I called him, told him to stay away, then went straight to his house and started clearing it out."

"The drugs."

Another memory. Peering into the bathroom cabinet, shining the torch, but not seeing anything. At first. But then – something right at the back, in the crack between the lower shelf and the rear of the cabinet. The excitement as I examined it with the magnifying glass, and realised what I was looking at. There's no bigger thrill than finding that one bit of evidence which is going to make the case.

"Yes. And anything else I didn't want you to find. The first coppers started turning up while I was still inside. I slipped out of the back while they were kicking in the front door, looking for him. Then I hung round a bit while they did the initial search. Helped set up the cordon. When you arrived to start doing the forensics I was trying to sneak off, but Grombert spotted me and sent me back." She grinned. "I heard him telling you to look out for La Paz – I nearly burst out laughing, since I had it all stuffed inside my jacket!" The smile turned to a frown. "Of course, I didn't know then that you were going to plant some anyway!"

"I didn't plant anything, Vera."

She sneered at me. "No, you didn't plant anything. And Grombert didn't lie in court, and that little snake Cadenti didn't betray Mickey to save his own neck, and that Judge didn't allow the false evidence and the lying statements!"

She was getting worked up again. I bit my lip and said nothing, whilst ahead of us the track started to rise up towards the hills.

Chapter 17

Symptoms of Concussion. These may include: being knocked out or struggling to remain awake, dizziness, nausea and vomiting, headache, memory loss, etc.

Around us, the fields were giving way to rough open country, dotted with sheep. I estimated that we were just about passing Frayhampton, on the other side of the ridge to our left.

I was pretty sure that I'd never come this way before, which surprised me. The track must surely appear on the Ordnance Survey maps, if nowhere else. I might not have come up from the bottom of the valley, having been put off by the apparent dead end at the farmhouse. But how come I hadn't found my way down from the hills by this route? It went much more directly back to my flat than any other way I knew of.

I glanced across at Vera. She seemed quite calm again, relaxed even. It was very hard to believe that she had murdered – what? Four, five, six people? I listed them, starting with the Gromberts and working backwards to Izzy and her boyfriend. Eight, I made it. That I knew of.

And that she was going to kill me as well, because she thought I'd planted evidence against Mickey. And Sam, because I'd told him about her. And because he was there.

He groaned, and stirred, as I was looking at him. "Sam!" I said, stopped the pick-up and turned to him. "Sam, look at me. Are you all right?"

He opened his eyes, and stared at me blankly. Then suddenly leaned forward and vomited into the footwell.

"Urrgh. That's disgusting," said Vera, and wound down her window.

"Sam – Sam!" I pulled out a tissue, started wiping the mess off his face. "Sam – can you hear me?"

His eyes had closed again and he was slumped forward, only held by his seatbelt.

"He's unconscious again," Vera pointed out. "So don't waste your breath. Keep driving, we've got a little way to go yet." She waved the stun gun at me, and tapped Sam on the side of the head.

"Go!"

I put the pick-up back into gear and drove on.

I needed some way to talk to Vera. To get through to her. Clearly, a straight out denial that I'd planted any drugs to incriminate Mickey wasn't going to get me anywhere. I needed to try something different. Desperately raking through my brain for inspiration, I remembered the tract that Pat from St Pat's had left. All about love.

"You must have been really in love with Mickey," I suggested tentatively.

Vera said nothing, but glancing across at her I saw a hint of a smile. A hopeful sign.

"I can understand that. He was – a bit of a charmer."

Vera sighed. "Look, I know what you're thinking. What people said about him. About how he was always chasing another bit of skirt... Well, he wasn't like that really. I mean, yes, he liked women. But he was just looking for the right one. His soul mate. And that was me. We... fitted together."

Yes, I thought. Crooked drug-addict cop and psycho serial killer. Perfect match.

"How did you meet?" I asked.

"At the station, of course. He came in to our office looking for a favour. Someone to help out, unofficially. He often did that sort of thing. He was always more interested in getting the job done than in going by the book. So he told me to see him when I got off shift... we spent hours in his car, watching some place where they suspected some dealing was happening. Taking notes on everybody who went in and out, car number plates, times. Usual sort of thing. And of course, we talked a lot." She sighed.

I recalled the rumour – Station gossip? - that Mickey often used a fake surveillance operation to seduce young female officers. Probably best not to mention that. (Was I finally learning sensitivity?).

"He told me about his plans. He was going places, was Mickey. He was in control of his life – not like most of the losers who just drift through. He was stronger than that, and just being near him was exciting."

"You certainly stuck with him when things went bad."

She nodded emphatically. "I told you. We were soul-mates. I don't think even he realised that, not until all the others failed him! All his so-called friends, all the ones who thought he'd be good for their careers – none of them, not one, were there when he needed them."

"So you hid him when the investigation started?"

"I kept him safe. Kept track of how the investigation was going. They never came near him."

I remembered the tract again. "You know, Vera – I think you loved him too much. I don't think Mickey deserved your love. You were too good for him."

She went very still. "Why do you say that?"

"Vera – think about it. Mickey – no matter what you say, Mickey was still working for Canoso. Taking money and feeding him information. Actively keeping police enquiries away from him. And taking his drugs!"

She stared across at me, suddenly cold faced. "You're still going along with that, are you? Why not admit the truth, at last, Alison? Or didn't they ever tell you the truth?"

"What truth?" I was genuinely puzzled. "The truth came out at his trial, Vera. The facts. You can't ignore that, ignore what he did."

"That trial was a farce, a mockery!" The anger in her was rising again. It was never far away. "Mickey was working with Canoso, yes – as part of a planned operation! One that was sanctioned by – guess who? - Vic Grombert! Mickey went to him when Canoso first made contact, and they set it up together. Mickey was going along with what Canoso wanted until he could get his trust and find out about his whole organisation. It was so much bigger than people realised. Canoso still had his contacts in Spain, he was planning to spread La Paz all over Europe – and Mickey was going to get them all!"

"I've never heard anything about that. It was never mentioned in court."

"Of course it wasn't. That stuck-up bitch June Henshaw – June Seaton now – she got herself involved in it. Her and her boyfriend – who, by the way, was working with Canoso but decided to sell him out! When things went wrong, they all dropped Mickey in it to cover their own backsides. So Grombert said nothing, Cadenti said nothing. You planted the drugs – yes, you did, don't bother denying it! Darnley made sure no awkward questions were asked at the trial – it was all a stitch up, start to finish!"

"And how do you know all this? Oh, don't bother. I can guess. Mickey told you, didn't he?"

She glared at me. "Oh, yes, he told me the whole thing. And I promised him that they'd suffer for it. You'll all pay for what you did to Mickey!"

"Cadenti, Darnley, Grombert. And me?"

She laughed. "Oh, you haven't worked it all out, have you? You missed off that little creep who was supposed to defend him in court."

"His lawyer? The one you pushed under a train? Yes, I knew about that."

She gave me an expressionless look, and my heart skipped a beat. There was no telling how Vera would react: she could flip into extreme violence without warning. I wished I hadn't mentioned the lawyer.

But then she laughed. Pleased, perhaps, at my recognition of her work.

"Nasty accident on the underground in London. People just get too close to the edge of the platform. That one was easy."

I found myself with no response. After a moment, Vera continued. "I was going to get the prosecution as well. But nature beat me to it. Heart attack. Pity, I felt a bit cheated. Still, I've done a good job on the rest, don't you think?"

"You'll get caught," I said grimly. "If I can put it together, so can someone else."

"No, I don't think so." Vera looked confident; her inner anger subdued by the thought of her success. "Serial killers make themselves obvious by using the same M.O. Of course, most of them are mentally ill, so you wouldn't expect them to think of that. But I make a point of doing something different every time. So: accident for the lawyer, burglary gone wrong for Cadenti. Bomb for the Judge – and look at Special Branch running around in pursuit of terrorists! Poison for the Gromberts. By the way, I printed out a suicide note for Vic, even got him to sign it by asking for his autograph! It doesn't explain the wife, I hadn't planned on her, but still, a nice touch, don't you think? Which just leaves you, your boyfriend, and the Seatons. I've saved them till last, because I want to do something really special. Perhaps a house fire?"

"Like your parents?"

"Oh, do you think anyone would make the connection?" She frowned, considering it. "No, that was too long ago, there's no link. Still, it's a good point. I'll have to be careful to make it different. An obvious arson, perhaps? Forced entry, multiple points of ignition. Maybe something distinctive for an accelerant?" She shook her head. "Ah, you've got me thinking about it now! But that's for another time. Let's just focus on you, eh?" She smiled brightly.

My people skills were just not adequate for this situation. I wished Sam was awake. He might have had a chance of talking us out of this.

The track, now no more than two parallel ruts, continued to climb. The valley was getting narrower, the walls on either side steeper. They were crowned with grey rock and the slopes were all scree. No easy way out on either side. The low autumn sun was already disappearing behind the western ridge, and we drove into shadow.

How far were we going? This little track had to run out soon – and then what? I focused hard on the driving, because I didn't want to think about that. I was aware that a huge bubble of panic had formed inside me: thinking too far ahead might burst it.

I had to keep Vera talking, I had to try and find a way through to her. Even at the risk of triggering her again. The thought about her parents suggested another approach.

"What happened to you as a kid..." I began tentatively. She was staring ahead, ignoring me. "Well, that was wrong. You didn't deserve that. Not from your parents, not from anyone."

Surprisingly, she laughed. "I see where you're going with this. Trying a bit of amateur psychology, are you Alison? What, did you think I'd be so moved by your sympathy and understanding that I'd just let you go?"

I shrugged. "Just thinking that it was a terrible way to bring up a child, that's all. If what I was told was true?"

"Oh, yes. It was true." She laughed again. "Well, some of it. But it wasn't as bad as all that. I learned some valuable life lessons from my parents."

"Such as?"

"Such as how to be in control. That's what Father taught me. And Mother taught me what happens when you're not in control." She looked across at me. "There's no more important lesson, Alison, but most people never realise it. Most people think about give and take, about compromise, about getting on. But that's just lazy. Or stupid. Ultimately, you have to be in control or you're nobody. Father – he was always in control. Always. Until – he wasn't. Then he was finished."

"You finished him!" I said, and bit my lip. Not the way I wanted this to go.

But Vera was nodding in agreement. "Exactly! I took control!"

"And Mickey? Was he in control?"

I was looking ahead, negotiating a particularly tricky bend in the track – we were right on the bank of a stream and there wasn't much room for manoeuvre – so I wasn't looking at her face. But I could hear something in her voice, something other than the normal rage.

"Mickey was the most in control man I ever knew. But the drugs... the side effects, the withdrawal symptoms. That was too much. Even for Mickey."

What was in her voice was grief. It hadn't occurred to me that she would feel that.

The track was taking us round a big outcrop of rock that jutted out from the side of the valley and nearly filled it. As we cleared it we came in sight of a building. Two storeys, perhaps fifty feet long by twenty wide, and apparently built out of the same grey rock that surrounded the valley. It blended in perfectly.

There was a metal gate across the track in front of us, with barbed wire wrapped round the top bar, and a barbed wire fence either side of it. The large sign - 'PRIVATE PROPERTY. No Trespassing. KEEP OUT' - seemed superfluous.

"Out you get," Vera ordered as I braked to a stop. "Open it up. Here's the key." She slid a padlock key on a chain across the dashboard. "I'll just stay here and look after Sam." The stun-gun was in her hand. She tapped it significantly against the side of Sam's head.

I got out, unlocked and opened the gate, and stood for a moment looking at Vera. Thinking to myself that this might be my last chance to do anything. Knowing that there was nothing I could do that wouldn't be disastrous for Sam. Vera smiled brightly as I got back behind the wheel and drove through.

"You can leave the gate," she announced. "I'll be coming back shortly. And we're here. Home sweet home. Pull up round the other side."

"Home sweet home?" It looked more like a place for storing animal fodder. There were windows in the upper storey, so perhaps it had some sort of shepherds accommodation as well, but homely wasn't the description I had in mind.

Though it did seem familiar. I'd seen it, or something like it, before.

"Yes, that's right," Vera confirmed. "It was Father's. Mine now. My inheritance, I suppose you'd say. Stop here."

I glanced the other way, up the valley. From this point it became much narrower and steeper. Steep even for walkers – if they could have got past the barbed wire fence. An unusually high fence. It looked like it was about ten feet of thickly woven strands, much more substantial than the usual barrier to stop sheep wandering. This was about security. It extended to the steep valley walls on either side – and there was no gate.

I had definitely seen that before. From the other side.

It had been a few years ago. I'd been all day up in the high hills, but the weather had changed, and I was keen to get down before it got dark. Looking on my map, I'd seen the valley that ran almost directly towards my home. No path marked, but no obvious barriers either.

Not until I'd come to the massive barbed wire fence, with the big angry signs warning off trespassers. And the weather beaten farm building beyond.

This building, in fact.

"Did your Dad put up the fence as well?" I asked.

"Oh, yes. Father was very keen on his privacy."

We sat and stared at each other. "What happens now?" I asked.

Thinking, if she gets out I can just start up and drive away. If she makes me get out first – then perhaps I can get round the front and slam the door into her as she gets out? Which might leave Sam vulnerable, but if I didn't do anything, we were both dead anyway.

"This is what happens," Vera said. She leaned over Sam and casually shoved the stun-gun into the side of my neck.

The pain was horrendous. My whole body in agony, muscles convulsing with the shock. And it didn't stop. She held it there, forcing my head against the window as the current surged through me. When she finally pulled it away, I was slumped against the door, twitching, confused, helpless.

I was dimly aware that she'd opened the door and undone my seatbelt. It only needed a quick shove and I toppled out and was lying in the mud, still unable to get my limbs to work properly, still unable to think clearly.

I heard a scream. It sounded like Sam.

After a while, she was standing over me. Black boots in front of my face.

"Come on, Alison. You should be able to get up now. Or at least start crawling." "Sam..."

"Oh, he's all right. Well, not exactly all right, but not dead, if that's what you mean. Not yet. I just gave him a little shock to make sure he stayed nice and quiet while I dragged him inside. See – I did all the hard work for you! The least you can do is give me a bit of help now. So come on, make an effort, Alison!"

The words were followed by a kick in the side. Not hard enough to break anything, but hard enough to hurt.

"I think there's still some charge in the stun gun, if you want some more of that?" she offered.

No. I didn't want any more of that. I managed to get my arms and legs moving. I couldn't manage to stand up at first, but I crawled to the front of the pick-up and pulled myself almost upright.

"That's good!" Vera encouraged. "Now straight ahead, through that door."

Worn grey planks, hanging open in front of a dark space. I didn't want to go in there, but I couldn't think of an alternative. I wanted to launch myself at Vera, drag her down, hammer her into the ground. I've never felt such a desire to attack another person. But I could barely stand, barely move. And she still had the stun-gun, the ASP, and full use of her body.

Besides which, Sam was there.

I stepped into the darkness.

Chapter 18

Checklist – dealing with dangerous or violent offenders:
1) Never confront a potentially violent person alone. 2) Always have a
way of escape available. 3) Be ready to call the police immediately if the
situation deteriorates.

The darkness stank. It smelled of animal droppings, of damp and decay and despair. Or perhaps that last one was just me, projecting.

There was some light. High up in the wall at each end was a window – well, a hole, at any rate. No frame, no glazing, just open squares. With bars, so not a way of escape, even if I could have reached them.

Outside, it was already dusk at the bottom of the valley, but there was enough light still in the sky to drift in through those window holes and show me – when my eyes adjusted – that the room was virtually empty. Bare walls of rough stone, perhaps once whitewashed but now just grey. Dirty flagstone floor. All down the long wall opposite the door and about four feet up was a metal bar: in front of me Sam was sitting on the floor with his back to the wall.

"What's this, a ballet class?" I asked. First thing that came into my head, seeing that bar. Or barre.

"So glad you still have your sense of humour, Alison," said Vera behind me. She pushed me, suddenly and hard, so that I staggered forward. My legs couldn't cope with it and I fell, knees and elbows making painful contact with the flagstones. "Probably something

233

agricultural," she continued. "Unless Father had it put in. Either way, it's very useful."

I was closer to Sam, at least. He had plastic bags round his hands and his wrists had been taped to the bar. He was still unconscious.

I pulled myself upright, looking round again. Hoping for something I could use as a weapon. Broom handle, rusty farm implement, anything I could fight back with.

Nothing like that, but in the shadows at the far end of the room I could make out stairs, and wondered what was up there. Perhaps I could make a dash for it? When my muscles were recovered enough to enable dashing.

Vera had come in behind me, carrying my rucksack, which she tossed into a corner. Seeing the direction of my gaze she shook her head. "Sorry, the penthouse suite is unavailable at present."

The fog was clearing from my brain, enough to make a belated connection. "Was that where you had Mickey hidden?"

"Some of the time. They did search the place once, but of course I knew well before it happened so I was able to get him out of the way. It was quite funny, actually, watching them run all over the country, chasing rumours, while he was sitting here, just a few miles from the station."

"I would have thought..." I began, then stopped, wondering if this was a direction I should take.

"What would you have thought?" Vera could switch moods in an instant. In this case, from pleasant reminiscences to deep suspicion.

"Just that – considering his drug problem – shouldn't he really have been in hospital? After all, that supply wasn't going to last forever, he was going to go cold turkey sooner or later. And those lappies, from what I heard, weren't just emotion suppressors. All sorts of junk in that mix, and long term use played havoc with major organs. In fact, that's what killed him, wasn't it? His whole body began to shut down after a while. But if you'd taken him to get help, they might have got him off the drugs soon enough to prevent that."

She glared at me. "I was getting him off! I'd cut his dose down, he was breaking free of the addiction!"

"Really?" I did my best to sound impressed. "That can't have been easy."

Her mood switched again. Now confident and assured, eager to demonstrate how in control she'd been. "Those capsules it came in? I started emptying some out before I gave them to him. He didn't know, but I'd got him down to half the amount he'd been on, with no side effects. Spread out like that, there was enough to last another year, and by that time I'd have got him off them completely. He would have been OK!"

I looked at her. Thinking, you idiot, you as good as killed him. But not daring to say it. "What went wrong?"

"I don't know! He crashed. Started showing withdrawal symptoms even though he was still taking the lappies. Shaking, sweats, mood swings. A lot of pain, stomach cramps. He was passing blood as well. I put his dose back up, but it didn't help. He was getting worse. So I had to take him in to hospital. Not the local one, of course – I drove him down to London, dropped him off at a place there. He gave them a false name, didn't mention La Paz or drugs at all. They managed to stabilise him. But someone recognised him from the news, and that bastard Grombert went down in person to arrest him. Mickey was still too weak to move, but Grombert had him handcuffed to the hospital bed!"

I hadn't known that. For a moment my sympathy was genuine. "That was a bit over the top."

"A bit! Considering Mickey was only in that state from doing his job, from going undercover and doing whatever it took to bring Canoso down!" She was back to angry again, which was probably her default setting. And back to the undercover cop story, I noticed.

"You're lucky they didn't catch you as well. I remember they were looking for anyone who had helped him."

"Oh, I'd kept out of the way. Sneaked in a couple of times, pretending to be visiting someone else. When Grombert arrived, I was watching from the corridor. Mickey saw me there, but he didn't say a word." She shook her head, looking sad and proud. "He never gave me up. Even when they were interviewing him, he didn't tell them about this place, or about who had helped him. He was still in control, you see. And he loved me. That was my Mickey."

I wondered if it had been love, or fear. Perhaps he was too scared to rat on her. Again, not a theory to mention.

"Must have been hard for you, going through that?"

She nodded. Then frowned. "You don't give up, do you? Still trying to get on my side? Not going to happen! I haven't forgotten your part in this, Alison." Suddenly, all business like. "So let's get on with it. Take off your coat. And that fleece as well."

"What? Why?"

"Just do it!" She hefted the stun-gun menacingly.

I removed them reluctantly. It was turning cold now, a sharp breeze was finding its way through those open holes, and I shivered when I was down to my t-shirt and trousers.

"That'll do," Vera decided. "I don't want to have to dress you completely."

"What's that supposed to mean?" I asked.

"Never mind. Throw your things over here." She kicked the coat and the fleece over towards the rucksack. "Now put this over your left hand." She tossed a plastic carrier bag to me.

As I obeyed, she pulled a roll of wide, silvery tape out of a pocket. The same tape that held Sam to the bar, I realised.

"Now tape the bag to your wrist, then your wrist to the bar." She handed the roll over to me.

"What's the bag for?" I asked as I did it.

"Oh, come on, Alison. You're a CSI, I shouldn't have to explain this to you."

I thought about it. "Tape instead of rope or cable ties so that it doesn't leave a mark to show that we were restrained. Plastic bags so that there are no traces of the adhesive on our skin or clothes."

"See? We've thought this through."

"We?" My hand was secured to the bar.

Vera shrugged. "Figure of speech. Hold still, I don't want to cut you. But I don't mind if I do."

She'd brought out a penknife, with which she cut off the roll of tape. Then pulled out another plastic bag and proceeded to secure my other hand.

"Father never used tape. He was a traditionalist, I suppose. He liked handcuffs. And of course, he was never concerned about forensics." She finished taping my wrist to the bar, and examined the other one. "Hmm. You didn't do a great job here, Alison. Let's just make that a bit tighter." She pulled more tape off the roll and set about making me secure.

"Your Father – used this place to, what, imprison people? You mean you?"

"He probably would have done, eventually. If I'd given him time. But he had this place long before

I was born. Before he was married, even. I don't know how many people he must have brought up here over the years." She finished securing me properly, stepped back and ran a critical eye over her work. "Yes, that's better."

"Why did he do that?"

"Wow, Alison, you're really into this amateur psychology thing aren't you? Perhaps you should have studied that instead of going into CSI!" Vera was smiling as she said it. Looking at me and Sam with the satisfaction of a job well done. "Well, of course Father liked control. But if you want my opinion, his big weakness was that he had to keep reminding himself he was in control. Mostly, he did that with myself and Mother, of course. But sometimes I think he needed a bit extra – I don't know, a more forceful reminder, perhaps? And I'm assuming that before Mother, he must have needed some other means of – ah – reassuring himself. So he had this place. And every so often he'd bring somebody up here."

"Who?"

"Oh, I don't know. Tramps, runaways – people who wouldn't be missed. People who didn't
matter."

I felt revulsion as a physical sickness. "What did he do with them?"

Vera looked irritated, as if I'd asked a stupid question. I suppose I had. "Whatever he wanted, of course. That was the *point!* He could do what he liked because he was in control."

"And – after he'd finished?"

She shrugged. "I don't know. He never went into details, but he did hint about somewhere where they wouldn't be found. I got the impression that he was talking about an old well, or maybe a cave in the rocks? There are a few round here, I believe."

She was so casual about it. That's what got to me. If her father had collected stamps or bred pigeons she would have used the same tone of voice.

"Did you say that he brought you here as well? And your mother?"

"I don't know about Mother. Perhaps, before I was born. She never talked about it, if he did. But then, she never talked much about anything. He only brought me here once. I think he'd realised that he was starting to lose control of me. Actually, he lost control a long time before, but I was careful not to let him realise it. But all that business at school, that you found out about, that made him suspicious. It took a while before he cottoned on, but he finally understood. So one day he brought me out here. Showed me the handcuffs and all the tools he used, explained how they worked. Never directly threatened me, but of course he didn't need to. We both knew what he meant. And that meant that I had to take control away from him. But there was already a plan in place for that."

"You mean the fire?"

"That's right. The same night, no point in hanging around." She sighed. "You know, before the fire service arrived, I was standing in the garden, staring up at their bedroom. I saw him at the window, trying to break it open. But he'd put in specially strengthened glass, and locks that he thought he had the keys to – I'd switched them, of course – so he couldn't get out. Just before the flames broke through into the bedroom he was looking down at me, and I like to think he understood what had happened, that he'd lost control and I'd taken it."

She nodded to herself, smiling gently at a pleasant memory, and I shuddered.

"But your mother..."

"Oh, she didn't matter. She never mattered to anyone."

And that seemed even worse than the fact that she'd been murdered. By her own daughter.

"Well, it's nice chatting, but I've really got to get on with things. Back in a moment!"

She went out of the door, and I started pulling. First one arm, then the other, then both together. The tape didn't budge. The bar was solid.

Vera came back in with a bucket. "Testing the restraints, are you? That's good. Gives me some peace of mind, knowing that you've tried and failed."

From the way she was carrying it, the bucket was full. She took it over to Sam.

"What are you doing?" I asked. "No, don't..." but she ignored me and emptied the bucket out over his head.

He jerked forward, gasping, shouting. "What... what..."

"Don't worry, it's just water," said Vera. "No running water up here, of course, but the rain butt outside is usually full. And there's the stream if we need more." She winked at me. "You're next! Back in a minute."

She went out of the door, and I looked across at Sam. "Are you awake?" I asked.

He looked round, blankly. "Alison? Where are we? What happened?"

"Vera happened," I explained, with a rush of relief that he was conscious again. "She got you with a stun gun as you went out of the door, then clocked you one over the head with an ASP that she shouldn't have. Then she made me drive you up here, and now..."

The door creaked open again, and Sam slumped back down, eyes shut. Vera came in with another bucketful of water.

"Oh, Sam's dropped right off again, I see. Poor love, he's well out of it, isn't he? Well, never mind. Perhaps for the best, right?"

She came towards me with the bucket and I braced myself. Even so, I couldn't stop myself gasping as she flung the contents over me. It felt like a deluge of ice.

"Nice bracing cold shower!" Vera laughed. It was a perfectly normal laugh, like someone had just told a good joke.

"Why?" I asked. My teeth had started chattering already, in response to the sudden drop in body temperature.

"Oh, really, Alison, must I explain everything?" Vera shook her head. "Look, you were cold already, now you're wet, and you've no chance of getting warm and dry again. Did you see the weather forecast? The wind's shifting, we're getting a strong northerly tonight. All that fresh air coming down from the Arctic, they're saying that we'll have the first frost of the year. A bit early, but the weather nowadays, eh?" She leant forward, peered directly into my face, and spoke earnestly. "You and Sam won't survive the night. Tomorrow, or perhaps the day after – whenever I have time – I'll be back to cut you down, put your clothes back on you, and take you off in the van. I'll dump your bodies in a nice remote spot. Probably drop Sam down a hill, or something like that, to account for the injuries. You'll be a few miles away. With your rucksack, of course, to add a bit of authenticity. Might be quite a while before they find you, but what a tragic story it'll be. Two young lovers out for a hike, he has an accident and she goes for help but loses her way... both dead of exposure. I expect they'll give you a nice write up."

She stepped back and stood up. "And while you're freezing to death, do take a few minutes to think about Mickey. After all, it's because of what you did to him that this is happening to you. If you hadn't planted those drugs in his house, I wouldn't be doing this. But as it is... justice, Alison. You're pretty keen on justice, aren't you. Working for the police, and so on. Well, so am I. Just remember that. Make it your last thought."

She turned back towards the door.

"Vera – wait!" I called out.

"Now what?" She sounded irritated. "Please tell me you're not going to start pleading for your life, are you?"

"N..no." The cold was setting in, I was having trouble speaking properly through the shivers. "Just some, something about the drugs I found, the Lappies."

"The ones you planted? Are you going to confess, then? Not that it'll make a difference, but if you want to clear your conscience, go ahead."

"I know who was responsible for them being there. Someone else you should target."

"Who?" She stepped back towards me, eyes narrowing.

"We never did find that hidden compartment you mentioned. I'm kicking myself for that. It must have been a good job, because I went over that cabinet really carefully."

She smiled. "I'm not surprised. You're not as good as you like to think, are you?"

"The thing is, I should have found it. Because those capsules I recovered – little white plastic capsules – they were wedged right in the back of the cabinet. Between the bottom shelf and the wall. What I thought was the wall, but from what you've told me, it must have been a false section, covering the hidden compartment. Those capsules were tightly wedged in there. Three of them. It was a real pig of a job to get them out. In fact, one of them broke while I was doing it. That's how I knew for sure it was La Paz I'd found, because of the powder that came out - pale pink, rather coarse. Just as described in the briefing. I was wearing a mask, of course, but I was still worried that I might inhale it. You wouldn't believe how careful I was to get every last bit of that powder, every fragment of the broken capsule. And to get the last two capsules out without damaging them."

"Yes, very professional of you. Is this going somewhere, Alison?" Vera was frowning, impatient, but still curious. Still listening.

"Bear with me. The thing is, I couldn't work out how those capsules had become so tightly wedged. They couldn't have just fallen in there like that. Of course, I understand now. They were like that because they'd fallen down while the hidden compartment was open, then the false section had been put in over the top of them. I wish I'd thought it through at the time, I might have found where the capsules had been hidden. But even with that clue, I still didn't find it."

"So?"

"So, if you'd left the lappies in there, I'd probably never have discovered them. But you'd got there before me. You'd opened the compartment, taken the capsules. I'm assuming that most of them were in some sort of container. But perhaps Mickey had left some loose. Which you knocked out, onto the bottom shelf of the cabinet. It's easy to understand how that happened. It was dark – I suppose you had a torch, but you'd have to be careful, you couldn't afford for the light to be seen. And you were in a hurry. The first responders were already outside by then, you knew that a search team would be in soon. So – you scooped up all the loose capsules you could find. But you missed the three that had dropped behind the shelf. Missed them and put the false section back in on top of them."

She was glaring at me now. "Shut up!" she snapped. "I've heard enough of this nonsense!"

I ignored her. "Three little capsules. They were the only physical evidence we had to connect Mickey to La Paz and Canoso. They were the main thing that put him away. And it was you who left them there, Vera. You who dropped those capsules and left them for me to find. Your fault that..."

"SHUT UP!" she snarled. The stun-gun was in her hand, contacts flaring, as she ran at me.

Three paces from the door, perhaps four.

She'd left the bucket on the floor, near my feet. I lashed out with my foot, kicking it directly at her. It caught her leg and she stumbled over it, putting out her hands to save herself as she fell on the floor directly in front of me.

Her right hand was just below me. I stamped down hard, putting all my fear and desperation into it, but she was already moving, twisting out of the way. I missed her hand, missed her fingers, and the stun-gun crunched under my boot.

She rolled away, out of my reach, started to get to her feet, glaring white hot fury at me. Then Sam hooked a leg round her neck, dragged her back and down against the other leg and holding her there. "Hold her, Sam!" I shouted. "Choke her!" But she was wriggling and twisting, tearing at his leg with one hand. And the

ASP was in her other hand. She flicked it open, full extension, and swung it at Sam. At his face.

At the angle she was holding it, she couldn't manage much force or accuracy. But it caught him on the cheekbone, just below his right eye, and he flinched, reflexively pulling backwards and giving her the opportunity to roll and wrench herself out of his grip. Finishing up on hands and knees in front of me.

I kicked at her face, trying to reach her, hurt her, at best knock her out cold, but I was at full stretch and she was already moving backwards and just the toe of my boot connected with her nose, snapping her head back. I couldn't follow through, I couldn't reach her any more and she scuttled back out of range.

We glared at each other. There was blood pouring from her nose. She wiped her face, smearing it across a cheek and stood up slowly, hefting the ASP.

"Come on, then, Vera," I said. Keeping my voice low and calm. "Come over here again."

She stared, knuckles white with the grip she had on her weapon. Then she shook her head. "Oh, no, Alison. It doesn't work like that. I'm the one in control. I decide where I go – and who I punish."

She stepped towards Sam. He raised his feet to fend her off, but from his position on the floor there was little he could do as she dodged past him and brought the ASP down hard on his lower right leg.

There was a horrible crack and Sam screamed, jerking at the restraints on his wrist as his whole body convulsed.

I shouted as well. "Get off him, leave him alone, you sicko, you sick murdering psycho, GET AWAY FROM HIM!"

She was away from him. Stepping back towards the door. But still swinging the ASP, and glaring at me.

Then she laughed.

"You know, you've been more trouble than all the others put together, Alison!"

I didn't have a reply to that. I just met her gaze and tried to put all my anger into it. If looks could kill... but instead, she kept on talking.

"I remember people used to talk about you, back when I was at the station. They'd say 'she's a strange one. She's 'a bit different'. Even 'she's special'. That was the nastiest one. Did you know they said that about you?"

I knew. I said nothing. Nothing to them, nothing to her.

"Well, don't worry about it. They said things about me as well. The difference is, I didn't let it pass. You can't, you see. You have to keep track of these things, deal with them. It's how you stay in control."

"I don't want a lesson in your sick philosophy of life!" I hissed at her.

She shrugged. "Too late to do you any good, anyway. What I was going to say, though, was that everyone thought you were a bit dangerous. Did you know? They all said 'Don't get on the wrong side of her! She's got a vicious streak. No telling what she might do!' How ironic is that? I was the one they should have been worried about, but they just ignored me!"

I hadn't known that people said that. I didn't realise that people thought that about me.

"Though, having said that, I have to admit that you've been dangerous to me. The only person who's caused me any worry at all!"

"I'm glad to hear it."

"Right. That's the spirit, Alison!" She grinned at me. A conspiratorial sort of grin, as if we were partners in some great enterprise. "But, I was just thinking back – when I saw you and Darnley on the steps of the courthouse together, I thought I was going to get two for the price of one! It was like Christmas had come early."

"Sorry to disappoint you," I said through gritted teeth. Partly from anger, partly because the adrenaline was wearing off and I was starting to shiver again.

"Well, I must admit it would have been so much more convenient. Or if you hadn't been so tricky when I tried to run you down, earlier. And just think, if I'd got you then, we wouldn't have had to involve poor Sam here, would we? So that's on you, I suppose."

I leaned back on the wall. Despair and exhaustion and cold were growing in me, leaving me with no energy for answers.

"Nothing to say? No last words? Well, no matter. Third time, Alison, and your luck's run out now. I'll get off, then. Things to do, people to see. I'll let you and Sam have your last minutes together in peace. Bye!"

She slammed the door shut behind her. I heard a chain rattling, and a padlock click shut. A few moments later the pick-up started. I listened as the sound of its engine faded into the distance, leaving us to the dark and the cold and the silence.

Chapter 19

Health and Safety Checklist – Dangers of rusty metal: 1) Rust can seriously weaken metal. Be especially aware of severe rust on load bearing structures. 2) Rusted metal can leave sharp or jagged edges. 3) Rust can encourage the growth of bacteria which, if allowed to enter the bloodstream through a break in the skin, may lead to tetanus. 4) Rust dust can be irritating to eyes or (if inhaled) lungs.

In the fading light, I looked across at Sam. He had closed his eyes again, but as I looked they flickered open.

"She's gone then?"

"Yes."

"Good. I couldn't really warm to her."

I felt a sob building up. "Sam, this is no time for trying to be funny."

"Can't imagine a better time." He even tried to laugh, but it wasn't very convincing. I could hear the strain in his voice.

"How is it? The leg?"

He didn't answer for a moment. "Broken, I think. Hurts like..." He broke off for a moment. "It's not too bad as long as I keep it still. And stretched out on the floor like this, that's the next best thing to a splint."

I didn't believe him. "How's the head?"

"Oh, I'd almost forgotten about that. But now you mention it, that hurts as well."

"Sorry."

"It's OK. Thinking about my head takes my mind off my leg."

"I meant, sorry about all this. About getting you into this."

"No. Don't be sorry about that. Alison..." He was looking at me. In the shadows, I couldn't see his eyes, but I felt them. I looked back at him. "Alison," he said again, "You didn't get me into anything. We're just in this together. And with you is where I choose to be. Now and always."

"Don't!" I said.

"Don't what?"

"Say things like that. Because I can't wipe my eyes just now."

"Oh. Sorry. I'll try and avoid the emotional stuff, then."

"Please."

"Except that I wish we'd gone to the Nook instead."

"Me too."

There was a long silence then. Sam rested his head back against the wall, and I think he'd closed his eyes.

"Sam! SAM!"

"What...?" He lifted his head again, and moved his leg a little, and stifled a gasp of pain.

"Sam, please don't fall asleep again. If you fall asleep, you might not wake up!"

"OK. Right. But I'm not sure how long I can keep awake for. You'd better hurry up."

"Hurry up with what?"

"With your plan for getting us out of here."

"My plan? Sam, I don't have one. I've no idea..." The despair that had been lurking inside finally burst through into a sob. And another.

"Alison! Ali! Get a grip!"

I choked down the sobs. "I'm sorry, but I really can't think of a way out of this."

"Well, I can't do much, can I? Even if I wasn't taped to the wall, I can barely move anyway. Besides which, I've thinking about the contents of my pockets and I haven't got a single thing that would help us. But I bet you have. Because you think of everything, Ali, and I know you'll work something out. You just need to focus and remember it."

There was silence for a while, as I took that in.

All down to me. Sam, trusting me to get him out of this. Kay and Liam, trusting me for a safe space. Ruth Darnley and the Gromberts and all Vera's other victims, trusting me for some justice.

Too much. Too much trust in a woman taped to a metal bar and slowly freezing to death. But what had Sam said? 'I haven't got a single thing that would help us. But I bet you have.'

What did I have?

I ran through a checklist.

Flat keys. Left behind – or had Vera taken them?

Wallet. In my coat, which was over by my rucksack, well out of reach. And not much use in any case.

Phone. Vera had taken that.

Small change. In my pocket. Could I saw through the tape with a coin? Possibly. Not very likely. And in any case, it was out of reach with my hands taped up.

Packet of tissues. Also in my pocket, and no conceivable use even if I could reach them.

Bottle of water. In my rucksack. There were a number of possibly useful items in there. Things like a torch, an emergency foil blanket, a knife - in fact a multi-tool gadget which included a knife - a first aid kit. I kept the rucksack stocked with things like that. Of course, Vera might have emptied them out when she was searching my flat. I hadn't had time to check. But in any case, it was on the other side of the room, out of reach.

Which left only... my spare key. Neatly tucked away in my belt. Because you never know, I might need it someday.

Today could be the day. It was a Yale, with a serrated edge. Like a saw. Enough like a saw to cut through tape, perhaps? If I could get to it.

The bar was just above waist height. The key might be in reach.

"Sam! I've got an idea!" I said.

There was no answer. Sam's head had dropped down on this chest, and he wasn't moving.

"SAM!" I shouted. No response. He was either asleep or unconscious and I had no idea how long he'd last like that.

The plastic bag round my hands was the first problem. But not a big problem. Fortunately, Vera hadn't gone for quality. It was just thin disposable plastic. Ecologically bad, but easy to poke a finger through, and then tear a hole big enough for my whole hand.

But then I had to reach the key in my belt.

I'd come across the belt with its cool little inside pocket in the Christmas Market down in Bath when I visited with my parents one year. I was supposed to be shopping for presents – for other people – but instead I brought three of the belts before I'd even thought about what I'd use the pocket for. I just had the idea that they'd come in handy.

The pocket was just to the right of the buckle. I twisted myself round as far as I could, pulling on the tape restraining my left hand, and simultaneously trying to bend my right hand round to reach the pocket.

I'm no contortionist, but I'm fairly flexible. I could get my hand round far enough, my body close enough, to just reach my belt. Just get a finger on it. Several inches away from the pocket.

I heaved against the tapes, twisted harder. Stood on tip-toe, leaned over backwards.

Had the tape stretched a little? I could just about get two fingertips on the belt. Still short of the pocket, short of the key.

I rested a moment, leaning back on the wall. There had to be some way of getting at that key.

I couldn't think of anything different, so tried again. Twisting round, pulling at the restraints. I tried steady pulls, sharp jerks. I tried pulling up, pulling down. Increasingly desperate, I hurled myself forward, put my feet on the wall and pushed.

"Come ON!" I shouted. "Come on, come on come ON!"

Just an inch or two. That's all I needed. Just a little bit of slippage on the bar, some stretch in the tape...

"Come on... Please!" I wrenched at the bar, put my hand round it and shook it.

The tape's adhesive was strong, well attached to the bar. It didn't shift a millimetre.

But under my fingers, something gave way.

At the back of the bar, out of sight, something crunched and broke, and left a hole.

The bar might have been painted once, but years and years of heavy use and damp conditions had worn that away. Rain had come in through the open windows. Some had fallen on the bar, run along it, dripped down it. Surface tension had kept little droplets clinging to the bottom, chemical reaction had slowly corroded the metal.

Steel expands up to ten times when it rusts. That causes rust blisters, patches where the metal has expanded. And in the process, lost its strength.

Underneath and behind, the bar was lumpy with rust blisters. One of these had crumbled away under the pressure of my fingers. It had left a hole that went right through the surface of the bar into its hollow centre.

I explored the hole with my fingertips. The surface was gritty with flaked rust, but at the edges, where the metal was still good, it was sharp.

I twisted my grip, feeling underneath. At the point where the tape went round the bar there was a big rust blister. It extended all the way under the tape. I felt round it, looking for vulnerabilities. Edges I could get my fingernails into. Then I started picking at it.

Some bits came away easily. Others, not so much. I changed tactics, squeezing on the bar, trying to force my fingers through the rust.

I felt some give at one point. My hands were aching with the effort. I paused, rested them for a moment. Flexed my fingers, then started again. Picking, poking, squeezing.

Gradually, the rust gave way. Sometimes in flakes, sometimes in powder. Then a whole lump of it came loose, but didn't fall. Didn't fall because some of it was stuck to the tape.

I pulled at it with my fingertips. Trying to grip it between my middle and index fingers, wriggling it away from the tape.

It was stuck really hard. I couldn't get much grip either, and my whole hand was aching.

I stopped again. Rested, leaning back against the wall. This was impossible.

But then again, what else did I have to do with my time?

"Sam?" I called. He didn't answer, didn't move.

I tugged against the bar, the tape, and something fell off. Exploring with my fingers, I found that most of the rust lump had crumbled away. What was left was tape, and jagged edges.

I got my fingers on the tape, pushed it against the sharp bit. Tried a sawing motion, but there wasn't much give in the tape, and I couldn't reach properly. Was I making any progress? I couldn't tell. I could only persist.

My index finger slipped off the tape and caught against the sharp edge. Painfully. The fingertip had gone right into the hole, and scraped against the edges as I withdrew it. When I tried to push against the tape again, it was slippery, and little pulses of pain rain up my hand.

"Just a small cut," I whispered to myself. "Don't be such a wimp."

I pushed again. Was it my imagination, or was the tape going deeper into the hole? Was it stretching, or had it started to tear?

Then there was a small shift under my fingers. Suddenly the tape was just a fraction looser.

"Yes!" I shouted, and renewed my efforts.

It was tearing. Just a little. But it had started.

I pushed myself forward again, felt the tape tear a little more. It was going more easily now...

Then it stopped.

I felt for the problem. Vera had put more than one layer of tape round the pipe, and where the torn section met the extra layers, it had stopped tearing.

But now I had a little more freedom of movement. It was easier to push that fresh tape against the jagged edges of metal, to force it in until it too started to tear.

A start, that's all I had. Then I couldn't reach any further.

A start was all I needed. A little chance and a little hope.

I pulled on my wrist again. Feet on the wall, heaving outwards, twisting and wrenching my wrist, knowing that the tape was starting to give, that it was weakened, tearing.

I screamed, a wild, inarticulate yell of fury. Changed my angle of pull, tried to drag the tape along the bar...

It moved. Slipped, shifted, then abruptly came free and I half collapsed onto the floor, staring in wonder and utter joy at my hand, wrapped in tape and plastic, smeared with blood and rust, but free and clear from its restraint.

"I did it Sam! I did it!"

Sam made no response, which reminded me that there was still a lot to do.

With my hand free, it was easy to reach the key in my belt. With the key, it was easy to saw through the tape holding my left hand. And with both hands free it was easy to get the rest of the tape and plastic off me.

I went over to Sam while I was doing that. "Sam? I've done it! I'm free."

He still didn't answer. I touched his face and it was cold. He was still breathing, short shallow breaths, but cold. So cold.

I ran back across the room to my rucksack. I'd repacked it back at the flat – had Vera taken anything out again?

The multi-tool was still in the side pocket, as was the emergency foil blanket. Torch in the other side which I switched on - the daylight was fading quickly now. I took them back over to Sam, opened the knife attachment and gently cut him free. As carefully as I could, but I couldn't avoid moving his leg and he woke with a scream of agony.

"It's OK, Sam, it's OK," I reassured him. "Sorry, but I need to lay you down properly, get you warm."

He looked at me, confused. "Alison? You're free?"

"Yes. I managed to get free. I need to get you warm, then go for help."

In spite of the pain he was in, he managed to smile. "Of course you did. Knew you would."

Impulsively, I kissed him.

"Warming me up nicely," he muttered.

"This'll do a better job," I said. I moved him away from the wall as gently as possible, opened up the foil blanket, laid it over him and tucked it under as best I could without touching the broken leg. Even so, he groaned.

"Is that better?" The foil could only reflect back the heat that was in his body, and there wasn't much of that. He still felt frighteningly cold, and was still wet.

"Yes, thank you. Cup of tea?" The words were cheerful, but the tone was strained.

"Working on that." I squeezed his hand, then went back to my rucksack. Action and adrenaline were keeping the cold at bay, but that was a short term solution, and I could feel body heat leaching out of the wet t-shirt. I stripped it off.

Spare clothing in the rucksack. I dug out a shirt and pulled it on. Dry fabric on cold wet skin. It felt like hope. Fleece and coat on top of that.

I picked up the rucksack and looked at the door. Then looked at the stairs. The impulse to rush out and get help was strong. But leaving Sam in that condition didn't seem right either. I wasn't sure that the foil blanket would be enough to avoid exposure. And there was his leg. People had died as a result of complications with a broken leg, and that was in hospital. At the least, if it wasn't set properly he could be crippled for life.

Plus which he probably still had concussion. I had to do more.

The stairs. The penthouse suite, Vera had called it. A joke, of course, but what was up there?

I went to investigate.

There was a wooden hatch at the top of the stairs. It was held shut with a padlock, but the screw heads on the hasp were exposed, and my useful little multi-tool had a screwdriver. Several, in fact, both flat and cross-head.

The screws were rusty, I discovered, but the wood was starting to rot, and they came out easily. I pushed the hatch open and went up.

Chapter 20

*Scene Examination Checklist: Wear Personal Protective Equipment as
appropriate. Look before touching. Avoid likely areas for footwear
marks. Consider physical evidence, possible DNA sources, surfaces
suitable for fingerprints. Photograph before recovery.*

Up to the place where Mickey Fayden had hidden out from the
police, being looked after by Vera and going through his own
private hell of addiction and withdrawal. I wondered which had
been worse. I wasn't being cynical, that was a genuine concern.
Between the devil and the deep blue sea, as the saying goes – and I
wasn't sure which was the devil.

I actually felt sorry for Mickey. But the thought reminded me
that this was a crime scene. Training and practice kicked in, and
I stood at the top of the steps, carefully examining and mentally
recording the room.

There were four windows, one in each wall. Glazed, but dirty.
Just clear enough for me to see that it was now fully dark outside.

A work surface ran the full length of the opposite wall. It looked
like it had been rescued from someone's kitchen renovation. Maybe
two kitchens – one end was a brown marble-effect surface, the other
a stained and grubby white. There was a plain wooden shelf below it.

On the work surface, looking from left to right, were a plastic
bowl, a small collection of mismatched crockery and kitchen utensils
and a litre bottle of what looked like mineral water. There was an
opened pack of the same bottles on the shelf underneath.

Further along was a single burner gas camping stove and a gas lantern – spare gas canisters underneath – with saucepans arranged in size order next to them. Some canned and packaged food followed. Underneath was something black and shiny. I had to get closer to see what it was. Black plastic bags – no, plastic sheeting. It looked thick, heavy duty, and there was a pile of it, next to an opened pack of silver tape. The same sort that Vera had used to attach us to the bar.

At the end of the work surface was a portable TV and a radio / CD player. On the shelf below was a small safe with a keypad in the door.

In the centre of the room was a folding table, with two chairs. There was a large toolbox on the table.

At the far end of the room, below the window, was a camp bed with a sleeping bag and a couple of blankets folded neatly on top of it. In the corner next to it was a large pedal bin with a broom and a dustpan next to it.

I'd seen worse hotel rooms. It looked like somewhere you could camp out quite comfortably for a while. No toilet or shower facilities, of course, no running water – but on the other hand, no neighbours or passing traffic. For a place within a few miles of town, it was as isolated as you could get.

It was also remarkably tidy. It didn't look like a place where a fugitive had been hiding. But then, it was a while since Mickey had been here. I had a suspicion that Vera had been using it since then, and the almost excessive neatness suggested someone who liked to be in control of their environment.

The tool box was particularly interesting. Touching it without gloves felt like sacrilege, but I compromised by using a clean tissue to flip it open.

The first thing I saw was a mobile phone. A rush of joy filled me as I grabbed it, heedless of fingerprints or DNA contamination

– followed by abrupt disappointment as I realised that it was just a plastic shell, with no actual phone inside.

I swore, loudly, and barely restrained the impulse to throw the useless thing across the room. But professionalism managed – barely – to prevail. Instead I looked more closely through the toolbox.

There were actually several mobile phones in the top tray – or more precisely, the remains of them. Plastic casing, circuit boards and components, none of them of any value.

I thought about it, considered the plastic sheeting and rolls of tape and recognised what I was seeing. This was Vera's bomb factory.

It had been generally assumed that the device that killed Ruth Darnley had been manufactured in a garage or workshop somewhere. But of course, it didn't have to have been. Vera had done most of the work up here, in this remote place, with the van parked outside. If some distant walker or shepherd had seen it, they would have thought little of it. No one would have come close enough to wonder why she was lining the inside with plastic sheets, held together with tape, or why she was putting propane gas bottles inside.

The mobile phone parts were her experiments, while she worked out exactly how to rig the detonator. Then she'd just had to wait for the opportunity. The main car-park closed - that had been in the news weeks before it happened, plenty of time to complete her preparations. And Darnley presiding over a case. Vera would already have known which car to target. She would have the note all prepared. When the time came, she just put the pieces together and drove into town. To the court.

This was an even more significant crime scene than I'd realised.

I carefully closed the tool box again, though not without noting the other items inside. Particularly the pair of bolt croppers. I was germinating an idea, for which they could be useful.

First things first, though, and the first thing was getting Sam up here where he could be warm and comfortable. I had an idea about that as well.

A few minutes later, I went back down stairs, carrying the gas lantern. Now lit, thanks to the matches Vera had left on the work surface. In a waterproof container – she thought of almost everything.

Sam appeared asleep or unconscious, but stirred as I came near, and squinted into the light.

"Alison?" he asked.

"Yes, of course. I've found some useful stuff upstairs."

"Thank goodness for that. I was afraid Vera had come back."

I put the lantern down beside him. "No sign of her. I don't think she'll be back until morning – she'll give us plenty of time to freeze. But that's not going to happen."

"Knew you'd think of something."

"More luck and desperation than thought."

He shook his head. "Whatever. I'll take it, and with thanks."

"Right. How are you feeling?"

"OK, under the circumstances. The blanket helps."

"I need to look at the leg, see how bad it is. Can you cope with that?"

He nodded. "Go for it."

I pulled the foil blanket out of the way, took out the multi-tool, and carefully cut up the trouser leg. Difficult, with the thick denim material of his jeans, but the knife was very sharp. I did it as gently as possible, but couldn't avoid moving the leg slightly. Sam clenched his teeth, but didn't make a sound.

"OK, then." I pulled the cut pieces of material aside. "Good news is, it looks like a clean break. The skin's not broken, no protruding bones. A simple fracture."

"Right. So what's the bad news?"

"You probably won't play at Wimbledon next year."

"That's disappointing. I was planning to get my first grand-slam." He shook his head, then groaned. "Mustn't do that. Head hurts more than the leg now."

There was a huge bruise developing over Sam's left temple, centred on a livid welt from where the shaft of the ASP had connected. Fortunately the ball on the end didn't seem to have made contact. All the same, it worried me more than his leg did. But there was nothing I could do about it now.

"We need to get you upstairs. It's a lot warmer there, and there's a bed. Let's do what we can with the leg.

I'd brought the broom handle. It made a good makeshift splint, and there was plenty of tape to hold it in place. With that done, I helped Sam to his feet and half carried him as we made our way slowly over to the stairs.

"Right, this is the difficult bit," I said. "Are you ready to give it a go?"

Sam looked up the staircase. "Got a better idea. Help me sit on the step."

I turned him round, and lowered him down. "That's it. Now then..." Pushing with his hands and his good leg, Sam moved his bottom up to the next step. Then the next, and so on. I held his broken leg to keep it from banging on the stairs as we slowly ascended.

Half-way up, he called for a pause. His face was white. "Just need a moment," he said.

"OK."

I went to get the lantern, took it past him up the stairs, and came back to sit beside him. He leaned against my shoulder and we sat in silence for a few minutes.

"What's the plan, then?" he asked.

"Get you settled in, then I'll go for help."

"How far is that? I don't have a clue where we are."

"You missed the journey. We're up in the hills. Top of the next valley along from Frayhampton. Brightrush, I think it's called."

"So you have to go back down the valley? How far?"

"Three or four miles to the first house, I think. But I'm not going that way."

He looked at me. "You know somewhere closer."

"Perhaps. I think. I've walked this area. Once, at least. It's only a mile or two at the most over the ridge and down to the next valley."

Down to where Kay and Liam lived. And where Vera might go next. If they hadn't got out when I told them to, if they'd looked for me but couldn't find me and gone home again... Vera knew what Kay had told me. I felt a cold certainty that she'd go after her old school friend – and Liam as well. She'd want to make sure they didn't tell anyone else the truth about her past.

So I had to get to them and warn them. I was hoping that Vera wouldn't rush. She'd think she had plenty of time. She'd want to get rid of the pick-up and my bike first. Then she'd need to collect her van from wherever she'd parked it. So I might have time to get to Kay, warn her and Liam, get an ambulance out to Sam and get the police looking for Vera.

It seemed like a good plan, but I was all too aware that it relied on Vera doing what I expected. If she didn't I could find myself in another confrontation. I didn't like that idea. I knew Sam wouldn't like it either. So I didn't mention it.

"Come on. Ready for another go?"

It took another ten minutes to get to the top of the stairs, then across to the camp bed. Sam collapsed back onto it. I couldn't get him properly into the sleeping bag, but with it and the blankets he was as close to comfortable as he was going to get.

I'd lit the gas stove before I went for Sam, and it and the lantern had made a significant difference to the room temperature. I offered him one of the bottles of water. He took a few sips and lay back.

"You'd better get going," he said quietly.

"In a moment. I want to make sure you're OK."

"OK as I'm going to get, outside of hospital." He reached out and touched my hand. "I don't deserve you, Alison."

"Hah. Nobody deserves me, but you're stuck with me anyway."

Sam had closed his eyes, but opened them again to stare at me. "You know what I mean."

"I... OK. Thanks. I don't deserve you either."

He smiled and shut his eyes again. "We need to discuss this further. But not now. I think I need to sleep. You've got some walking to do. See you later." "See you later." I squeezed his hand and stood up.

First, back to the toolbox for the bolt croppers. Then...

I looked round the room again. Something was niggling at me.

Sam seemed to have fallen properly asleep. There was nothing more I could do for him. But I felt like I was missing something. Something significant.

I can't always trust feelings like that. But there was a pattern here. A clue.

I was impatient to get going. Time was running out.

I took one more look round. Carefully ticking off significant items. Food, water, toolbox, tape, TV, radio, safe.

I walked over to the safe, took out my torch and examined it more closely.

I hadn't bothered before. I wasn't likely to be able to get into it, the police could check it later. But now I was looking properly, there was something wrong with it.

It was just a typical small safe, as found in thousands of houses. The sort of thing used for money, jewellery, important papers. About a foot wide, a bit less than that in height and depth, with a large handle on the right and a keypad in the middle.

But the keypad was damaged, the face of it bent inwards. There were other marks all round the door and frame. The sort of marks you get when someone's trying to force an entry.

Tool marks are usually quite distinctive. Any CSI can tell at a glance if someone's used a flat head screwdriver, a crowbar or a hammer. These marks were different from any of the usual ones. Arc shaped indentations. Not very deep, but enough to show on the painted steel surface.

I made a mental estimate. If you extended the arc round to a full circle, it would be about three inches in diameter. Seven to eight centimetres. About the size of a standard tin can.

The marks were consistent with someone trying to smash their way into the safe with a can of beans or something similar.

Forensic evidence is like a story with a lot of the details hidden. All you have left are the highlights. The trick is discerning the pattern that link those highlights together. If you can see the pattern, you know where to look for the next highlight. For example, if you see the marks of a ladder below a window, the next place to examine is the window itself. Tool marks on the window frame, footwear marks on the sill or the floor below.

I knew where to look for the next highlight. I brought out my tissue again, and carefully tried the handle of the safe.

It turned. A little reluctantly at first, but it turned, and the door swung open.

Inside was a clear plastic container, about six inches high and three across. It was a quarter full of plain white medicine capsules.

The story was becoming very clear in my mind now. It fitted in with things I already knew, such as the long term effects and withdrawal symptoms of La Paz. And Vera's failed attempt to get Mickey off them.

La Paz - 'lappies' on the street – had started out as a legitimate attempt to make a drug to help busy people de-stress. What they got was something that inhibited emotions. Someone under its influence felt nothing. No love, no fear, no inhibitions, no humanity. It stripped them down to basic drives. In that condition people would take ridiculous risks or commit horrendous crimes without a spark of emotional response.

The results were appalling. But even worse was the intensely addictive nature of the drug. After only a few uses, a person would be hooked. The typical cycle was that after taking a dose, the drug would kick in almost at once, and its effects would last for several hours, before the recipient began to slowly recover their emotions. Often a confusing period, especially as they began to recall what they had done under the influence of La Paz. Then there would be a longer time, perhaps a day or so, when they were more or less normal.

But after that, they started to experience withdrawal symptoms. Physically there would be sweating, stomach cramps, headaches. Emotionally there would be increasingly violent mood swings. Another dose would keep these at bay. But the more a person took, the worse the withdrawal symptoms would become.

And here was Mickey, who had been taking La Paz for a while. Months, at least. He was well hooked. And Vera was trying to get him off, decreasing his dosage.

She'd gone too far, too soon. It had triggered the worst stage of the withdrawal.

He knew where the lappies were. She'd kept them in the safe. He didn't know the combination.

And when the mood swing took him into fury, he'd taken a tin and hammered away at the safe. It was the only tool he had, and of course it was quite ineffectual.

Vera had come back at some point. Perhaps his mood had flipped out of rage and into despair. Or perhaps she'd used the stun-gun on

him. In any case, he'd been restrained, subdued. And she'd managed
to open the damaged safe, give him some more lappies. But by then
it was obvious that her programme wasn't working. Perhaps she
increased the dose, and it still didn't work, didn't bring him out of
withdrawal. He was too far gone.

So she loaded him into a vehicle, and set off to find a hospital
where he could be left, where he might finally get the professional
treatment he needed. Too late. The damage done was irreparable. He
stood trial, went to prison, but never fully recovered.

That was the story told by the safe, the marks, the capsules. Just
one thing was needed to confirm the story.

I opened the container, shook out a few of the capsules. They
looked exactly like the ones I'd recovered from Mickey's house. I
slipped a few into my pocket. Evidence to help persuade the police
how serious this was. If needed.

But I had to be able to say as definitely as possible that this was La
Paz. In my mind, I was already writing the statement, and 'I thought
they looked the same' wasn't strong enough.

I took a capsule and broke it open. White powder poured out
onto the floor. Fine white powder. Not coarse, pinkish powder. Not
La Paz.

Tentatively, I dipped my finger in the powder, then touched the
tip to my tongue. The sort of thing detectives do all the time on TV,
but no one ever does in real life. Except now I did, because I had to
know what I was dealing with here, and the lab wasn't available.

The taste was distinctive. It was aspirin.

Which meant that my story was wrong. There was part of the
pattern that I was not seeing.

Chapter 21

Rules for night walks: 1) Wear light and/or fluorescent clothing (be visible, be safe!). 2) Stay on known or well-marked paths. 3) Carry a torch but be wary of using it as this will impede your night vision. 4) Don't walk alone at night!

Vera had put a chain on the outside of the door and secured it with a padlock. Neither the chain nor the padlock were very heavy duty: I doubt if she ever expected us to get free of the bar. There was enough slack in the chain for me to push the door open a few inches and reach through with the bolt croppers.

I walked up the hill to the wire fence, and went along it, trying to remember back five years or so. I'd come down the hill then, and walked along the outside of the fence, looking for a gate. Failing that, a place where I could push through or climb over. But the fence was high, and solidly constructed with a lot of barbed wire. Eventually, and having established that the fence ran all the way across the valley, I'd given up and turned back.

Of course, I hadn't had any bolt croppers then.

I couldn't be sure exactly how far along the fence I'd searched, but it must have been getting close to the valley wall. I picked a spot and set about cutting my way through. The bolt croppers worked with marvellous efficiency, and I resolved to get myself a pair. Or maybe keep these, though technically they were part of a crime scene and would have to be entered into evidence.

Five minutes and I was on the other side. I put the bolt croppers in my rucksack – too useful to leave behind – and started up the slope.

To my left, a twenty foot high cliff marked the side of the valley. It ran for over a mile before diminishing to an embankment and then disappearing completely as the valley opened out onto a plateau. However, five years ago I'd come across another way. Not a proper path, more of a sheep track, but it had got me up onto the ridge a lot sooner than if I'd had to go all the way back up the valley.

The question was, could I find it again? Especially in the dark. The sky was clear, stars hard and bright above me, the moon riding high and only just past full. But it wasn't anything like full daylight.

There had been a sort of rocky outcrop from the valley wall, I remembered. I could see something like that up ahead, the pale rock catching the moonlight and standing out against the shadows. Unfortunately, the actual path was somewhere in those shadows. Had it been before the outcrop or after it? I couldn't remember.

The rock loomed above me as I got closer. There were no signs of a path on the downhill side, just a steep slope of scree. Impossible to climb, dangerous to attempt.

I followed the base of the rock. It was cracked and fissured in many places, and in the moonlight the effect was bizarre and confusing, the ground littered with rockfalls. I moved away from it, wary of my footing. A twisted ankle would be the end of my escape attempt.

I reached the other side of the outcrop, where it merged back into the valley wall and found it to be sheer, without a hint of a path.

There was a clenching in my guts as I looked at it. If I couldn't find the path, then I should probably turn back and go down the valley. But anything might happen to Kay and Liam in the time that took me.

Or perhaps I'd misremembered? Perhaps the path was marked by another outcrop? Maybe it was less obvious than I'd remembered. Should I keep going for a bit, explore further?

I shut my eyes, trying to think back. There had been a rock, I was sure. In fact, there had been rock on both sides of me as I climbed up.

Or had that been another path, another place altogether?

I went back along the face of the outcrop, peering into the various fissures. Some looked deeper than others.

I took out my torch, reluctantly sacrificing my night vision for a better look into the shadows. Most of the cracks were only that, extending only a short distance. Some were deeper, disappearing from sight through narrowing fissures and round sharp turns. Some seemed to lead down into shadows.

One had sheep droppings. Well inside and up on a ledge.

I couldn't see beyond the ledge but it seemed familiar. Or was that just wishful thinking?

I wriggled my way into the fissure. It wasn't the widest I'd seen, but that seemed familiar as well. I'd had difficulty getting through before. With a bit of a scramble, I managed to hoist my way up onto the ledge, and experienced a heady rush of relief when I saw a way opening up in front of me, climbing up through the rock to the ridge above.

Five minutes later, I emerged onto open ground.

Below, I could see lantern-light spilling out of the windows of our prison. Where Sam was. Waiting for me. I blew him a kiss, and felt embarrassed by the pointless gesture, but I wanted to do it again anyway.

Instead I looked down the valley. Distant lights, farmhouses and villages. Home was somewhere in that general direction. I wondered if Oliver had found his way back yet?

Above was clear skies, stars and moonlight. Cold and hard and beautiful. Any other night I would have paused to stare and wonder.

Instead, I turned and looked up at the ridge. All shadows and shades of black or dark blue.

The north wind was strengthening as I stood there. It carried ice with it, a freezing touch that reminded me of the fate Vera had intended.

"Not happening!" I said to myself. And to her. "Not that easy!"

I started up the slope towards the crest of the ridge.

It had been hard going in daylight. The slope was gentle enough, but the ground was rough. Thick tussocky grass mingled with loose stones, sharp edges of rock poking up through the earth. Easy to stumble, to twist or even break an ankle with a careless or unlucky step. Even easier by moonlight, while desperate urgency compels a faster pace than is wise.

I tried to find a compromise between need and caution. Watching every step but also looking round, trying to navigate. I couldn't remember any landmarks from five years ago, probably couldn't see them if I did. The valley behind me was soon lost in the darkness. The stars were clear, and I had no trouble finding Polaris, but stellar navigation is more suited to the sea or the desert than a rough hillside.

Mostly, I tried to stay at right-angles to the slope of the ground, hoping that would take me in the general direction that I needed to go.

How far was it? A mile or two, I'd told Sam. Couldn't be far off that. How long would it take me?

Hadn't seemed very long before. In daylight. Three miles an hour is average walking speed. I can usually do much better than that. But perhaps not in these conditions. All the same, it shouldn't take more than an hour. And I'd done the hard part.

The exertion was keeping me warm enough, though the biting cold was numbing my face and fingers. I usually had a woolly hat in my rucksack, but it wasn't one of the things I'd put back in after Vera emptied it. I hadn't been thinking of a night walk then. I didn't have a hood in this coat. No gloves either. I tried putting my hands in my pockets, but the dangers of stumbling were too great, I needed them out to catch myself if I fell.

I pushed on through the silver-edged darkness and tried to keep my mind off the cold by thinking about the capsules. Discovering aspirin where I should have found La Paz was niggling at me. It didn't fit the pattern that I'd been seeing. I knew that Vera had been adjusting the dosages, but switching it for aspirin suggested that she'd tried to make Mickey go cold turkey. A pretty desperate move, and it wasn't surprising that he'd suffered from extreme withdrawal as a result. Perhaps they'd run out of the real stuff and she'd tried using the aspirin as a placebo? Possible, but it didn't feel like Vera. Too chancy a strategy for someone who liked to be in total control.

It was hard to follow a train of thought while having to watch every step. Especially as the slope was getting steeper. Steeper than I remembered.

There was a sort of a hummock in the middle of the ridge. Or had that been this ridge? I thought it was. Five years ago, I'd gone round it, but I couldn't remember which way. Left or right? Or I could just keep going up, but if it got any steeper I'd be climbing on all fours.

I took a decision, and went left.

The going got easier, the slope easing out. Now I'd avoided the hummock, I must be near the top of the ridge.

The ground under my feet began to feel squishy. My footsteps splashed. I was walking into a bog.

I stopped. And swore. It always amazed me how water could collect at the top of a hill, but it had caught me out more than once. But what to do now? I was sure I didn't remember this from last time, so perhaps I should try back the other way. It would cost me time, but if I carried on I could find myself knee deep and struggling in mud and water. I might even manage to fulfil Vera's plans for me, by getting stuck, getting wet and dying of exposure.

How far did this marshy area extend? The moonlight couldn't tell me. I would have to get my torch out and lose my night vision again.

LED technology has made torches so much more powerful than they used to be. The bright beam cut through the gloom, reflecting off water as far as I could see to right and left.

But just before me, just twenty or thirty feet away, there was a rise in the ground level. It looked drier, at least.

I picked my way carefully over to it, using the torch to guide me as I stepped from tussock to rock to only slightly muddy patch, and managed to reach the rise without going more than ankle deep, finally stepping up to drier ground with considerable relief.

Which turned to actual joy when I realised I had discovered a farmer's track – narrow and unpaved, but firm, dry and relatively free of obstacles. What was more, it ran in approximately the right direction. I switched off the torch, let my eyes adjust, then set out at a much better pace than I'd been managing before.

Ten minutes, then I was looking out over another valley. In the distance, the lights of the town glowed. There was a dark area near the middle which probably marked the Delford Mills Project area. Off to the south a patch of brilliant illumination would be The Castle, home ground of our local football club, Delford Vale. Looked like they had an evening match on.

Much closer was a small cluster of lights that marked Frayhampton. And, almost directly below me, a single small light. Which was in about the right place to be Kay and Liam's house.

Going the wrong way round the hummock had been serendipitous. I had expected to have to find my way through the ruins of the old mill buildings – as I had five years ago. It hadn't been easy in daylight; it would have been a lot harder this time. But instead I'd come out almost in spitting distance.

The downside was that the light suggested that they were still there. They hadn't taken my advice to get out. As yet, there were no headlights showing between them and Frayhampton. Nobody driving up the lane which led to their hamlet. There was still time. I just needed to find my way down to them.

That looked like a problem at first – the slope behind the houses was quite steep and, as I remembered from my previous visit, thick with brambles. Fortunately, the farmer's track came to my rescue once more, as it turned and ran across the slope, descending to join the Frayhampton lane further down the valley.

I followed it until I came to a point where the slope was easier and clear of brambles, then half-slid, half-climbed the rest of the way down. I reached the lane about a hundred yards below the houses, and started back up, almost running now in my eagerness to reach Kay and Liam.

On the way I was rehearsing what I needed to say. "Vera knows where you are, she's already tried to kill me twice today and she could be on her way here now! Don't take time to pack, get in your car and..."

I stopped. Stopped talking, stopped walking. Because I could now see the front of the houses more clearly, and the light from the window was falling on the vehicles parked there.

One car which I recognised as Liam's. And a pick-up.

Vera had not done as I'd expected. She hadn't spent any time getting rid of the pick-up. She'd come straight here. Which meant that she'd been here for some time.

Kay and Liam might already be dead. Or if not – what might Vera be doing to them now? How far would her vindictiveness take her if she felt betrayed by her old school friend?

Part of me wanted to rush straight in and put a stop to it, whatever was happening. But another part urged caution. Vera was not to be taken lightly. I'd be at a disadvantage, in that she would use Kay and Liam against me, as she had with Sam. I'd have to catch her by surprise and disable her before she could react, and with her there was no guarantee that it would work.

Plus which, there was that shotgun Liam had mentioned. If he'd found it, then there was a good chance that Vera had it now. Charging in there without knowing would be stupid. And as soon as Vera saw me Sam would be in renewed danger as well. If I failed to take her down, then her first response would be to go back to the farm building and deal with him.

So what then? I glanced back down the lane. Fifteen or twenty minutes to get down to Frayhampton and find a phone. And how long for a copper to get up here? If I mentioned the shotgun, they'd send Armed Response – which might take longer, if there were no units immediately available. But I couldn't not mention it. I couldn't risk sending an unarmed officer in against Vera with a shotgun.

Best case scenario, it might be the best part of an hour before something could happen. And every moment that passed increased the risk that Kay and her brother would be dead.

But perhaps there was another solution. A line of telephone poles ran alongside the lane. Telephone wires connected to some of the houses – specifically, the last three houses in the row.

I carried on up the lane, but more cautiously, keeping to the side of the road and ready to duck down if someone came out.

Liam had said that the house on the end belonged to someone from London who only came up in the summer. Or something like that. So probably empty just now.

Empty but secure. As I got closer, I could see a white box fixed to the front of the house. A white box with a little blue light that flashed at regular intervals. The man from London had installed an alarm. Professionally, that was something I approved of. Personally, I could have done without it just now. There was no way I could risk setting the alarm off and alerting Vera.

The other side of Kay's house was the old lady Liam had mentioned. Mrs Denny? Mrs Derry? It didn't matter, anyway. The point was that she'd gone to hospital and wasn't likely to be coming back. So the house was empty. It didn't seem to have an alarm fitted, but it did have a telephone line.

Next in line was the Sales Rep. Hardly ever there, according to Liam. No lights on, so tonight wasn't an exception. No telephone line either. Perhaps he wasn't there often enough to justify it. Or if he was there, he didn't want anyone calling him. Either way, there was no point in trying it.

The two end houses were empty, and boarded up. So the only possibility was Mrs D's.

Of course, it might well be locked. But Liam had said that they were looking after the house. Perhaps they might have left a window open? Or a key somewhere nearby. Round these parts people often leave a key near the door – under a plant pot or something like that.

Not the front door, though. The light was on in Kay's front-room, if Vera was there she'd only have to look out to see me at the neighbour's front door, just a few yards away.

I'd try round the back. If it worked, if I could get in and if I found a working phone, it would save time and perhaps lives. And then I'd be on hand if things seemed to be kicking off. Intervening would be less risky if there was backup on the way.

If it didn't work then Frayhampton was the only option, and I'd just have to get down there as fast as I could.

A track ran round to the back of the houses. It had been gravelled once, but the stones had sunk into the soil leaving just mud and puddles. And it was very dark, between the houses on one side and the steep slope on the other. I crept up, feeling my way, not daring to use my torch in case Vera should happen to look out of the back.

There was a faint glow in Kay's back window, something leaking through from the front, perhaps. Useful, though, since it told me where I was. The next door along would be Mrs. D's.

There was only a short paved yard between the track and the back door. No fence, wall or gate to negotiate. There was a rubbish bin – black plastic in dark shadow, invisible. I bumped into it with my knee, something fell off with a dull thump.

I stood absolutely still, holding my breath and listening.

No sounds. Just night noises. Wind gusting in the rooftops and through the trees further up the valley. Something rustling in the brambles on the hillside.

After a moment I started to breathe again. I carefully side-stepped the bin and took the last few paces up to the door. Fumbled around for the handle, and tried it. Gently.

There was a squeak of protest from the under-oiled mechanism, but it turned. And the door swung easily open.

Too easily. Before I could stop it it had hit something that clattered.

I froze again.

Silence. Silence and darkness, and a slightly musty smell from inside the house.

I'd had enough of creeping around in the dark. I took out my torch, and shielded with my hand to release just a narrow beam of light.

I was standing in a rather cramped little kitchen, with a sink, a cooker and a fridge squeezed in below the window and a small table by the opposite wall. Blue Formica top and two matching chairs. Cupboards along the wall above, mugs hanging off hooks. A door to the right probably led to a downstairs bathroom that ran out into an extension behind the house. There was another door directly ahead.

In spite of the musty smell, which was probably ingrained into the ancient lino floor, it looked clean and tidy. Apart from the saucepan behind the door, which is what had clattered. But the important point was, there was no telephone.

I closed the door very gently behind me, and opened the one ahead.

As in Kay's house, there was a short hallway that ran to the front door. Stairs on the right to the first floor. Door on my left into the front room. But no telephone, just a few faded pictures on the walls.

Front room it was, then. I opened it with caution.

I could hear faint music. After a moment, I realised that it must be coming from next door. From Kay's house. They had the radio on, perhaps. I wondered what was happening there. No shouting, no screaming. Were they already dead? Or unconscious? I tried to imagine what Vera might decide to do, and failed. I couldn't put myself into her mind.

Mrs D's front room was neat and tidy. Just opposite me was a large leather sofa. There were pillows and blankets on it, neatly folded. Perhaps she'd taken to sleeping down here before she went to hospital. Many older people did that when the stairs became too much for them.

I looked further. Large chest of drawers on my left at the back of the room, with a radio on it. A coffee table in front of the sofa. There were several books there, plus a notebook and pencil, all carefully lined up. A larger table by the window had clothing laid out across it in neat, orderly piles.

There was something about that order, that precision that seemed familiar to me. Familiar and threatening. I felt a pattern developing. But I couldn't see what it was.

I stepped into the room, looking more closely at the table. The clothes were not what you'd expect in a house where an old lady lived alone. Jeans, t-shirts. Socks, female underwear. Nothing flash, all sober colours and sensible styles. But not old.

And yes! There was a telephone! Right at the back of the table. It was old, so old that the plastic had turned yellow, but it seemed to be plugged in.

I walked over to it, and flicked my torch into the corners as I did so. An ancient TV was next to the table – bulky cathode-ray, and probably not even working because there was a coat stand in front of it.

That looked to be the same vintage as the TV and the phone. Varnished wood, badly chipped and scraped from long use. It had an umbrella rack at the bottom and several large hooks round the top.

There was something brown on the coat stand. Other things as well, but what caught my eye was something brown. Hanging by its hood.

In my mind, I felt patterns shifting.

I forgot the phone, went to the coat stand. Took hold of the brown garment and stretched it out.

It was a cagoule. A brown cagoule.

Of course, a lot of people might have brown cagoules. Mrs D. might have had one. But there was a green gilet underneath it.

I dropped the cagoule, stepped back from it. There was a roaring in my head and ice on my back.

Vera? How could it be Vera's? Unless she'd been hiding out here, all this time? Right next to Kay and Liam without them knowing about it?

No. of course not. That wasn't credible.

Not without them knowing about it.

Paradigm shift, and now I saw it clearly. Vera, her first day at school. After being totally isolated all her life, suddenly finding herself with hundreds of other kids. Children screaming, running, shouting – talking to her. Terrifying.

But there's Kay. The girl next door. Who she actually knows, at least by sight. Big, strong, confident Kay. Who looks after her, takes care of her.

Who's the leader in that scenario?

There was a click from behind me and the lights came on. Dazzlingly bright after only moonlight or torchlight for the past few hours. I turned, blinking, and made out a figure in the doorway. It moved towards me, and as I strained my eyes it resolved into Liam. He had a shotgun, and was pointing it at me.

"I found some ammunition!" he announced. Rather proudly. "Tried it out and it still works fine!"

"What he's saying, Alison, is that you shouldn't move. Or he'll shoot you." That was Kay, coming into the room after him.

"These walls are paper thin. You can hear everything that happens next door."

And that was Vera behind her.

"We couldn't find a key for the back – I don't think the old lady ever locked it – so I left a saucepan behind the door. Just in case any of the local lads decided to have a look round, once they heard she was in hospital. Never expected it to catch you!"

A moment ago seeing Vera would have been a shock. But now it wasn't even surprising.

Chapter 22

Forensic Examination of Firearm Discharges (personal notes): 1) If a shotgun has been used, take care to photograph and diagram the spread of shot as this gives an indication of range. 2) If a person has been hit at close range, look for and photograph / document both entry and possible exit wounds. 3) If the weapon is still at the scene, ensure that it has been made safe by Firearms Officers before recovery.

The shotgun looked old, with worn woodwork and exterior hammers. My knowledge of such things is limited, I've only done a basic firearms and ballistics course, but I guessed it might be a 410. Small for a shotgun, but at this range it could do some serious damage, and the hammers were cocked.

"Really, Alison, you are being difficult!" said Vera. She sounded annoyed. "That's three times I've tried to kill you now. How did you get away?"

I dragged my attention away from the shotgun. "My secret! Sorry to be so awkward, but I'm just not the compliant type." I turned to Kay. "Everything you told me was a lie."

As I said it, I was thinking about the capsules in my pocket. Supposed to be La Paz. Actually aspirin. They told a lie.

She shook her head. "Not everything. In fact, most of it was the truth. I just gave it a slightly different slant."

"All those things that happened at school..."

"Yes, they all happened."

"But it wasn't Vera who made you do them."

Kay laughed. She glanced across at Vera, and they both laughed. Old school friends, sharing memories. "No," she agreed. "It was more of a joint enterprise thing."

"And Izzy?"

"Just like I told you. Apart from the fact that it was me who actually set off the gas, whilst Vera was holding the sign up to the door."

I shook my head. "And the..." I touched the side of my face.

Kay mirrored my action, touching the scar tissue that marred her skin. "The acid? Oh, that really was an accident. We went in there to get it, but someone had moved things around. I had to reach for it, climb on a shelf, and the whole lot gave way."

"Your parents?" I looked at Vera.

She shrugged. "You know all about that. The fire worked perfectly but then things went a bit wrong. We'd planned that I'd move in with Kay, but of course she was in hospital, and I got sent off to relatives down in London. It wasn't easy staying in touch. We didn't get back together again until I moved back up here and joined the Force."

I looked at Liam. "And you knew about all this? You're OK with it all?"

He nodded. "Kay told me."

"Liam's a good kid!" Kay put a firm hand on his shoulder. "A good little brother, aren't you?"

He gave a little half smile and shrugged.

"Kay's done a good job of bringing him up," Vera put in. "He's very useful."

"I'm sure of it. And what about Mickey? Was he useful?"

I was speaking to Vera, but I was looking at Kay. And I saw something in her eyes. A shadow, perhaps. Or more prosaically, a tightening of the muscles round her eyes. Just for a fraction of a second. But it was enough. The final part of the pattern, and now I knew the whole story.

"Of course. We had some big plans." Vera looked whimsical. "Me and Mickey – and Kay, and Liam of course. We could do so much together. If things had worked out right, Mickey would have been well on his way up in the Force, and that would have opened up so many possibilities for us all." She frowned, another one of her mercurial mood swings. "But you spoiled that, you and the others!"

"So you hid Mickey in that farm building. You know, I was wondering how you managed to look after him and still keep up your PCSO duties. But of course, you had Kay to help out. Yes, I see how it worked. And then, after you left the Force you started working on your revenge."

"Not straight off," said Liam, "On account of..."

"Shut up, Liam," said both Kay and Vera simultaneously.

"Well, whatever. But you've been living here?" I asked Vera.

"Had to get the old girl out anyway," she explained. "She was a bit nosey, she started asking questions about me. Didn't want her to start gossiping. Wasn't a problem, she shouldn't have been here on her own anyway at her age. She's just lucky that the fall didn't kill her."

"Why didn't it? Or do you draw the line at old women?"

Vera looked puzzled. "Why would we? No, if we'd killed her, then the house might have been sold.

So she just got taken to hospital, and I moved in for a bit. Worked out well for everybody, really."

I shook my head. "And you were here when Kay was telling me her amended history?"

"Actually, I was in Kay's kitchen. I could hear every word. I had a struggle not to laugh sometimes, though. Kay was brilliant, wasn't she? Especially that bit where you thought you were persuading her to carry on - while she was just dangling the bait! Considering we only had a little while to put the story together while Liam went to get you, she was so convincing. I almost believed it myself. Liam was quite convincing as well. And that whole hiding in the dark thing – that was my idea, great atmosphere!"

I was careful to keep my voice steady, my face calm. Not to give them the satisfaction of seeing my anger. "Yes. Impressive. And how come you didn't just kill me then?"

"We did consider it, didn't we?" Vera looked over at Kay for confirmation.

"That we did," Kay said in agreement. "Wish we had, now. Would have been a lot simpler. But we thought it might be useful to have you onside. So I gave you the sob story, made out I was the weak little victim. I knew you'd keep in touch, let me know how the investigations were going, how much you knew, and who you'd told."

"And where you lived," Liam put in. "I followed you back - you didn't see me!"

"But the house you went to wasn't yours after all." Vera looked annoyed by my inconsideration.

"I went to Sam's. Sam's parents, that is." A small light bulb moment. "Ah! That's why you rang me, Liam. To find out where I was."

"Yeah, well, Kay and I were watching this other place, and we saw people come and go, but you weren't there. So we needed to track you down. Or get you out here, but you wouldn't come. So it was good of you to let me know your address."

"Which you then passed to Vera. Of course. So that after she failed to run me down, she went to my flat, tossed the place, and waited for me to turn up."

"Eventful day!" Vera said breezily. "But it's really been a bit much. We need to wrap this up now."

"What, put me back to carry on freezing?"

"Well no. We've had second thoughts on that," Kay announced. "Not that the original plan was bad -" she nodded at Vera "- but on the whole we decided that it would be better if you and Sam just disappeared altogether. Fortunately, Vera's Dad had a way to make that sort of thing happen. Did she tell you? He must have made over a dozen people disappear over the years. We think he had a cave in the rocks to dump the bodies."

I thought of the fissure up which I'd climbed earlier, and considered what other formations there might be in that area. Probably more than one that would be big enough for dumping bodies.

Vera saw the look on my face, and chuckled. "Yes, neat, isn't it? And the good thing is that now we don't have to worry about how we kill you, since no-one's going to find the body. So we'll just take you outside – Liam's been itching to try out that shotgun – and then drive you back up there. Might have to search for the right hole in the ground, but once we've found it, you and Sam can go down there together. Romantic, don't you think?"

My throat had gone very dry. "Liam... you don't have to be part of this. They're murderers, but..."

"Of course he's part of this!" Kay said firmly. "It's his initiation, if you like."

"What she says. It's not personal." Liam gave me an earnest look. Like he wanted me to know there was no hard feelings on his part, at least.

"I think we've had enough talking," said Vera. "And I'm really quite fed up with seeing you still alive when you should have been dead three times over! So now we're going outside. Out the front."

"What, just to spare you a mess in here?"

"Of course." Vera looked at Kay. "What do you think – shall we do it in the pick-up? We'll be torching it later anyway, along with her moped, so that'll deal with any forensics."

"Sounds like a plan," Kay agreed. "Come on then, Alison. Let's have some cooperation this time. If you make things awkward for us, then we'll toss your Sam in the hole alive and let him die wrapped up in your body. How does that sound?"

Vera giggled.

I closed my eyes. I put aside despair. There was so much I wanted to say, but I didn't have time for anger, or insults, or any wasted words. I had to get a message across to them and I'd only have one chance. I needed to speak clearly and carefully. And quickly.

What had Ruth Darnley said?

'Be clear concise and accurate. Court rules.'

Right then.

"OK. I'll cooperate. But – Vera, I owe you an apology."

She raised an eyebrow. "Bit late for that."

"Yes. Probably. But – the thing is, I accused you of causing Mickey's death. By trying to get him off the lappies. I shouldn't have said that. I was wrong."

"OK, then. Apology accepted."

"I know I was wrong, because I found these."

I reached into my pocket and tossed a few of the white medicine capsules onto the floor.

"You found the lappies?" Vera was frowning. "So what?"

Kay was frowning as well. In fact she was looking worried. "It doesn't matter. We're wasting time. Get her out of here!"

"They're not lappies," I said.

I'd kept one of the capsules in my hand. I broke it open, and poured out the white powder into my palm.

"Aspirin, Vera. Someone switched La Paz for aspirin."

"Shoot her Liam! Shoot her now!" Kay shouted. Liam looked at his sister, puzzled.

"I thought you wanted it doing in the pick-up," he said and glanced at Vera. Who had turned as white as the aspirin.

"No wonder Mickey was having withdrawal symptoms," I continued. "You thought you were giving him the drug, but in smaller amounts. Weaning him off it. But someone was messing with the capsules. Altering the dosage. I think he'd probably been having massive hits of La Paz, then suddenly he was switched to aspirin. No wonder he went into withdrawal. But who could have done that? Who could have doctored the capsules?"

"SHOOT HER!" Kay screamed and snatched at the shotgun. But Vera had pulled Liam out of the way, and grabbed her first. Both fists gripping her clothes.

"What did you do?" Vera asked. In a normal sort of voice. Then again, "What did you do?" This time, it was a shriek. She started to shake Kay. "WHAT DID YOU DO?!"

"He was no good for you, no good for us!" Kay shouted. "Vera – he was bringing us down, we didn't need him, he was..."

She didn't get a chance to finish. Vera pushed her away, and had her ASP out and extended as Kay stumbled backwards.

Liam was looking at them both with his mouth gaping. "Vera – stop..."

Kay got her balance, and stood still, holding out her hands. "Vera..." she said.

Vera ignored them both. She didn't say anything else. Just swung the ASP, brought it down on Kay's head with all the strength of her arm.

It connected just above the temple. Not the shaft that had impacted on Sam's head, but the weighted ball at the end. It crunched as it hit and Kay dropped. Like all her muscles had been cut at once.

And Liam screamed her name, screamed like a child, stepping forward as Vera turned towards him, jabbing her in the chest with the shotgun and firing both barrels at once.

A bang. Loud, but muffled, and Vera was hurled backwards, crashing down on the sofa where she'd been sleeping. Red across her chest, red over the wall behind her. She looked at me. For a brief fraction of a second she held my gaze, then in an indefinable moment she wasn't looking any more, though her eyes were still open. But there was nobody behind them.

There were no echoes in that little room, but the sounds of the shot and the scream seemed to hang in the air for a long time, while in the other house faint music still played. Liam had dropped the shotgun and was kneeling next to Kay, tentatively touching her face and whispering her name over and over. I couldn't see the impact point on her head, or any blood, but some clear fluid was leaking out of her ear.

I picked up the shotgun, broke it open and tossed it onto the table. The phone was just behind it. I picked up the handset and was relieved to get a dialling tone. My fingers were shaking, it took me several attempts to dial 999.

"Emergency, which service please?"

For a moment I froze. Looking round me, seeing what had happened here and knowing all that had happened before. I knew the full story now. But how to tell it? Where to start?

Court Rules.

"Hello? Which service please?"

I took a deep breath. "I need an ambulance at this location, for one gunshot victim and one serious head injury. Also at another location for one person with suspected concussion and a broken leg."

After that it was only a matter of answering questions. Just like in court.

Chapter 23

*Funeral Attire Check-list: Respectful, neat, modest, clean. And black.
Other colours may be acceptable, but black is safe.*

I'm not a big fan of social occasions, but over the next month I
went to four funerals.

The first was easily the biggest and best attended. It was for
Her Honour Judge Ruth Darnley, it took place in the town's largest
church, and it had some serious press coverage, including TV
reporters outside.

Part of that was due to the political dimension. The Government
had made a huge thing out of the supposed terrorist bomb. Outrage
over the 'attack' had been fuelling their push for an entire raft of
tough new legislation. When the truth behind Ruth's death came
out it led to considerable high-level embarrassment and some hasty
ministerial back-tracking. Word was that Heads Would Roll. Not
Government heads, of course, but the search for scapegoats was well
under way. Rumour had it it that the blame had been passed down
the line from Home Office to the police to Special Branch and was
likely to end up with DI Halse, which was blatantly unfair.

But, apart from that, there were a great many people who had
had genuine affection for Ruth Darnley. In a quiet way, and often
unconnected with her work as a judge, she had touched a lot of lives.
The local paper had given over an entire issue to accommodate all
the testimonials that had been sent in, and a lot more had appeared

online. The Church was packed, and mourners filled the adjoining Church Hall and the grounds.

Not surprisingly there was a long list of people who wanted to speak. The service was taken by the Bishop, the main eulogy was delivered by her brother, but he was followed by the local MP (not a member of the Government), the Chief Constable – and myself.

That was a surprise for many. A shock for me. The request to 'say a few words' came directly from Ruth's family. Apparently because I was both the last person to see her alive and the one responsible for finding her killer. How they had decided that this made me a suitable person to speak at her funeral I had no idea, but I desperately wished they hadn't, and yet couldn't refuse.

So I referred once more to her advice. Clear, concise and accurate. Court rules.

It was terrifying to stand at the lectern in front of so many people who had known Ruth Darnley, and known her better than I had. Anyone of them had better reason to speak about her and would have had better things to say. The Chief Constable, resplendent in full uniform, was directly in front of me. D.I. Halse was sitting next to him, stony faced and staring past me. Probably trying to ignore my presence completely.

I wasn't in uniform. CSIs don't get uniforms suitable for funerals. I couldn't stand up there in my well-worn fleece with faint but ineradicable crime scene stains. Instead, I'd bought a black suit, and had to force myself to stop fiddling with the buttons or trying to straighten my jacket.

My words were written out on an A5 card, which I placed carefully in front of me. I focused on the words. I didn't look up. Ignored my dry mouth.

"Out of the last ten minutes of her life, Ruth Darnley spent five of them talking to me. In that time she made me her friend and gave me some wise, practical advice for life. I so deeply regret that I did not have more time to talk to her. I so deeply regret…"

I paused. Suddenly unable to read my card. I had more written down, but I couldn't remember what it was. Instead I stood silent, trying to swallow the lump in my throat, and finally looked up, looked out at all the faces, and spoke my heart.

"I miss you, Ruth. I was only your friend for a few minutes, but I will miss you for the rest of my life."

I left it at that. I didn't have much more to say anyway. I went back to my seat, and when the coffin was carried out – it was to be taken a short distance through town, to allow the many other mourners to pay their respects, before a private, family only committal at the crematorium – I slipped away.

A week later, Vic Grombert and his wife – Sharon, I hadn't known her name before – were buried in the churchyard at St Patrick's. They had a family plot. Apparently there had been Gromberts resident in Warkestone Abbey for several generations, and in the area for much longer than that.

The Gromberts' funeral didn't have the same national significance as Ruth Darnley's had had, but St Patrick's is a smaller church and it was just as packed. Mostly by police officers, reflecting Vic Grombert's long and distinguished career. Sharon Grombert had had her own career in medicine, and another large group of mourners reflected that.

The Chief Constable spoke again. Fortunately, I was not called upon this time. All the same I did my best to escape unnoticed when everyone else was going over to the church hall for drinks and snacks, but I was intercepted by my neighbour the Curate. Pat from St Pat's. She'd been very helpful in the past few weeks, especially in sorting out the mess Vera had left of my flat, so I stopped to talk.

"How are you feeling about this?" she asked. I wondered how some people could manage to ask direct questions like that without causing offence. But Pat had a gentle way about her that didn't strike sparks the way I usually did.

But it was still a difficult question to answer honestly.

"Regretful," I decided after a moment's thought. "Deeply, bitterly regretful. So much pain from one person taking it upon themselves to administer justice."

"Or get revenge," Pat suggested.

"I don't think Vera saw a difference."

"No, probably not. But what I was thinking was, I hope you're not feeling any guilt over this?"

I raised an eyebrow. "Professional concern?"

"Sort of." Pat grinned. "I suppose it is a bit of a theme, in churches. But only because we know it can do so much damage. Guilt can destroy people, Alison, and often the ones who are least deserving of it. Dealing with that is sort of our core business."

I thought some more, and slowly shook my head. "I wish I'd got to the Gromberts a bit sooner. I might have prevented this. I wish I'd realised that they'd be on Vera's list. But I didn't, and I'm not taking it on board that I didn't. If there's guilt to be had, it's Vera's. Perhaps Kay's as well. Or it would be if they were around to take it on. But that's your department, I don't know how it works."

"I don't claim to know how it works myself. The fine details of Justice at that level are above my pay grade! And from what I've read, poor Vic and his wife were always going to be targeted at some point. There was nothing you could have done about that – it's just fortunate that you stopped Vera and Kay when you did, before they killed anyone else. And without getting killed yourself."

Vera's notebook – the same one that I'd seen on the table in Mrs D's house – had included meticulous plans for the deaths of everyone she blamed for Mickey's arrest and conviction. The police hadn't released details, but the general outlines of her campaign were out there. I wondered if Rob and June Seaton knew that they'd been next on her list after me.

"Anyway, if you want to talk any time, you know where to find me. Not just about all this. Just if you want a chat and a coffee. Or I might come to you, I sometimes need to talk to someone with your sensible outlook on life!" She waved good bye and scurried off to the Church Hall, leaving me wondering how she saw me as sensible.

Well, I'd been called worse. Perhaps I'd got another friend to replace the one I'd had and lost so quickly.

Sam came with me to the next funeral. He hadn't attended the first two, mostly due to considerations of space. Especially because he was taking up quite a lot of it with his crutches. His leg was in plaster and apparently healing well, and the bruises on his head, spectacular in their heyday, were now almost faded. Apart from some holes in his memory he'd suffered no long term effects from Vera's attack.

Whereas Kay had never recovered consciousness. Eventually they turned off the life-support.

Her funeral was a much smaller affair. Apart from Sam and myself, there was only Liam with a prison officer and a few family members. I recognised Jackie, the goth from the shop, and deduced that the others with her were Liam's uncle, aunt and nephews.

I didn't need to be there myself, of course. Except that I did, somehow. Call it a need for closure. A way of completing the pattern, so that it could, finally, be the past.

The crematorium chapel wasn't big, but it still seemed almost empty. It was a short service, just the basic funeral liturgy. Nobody gave a eulogy. I suppose there was very little that could be said. Afterwards Jackie's family hurried out without speaking to anyone.

Liam watched them go with a lost and bewildered look, which turned almost frightened when I approached him. He whispered something to the prison officer, who shook his head at me before walking Liam out and back to the prison van that brought him.

"What were you going to say to him?" Sam asked.

"I've no idea," I admitted. "What do you say to someone who was going to shoot you a few weeks ago?"

"He doesn't look like a killer, does he?"

"I don't think he was, really. Just an ordinary lad. A bit simple, perhaps. But totally dominated by his sister. He would have done anything for her."

Liam had pleaded guilty to murder, being an accessory to murder and various other crimes including possessing an unlicensed firearm. Sentencing had been delayed while various psychiatric reports were considered.

"Any word on what might happen to him?" Sam asked.

"Nothing definite. Worst case is that he goes into the general prison population, which might destroy him. It might sound harsh, but I honestly think that his best hope is probably long-term committal to a secure institution."

A week later we were back in the crematorium. This time the gathering was even smaller. Myself, Sam and a young woman with a baby were the only ones who came to see Vera off.

An ending. Last item on the list.

Vera had been dead long before the ambulance arrived. Shot through the heart. The body had been retained for a while after post mortem in case any further forensic tests were needed – usual police caution, there was really nothing more to be learned from her. But in view of her status as a serial killer, nobody wanted to rush things.

The baby had come to light during the follow-up investigation. It was the final piece of the pattern. It explained the timing of Vera's vengeance.

Sam and I looked at the little bundle and at each other.

"What a place to be conceived," he whispered. "Desolate little farm building out in the middle of nowhere."

"And a place with a history," I whispered back.

There had been a thorough search of the surrounding area for places where bodies might have been hidden. So far, eight skeletons had been recovered from two holes. Courtesy of Vera's father. None yet identified.

"I hope the poor kid never finds out about it," Sam said. "Who's the woman with him?"

"Laura Staysworth, Vera's cousin. From the London branch of the family, where Vera was fostered after she killed her parents."

"The one you met on Eel Pie Island?"

"Yes, that's her. It seems that, not long after Mickey died in prison, Vera suddenly turned up at her relatives' house with the baby. He was just a few months old. She gave him to her cousin to look after – *ordered* her to look after him – and said she'd be back to collect him when she'd finished some business. A day or so later the lawyer went under a train at Victoria Underground station."

"Will she keep him?"

"I doubt it. He'll go into care and then for adoption, I imagine. I hope he finds a family that'll love him and give him a future."

"And protect him from his past."

"Absolutely."

Vera's coffin went out of sight. I looked over at a Vera's cousin as we turned to go. She met my gaze, but showed no sign of recognition and hurried out.

Sam wasn't up to hurrying. We took our time as he got his crutches under him. Cousin and baby were gone when we got outside.

The Crematorium is in open country to the south of the town. As we stood in the doorway, we could see Monument Hill in the far distance. Nearer, the crematorium car park was fringed with trees that were now in the full glory of their autumn colours. The air was still, a little damp under grey overcast skies, and there was a rich smell of leaf mould hanging in the air.

I took some deep breaths, flushing my lungs with the freshness of it.

"I read something about love recently," I said after a while. "Pat the Curate gave me a leaflet. Asking about who deserved our love."

We started across the car park to where my car was parked. I'd decided that I didn't want to get around by moped any more, I just didn't feel safe on it now. So I'd traded up to a little Fiat, which as well as feeling more secure was also more comfortable now that winter was approaching. Plus it had the additional advantage that I could ferry Sam around until he was out of the plaster.

"So who does deserve love?"

"That's just it. I think it's the wrong question. Love isn't about deserving, it's about needing. We need to be loved, we need to be able to love. If Vera had had proper love from her parents, she probably wouldn't have turned out the way she did." I paused, reflecting on my own difficult relationship with my parents. "Though they can't take all the blame. I felt like killing my parents sometimes, but I would never have actually done it."

Sam nodded. "Murder is a bit of an extreme response. Especially cold-blooded, pre-meditated murder. But what about Kay? Nothing wrong with her parenting, as far as we know."

I considered it. "I think Kay wanted something more than her parents' love. I don't know why, but in Vera she saw a way of satisfying that. Vera needed Kay, and Kay liked to be needed. Later on, Liam met that need, perhaps. When Vera came back, Kay had everything she wanted."

"Until Mickey happened." We reached the car, and Sam leant against it while I opened the door and put his crutches inside. "That wrecked it, as far as Kay was concerned."

"Yes. I'm pretty sure she would have found a way to be rid of Mickey eventually. Circumstances gave her the opportunity."

"Vera's love for Mickey set her off on a campaign of revenge."

"Which Kay was happy to help with. Because afterwards she would have Vera back."

Sam eased himself carefully into the passenger seat. He had to have it all the way back to fit his leg in. "When did you work all this out?"

I went round and got behind the wheel. "I didn't work it out. I saw it. In the moment when I realised that Kay and Vera were working together. Everything became clear. Then when I mentioned Mickey, there was something in Kay's eyes that confirmed it. That's when I understood about the aspirin."

"Did you know what would happen when you showed them what was in the capsules?" Sam asked quietly.

I put on my seatbelt and started the engine. "Not exactly. Not in detail, of course. But – given how volatile Vera was, I knew something would happen. I thought it would give me a chance. Perhaps to grab the shotgun, perhaps to escape." I shook my head. "Strange thing about Vera. She was so obsessed with control – control of her environment, control of people – but she had no control over herself. Superficially, perhaps, but inside she was all over the place."

"Strange thing about love," mused Sam. "That it could lead to such things."

"Well, I'm no expert on the subject. But I think there's love, and there's love. Like, for example – I love this car. It's comfortable, it drives well, it's got a good music system and a built in sat-nav and I feel safer in it than I did on my moped. I love it, because of what it does for me. And that's how Kay and Vera loved each other. For what their relationship did for them."

"OK to love cars like that," Sam suggested. "Not people." He looked at me with a smile.

I'm learning to understand Sam's smiles. At first, they all seem the same – bright, slightly lopsided, cheerful and endearing. But sometimes, the smiles are just smiles. And other times, they are the way he covers something deeper.

Like now, when there was a question beneath the smile.

I returned the smile and considered the question.

"I think..." I tapped thoughtfully on the steering wheel. "I think that love between people isn't something that should be too casually defined. It shouldn't be reduced to a set of expectations. It can't be rigid. I think it needs to be worked out step by step. Or better yet, crafted. Carefully, over time. With the shared desire to bring out the best in each other. And..." I thought back to the leaflet. "And the willingness to make sacrifices to be together." I glanced over at him. "Does that make sense?"

"It makes a lot of sense to me," he agreed. "Especially that bit about taking time to work things out."

"Good. How about we take a little time down at the Nook and do some work on it over coffee and cake?"

"Love that plan!" Sam said.

CHECKLIST: HOW ARE you doing, Alison?
Good. Very good.

The Author

Paul Trembling started making up stories before he could read or write and has never been able to get out of the habit. His varied career path includes being a seaman, a missionary, a janitor, an administrator and a Crime Scene Investigator (CSI).

To date he has published twelve novels and short story collections. When not writing, he enjoys walking, photography and, of course, reading. He currently lives in Bath with Annie and their two dogs, Edna and Willow.

Drawing on his extensive CSI career, his latest contemporary crime thriller, *Local Killer,* is the fourth book in the gripping *Local* series.

More details on this and his other books can be found on his website,

https://yearningblue.weebly.com/[1]

For up-to-date news of his writing, take a look at Paul Trembling - Writing on Facebook

---

1.   https://yearningblue.weebly.com/#inbox_6666cd76f96956469e7be39d750cc7d9__bl
ank

Resolute Books - who are we?

We are a co-operative group of like minded writers seeking to give mutual support and assistance to each other by sharing knowledge and information on the writing and production of our books, and by promoting each others books in all areas open to us. We aim to produce books of the the highest possible quality both in terms of writing and production.

You can find out more us and our books at: https://www.resolutebooks.co.uk/

Other books in the Local Series by Paul Trembling

R OB SEATON KILLED A WOMAN.
Rob doesn't know Laney Grey. But when she steps out in front of his van and dies on impact, his life will never be the same. He has to know who she was, why she chose to die, and why he had to be part of her death.

To understand her, he must learn to read her poetry. To know her, he must unravel the mysteries of her past.

As Laney's dark secret starts to come to light, and Rob's innocence is questioned, he must learn the full truth.

But truth comes at a cost... Will Rob be the one who has to pay?

THE POLICE CALL CAME AT 4:00 AM.

A possible burglary that turns out to be a particularly nasty murder. Sandra Deeson, the Librarian who finds the bloodied body, is deeply shaken.

Then the nightmares begin- because what the police don't know is that this is not the first time she has found a corpse.

One of Sandra's colleagues is missing. The Police investigation starts and then stalls. There may be a clue in the painting someone left for Sandra - but the picture brings back memories she's tried to keep buried.

Two unidentified bodies, thirty years apart, and the only connection is Sandra herself. Last time, it cost her dearly. This time the price may be even steeper.

IT WAS HIM; GRAHAM was sure of it. He might not have seen Adi Varney for years, but no one forgets their oldest friend's face.

As a football player and manager, Adi had taken his club from victory to victory before suddenly leaving it all behind. No one understood why.

But now he was back... or was he? If it was Adi, why was he avoiding everyone who knew him?

Convinced that something is very wrong Graham is determined to work out what has happened to his friend. The game he uncovers is deadly - but if he doesn't play, lives will be on the line.

Milton Keynes UK
Ingram Content Group UK Ltd.
UKHW021836160923
428824UK00003B/13